THE LAST RUN

R. RIVERA

Copyright © 2026 R. Rivera

All rights reserved. No part of this publication may be reproduced, distributed, or transmitted in any form or by any means, including photocopying, recording, or other electronic or mechanical methods, without the prior written permission of the publisher, except in the case of brief quotations embodied in critical reviews and certain other noncommercial uses permitted by copyright law. For permission requests, write to the publisher, addressed "Attention: Permissions Coordinator," at the address below.

ISBN: 979-8-9933808-0-3 (Paperback)

Library of Congress Control Number: 2025921770

Cover design by Miblart. www.miblart.com

Any references to historical events, real people, or real places are used fictitiously. Names, characters, and places are products of the author's imagination.

Ryan Rivera

Uvalde, Texas

For every girl who ran and wasn't believed. This is your finish line.

"To be silent is to be passive. To be passive is to be dead."

Jeanette Winterson

Preface

The Last Run came from a place that would not leave me alone. It began as a fragment of dread, a quiet sense that danger does not always come from strangers. Sometimes it lives inside a home, behind routine, silence, and the faces people trust most.

Hollow's Edge is a town built on appearances. On what people choose to see, and what they choose to ignore. Beneath that surface, this story asks what happens when fear is mistaken for loyalty, when control wears the mask of care, and when the truth arrives too late for the people who needed it most.

As you enter this story, remember this: silence protects more than secrets. Sometimes, it protects the wrong person.

Contents

Prologue

Olivia Harper ran even when no one chased her.

The track lay empty beneath the night sky, the stadium lights dimmed hours ago. Her shoes slapped against the lane, each step a drumbeat in the dark. Breath tore at her chest, sharp and cold, but she pushed harder. She wasn't racing anyone. She was racing the silence, the weight of the house waiting for her, the rules that wrapped tighter every day.

She slowed near the curve, her legs trembling. The stands stretched around her like shadows, every seat empty yet watching. She bent forward, hands on her knees, the chill of the air clinging to her sweat. For a moment she let her eyes close, imagining the sound of a crowd cheering, voices lifting her up instead of pressing her down.

But the only sound was her own pulse in her ears.

Her phone buzzed in her jacket pocket. She froze; the sound louder than it should have been. Slowly, she pulled it out. One message. His name on the screen.

Where are you?

Olivia's thumb hovered over the reply box. She thought about typing *Just out,* but the words stuck. Instead, she locked the phone and shoved it back into her pocket.

She knew he would ask when she got home. He always asked. He said it was because he cared, because the world was dangerous, because girls like her couldn't be too careful.

But it wasn't the world she feared.

The night wind stirred, carrying the faint rustle of leaves. Olivia looked down the lane once more, the white lines bright against the black surface. She imagined her body crossing the finish line, the moment the race ended, when her chest broke the tape and she finally got to breathe.

She stood straighter, wiping her forehead with the back of her sleeve. Her legs shook, but she took another step, then another, pushing herself forward again. Running meant movement. Running meant not being still, not being caught.

Her phone buzzed a second time.

Answer me.

The words sat on the screen like a weight. Her throat tightened. She pressed the power button until the screen went black, tucking the phone deeper into her pocket.

A shadow shifted near the chain link fence at the edge of the track. Her breath caught, every muscle went stiff. For a second she thought someone had followed her, but it was only a towel snagged on the fence, moving in the wind.

Still, her skin crawled. She grabbed her bag and zipped her jacket to her throat. She couldn't shake the feeling of eyes on her.

The rules came back to her one by one, echoing in her head. Text when you get to school. Call at lunch. Phone stays in the kitchen overnight. No exceptions. He said they were for her safety. She knew better.

Olivia left the track and cut across the grass, her shoes wet with dew. The streetlights ahead glowed faintly, guiding her back toward the neighborhood. Each step closer to home made her chest tighten. She wanted to keep running, past the lights, past the houses, past the pull of his voice waiting inside.

But her feet turned toward the street she knew. Toward the house where the windows always glowed, where the curtains were never left open, where silence was heavier than walls.

At the front door she paused, her key trembling in her hand. For a moment she thought of Riley, of Danny, of the way their voices carried hope she couldn't seem to hold. She wished she could step into their world instead of this one.

She unlocked the door. The hinges creaked.

The house breathed differently at night. The air was thick, still, like it listened. She shut the door softly, slipping her shoes off by the mat. Her phone buzzed again in her pocket.

From upstairs, his voice called down. Calm, steady, practiced. "Olivia?"

Her pulse stumbled. She forced her voice even. "I'm here."

She walked toward the stairs, her legs heavy as if the race had never ended.

And deep down, she knew it never would.

Part I

The Starting Line

Chapter One

Between the Lines

The Empty Victory

The bleachers at Hollow's Edge High were nearly empty now. Late sunlight stretched long shadows across the track, splitting the lanes into uneven strips of gold and gray. A few banners still hung from the fences, fluttering like tired flags each time the wind picked up. Somewhere near the field house, a door clanged shut. The sound echoed once, then died fast.

The air tasted like effort. Sweat, dust, and rubber from the track clung to Olivia's skin and hair, as if the race refused to let go. She walked slowly along the fence line, her duffle bag bumping her hip with each step. A half-empty water bottle swung from her hand. Her legs still buzzed with that fading afterburn.

She had won.

The medal ribbon pressed against the back of her neck beneath her hoodie. She could still feel its weight, even though the fabric. It should have burned in her chest. It should have filled her up. Instead, it felt like a coin in an empty pocket.

Olivia glanced back at the finish line. The chalk marks were already smudged. A volunteer dragged cones toward a cart while Coach Mendez spoke to the meet official in a low voice. No one looked her way.

She tried to hold on to the moment anyway. In her mind, she replayed the last few seconds of the race. Riley at her shoulder. Their spikes hitting in perfect rhythm. The roar of the crowd swelling as they drove toward the line. Olivia had leaned first, barely enough to count.

Still enough.

"I had you at the start," Riley said.

Olivia looked over as Riley Mercer fell into step beside her. Her cheeks were flushed and blotchy from the heat. Damp strands of hair clung to her forehead. She wiped her brow with her forearm and made a face like the whole thing still annoyed her.

Olivia kept her eyes forward and let her mouth lift into a small smirk. "But the finish is what counts."

Riley gave a short laugh that sounded more tired than amused. "Barely."

The word came out under her breath, but the corner of her mouth still lifted. That was how it always was between them. Sharp edges. Careful distance. A rivalry balanced on trust neither of them ever named.

But today felt different.

Riley's gaze flicked to Olivia's medal, then away, like it burned. Her shoulders sagged as they walked, and not just from the race. Olivia could feel the shift in the air between them, in the quiet after the crowd, in the way Riley's joke landed softer than usual.

Olivia slowed near the gate, her sneakers scuffing the asphalt. "What is it?"

Riley shrugged, but it looked forced. "Nothing."

"This isn't your nothing."

Riley let out a breath through her nose. Her eyes narrowed, then softened again. "It's just... you keep winning."

Olivia blinked. That was not an insult. Not from Riley. "I work for it."

"I know." Riley's voice dropped. She picked at the strap of her bag. "I'm not saying you don't."

Olivia stayed quiet. She knew Riley well enough to wait.

Riley glanced past the parking lot toward the road behind the school. "Your dad coming?"

The question landed like a slap to the chest. Small, but sharp enough to sting.

Olivia tightened her grip on the bottle. "It's fine."

"That's not an answer," Riley said.

Olivia forced a lighter tone than she felt. "He's busy. He'll be here."

Riley watched her for a long second. Her face held that look she got sometimes, the one that said she thought she had already said too much. Olivia's stomach tightened anyway.

Then Riley looked down. "Guess that's what I'm good for."

The words sounded casual. The look on her face didn't.

Olivia opened her mouth, ready to argue, ready to tell her that was not true, but Riley's mom honked from the lot before she could say it.

Riley flinched and lifted a hand in a tired wave. "See you Monday, Speed Queen."

She started to walk away, then paused and glanced back. "Just... be careful, Olivia."

Olivia's chest tightened again, "About what?"

Riley didn't answer. She turned and jogged toward the car.

Olivia stayed by the gate and watched her go. The last of the crowd noise had faded now. Only the wind and distant traffic were left. She looked toward the teacher lot.

Her father's truck was not there.

Again.

A sour taste rose in her throat. Dust, sweat, and something too close to disappointment. She shifted the duffle higher on her shoulder. The medal tapped lightly against her chest with a soft, hollow clink.

The Walk Home

The streets grew quieter as Olivia left the school behind. The energy of the track faded with every block. The cheers were gone, swallowed fast by the kind of silence that always seemed to rush in too quickly once the good part ended.

Her sneakers crunched over cracked sidewalk. Small stones shifted under her soles. Each step carried her farther from the lights and closer to the dimmer parts of town. Hollow's Edge always looked older at dusk, as if the whole place sagged under its own weight. Storefronts sat dark behind dusty glass. Closed signs hung crooked in the windows, faded white by the sun.

A rusted bike leaned against a fence with both tires gone, its rims bare and bent. Somewhere in the distance, a porch-swing creaked, though no one sat in it. A dog barked once behind a wooden gate, then fell silent. The quiet that followed felt heavier than the sound.

The air smelled like cut grass and gasoline. Something sour drifted from the diner dumpsters, mixed with fryer grease and old oil. It made her stomach turn. Olivia tugged her hoodie tighter. The cuffs were still damp. Sweat cooled against her skin and left her shivering even though the evening air was warm.

Her legs ached in that steady, familiar way. It should have felt good. It should have felt earned. A clean kind of pain. A reminder that she had done something real. Instead, it felt like a warning.

She passed a row of houses with sagging porches and peeling paint. Yards were patchy and brown, choked with weeds and dead spots. Some had old toys half-buried in the dirt. Olivia tried not to stare.

She told herself she didn't mind walking home. It gave her time to stretch the win, time to stay away from questions, time to put off whatever waited for her inside that house. But her chest tightened anyway. Each block felt like a rope pulling her back toward something she didn't want to face.

Her father wasn't cruel. Not in the ways people noticed. He worked hard. He paid the bills. He kept food in the kitchen. But the house had changed. Or maybe she had.

Some nights it felt like the walls listened. Like the air held its breath. Like one wrong word could turn the whole place sharp.

By the time she reached her street, porch lights had started to flicker on. They glowed in uneven rows, small squares of light that looked almost like eyes. Olivia slowed near her yard. Weeds pushed through the cracks in the walkway. The grass was patchy and overgrown near the steps. The porch light shone steady against the dark.

The siding looked gray under the bulb. Paint curled off the edges in thin flakes. From the street, the house looked safe.

It looked normal.

Olivia climbed the steps anyway, though her hand hovered the doorknob for a second longer than it should have. For one small, ugly moment, she wished she could turn around.

Then she opened the door.

Just Another Night

The smell hit her first. Citrus cleaner and oil. Warm food that had sat too long on a plate.

"Olivia?" her father called from the kitchen.

His voice sounded steady, but it carried a weight she could feel. The kind that came home with a man after a long day and never quite left him.

"Yeah," Olivia said. "I'm back."

Ethan Harper stepped into the hall, wiping his hands on a stained shop rag. His dark blue work shirt hung loose at the shoulders. His name was stitched above the pocket in white thread. Grease marked the fabric near the collar, and a chemical tang clung to him beneath the cleaner. Gasoline. Soap. Metal. Work.

He looked tired in the eyes. The kind of tired that sleep didn't fix.

"How was practice?" he asked.

Olivia paused in the door. The medal was hidden under her hoodie now, but she still felt it like a bruise. "It wasn't practice. It was the meet. The one I qualified for."

Ethan blinked, as if the word *meet* had to catch up with him. "That was today?"

"Yeah." Her voice came out flat. Not angry. Just worn thin.

He rubbed the back of his neck with the rag. "Damn. Sorry kiddo. The shop's been hell this week."

Olivia made herself smile. It tugged at her mouth, not her eyes. "It's fine."

Ethan crossed the space between them in three long steps and pulled her into a hug. It was too tight. His arms locked around her like a clamp, his chin pressing into her hair. For one second, she felt small again, eight years old and safe the way she used to be.

Then the pressure lingered too long, and her lungs wanted more space.

Her arms stayed stiff at her sides. She patted his back once, then let her hands fall away.

"You're still my champion," Ethan murmured, his voice low and heavy. "Always will be."

Olivia swallowed. Her throat felt dry.

When he finally pulled back, he cupped her face in both hands. His thumbs were rough and calloused. They brushed her cheeks and left faint smudges behind. His eyes moved over her face, searching.

Not warm. Not cold either. But measured.

"I mean it," he said. "And don't let that Mercer girl fill your head."

Olivia's stomach tightened. Riley. Always Riley.

"She's good company," Ethan went on. "But she's not family."

Olivia let out a thin laugh. "It was just a race, Dad."

Ethan held her gaze for a long, unreadable moment. Then his mouth curved into a smile that never quite reached his eyes.

"It's never just a race," he said.

The words landed softly, but they carried a hook.

Olivia glanced toward the kitchen. The T.V. buzzed from the living room with the volume low, filling the house with a thin layer of noise. Like silence had to be kept out. Ethan's eyes followed her glance, then returned to her.

"Go shower," he said. "I saved you some dinner."

"Okay," Olivia whispered.

She slipped past him and headed for her room. The duffle felt heavier now, as if it carried more than clothes. Behind her, Ethan returned to the kitchen. His footsteps were slow and even, and the house seemed to settle around him.

She showered, changed, and later picked at the plate he had left for her, barely tasting any of it. By the time she carried it back to the sink, the house felt quieter than before, the television still murmuring from the next room like it was filling space neither of them wanted to touch.

Restless

Later that night, Olivia sat on her bed in an old T-shirt and sleep shorts, her hair still damp from the shower. Her socks were gone now, but the chill in her room still found her skin. Her track clothes lay in a loose pile near the hamper, and her shoes had been kicked aside by the dresser, like she could not stand to look at them anymore.

The medal rested on her nightstand. Its shine had been swallowed by shadow, though now and then the lamp caught it just enough to make it glint. The room felt too quiet. Not silent, but close to it. The kind of quiet that pressed at the edges, waiting for something to break it.

Outside, the porch light hummed through the wall. The T.V. still murmured in the other room. Her dad always left it on. Once, when she was younger, he told her silence wasn't safe. Tonight, the sound didn't help. It only made the house feel more awake.

Olivia leaned back against the headboard and stared at the ceiling fan as it turned above her, slow and steady and endless. Each lazy rotation felt like a starting pistol going off inside her head. She had showered. She had eaten a few bites. She had done everything she was supposed to do. None of it had made the day feel any less wrong.

Her phone vibrated on the blanket beside her.

The glow lit her face in the dark. It was from Danny.

Speed Queen. You crushed it today. Proud of you. Let's talk soon. Maybe about getting you out of there.

Olivia's stomach tightened. Danny always seemed to know the right words. Or maybe the right hooks. He had a way of making her feel seen, like he noticed the things everyone else missed. Riley didn't trust him. She had called him slippery once, with a laugh that didn't sound much like a joke.

Olivia read the message again. Then again.

Her thumbs hovered over the screen. She could picture him typing it, calm and sure of himself. Sure, of her too, which somehow made it worse.

She started to reply, then stopped. The half formed words sat there for a second, before she deleted them. Instead, she set the phone down faceup, like she wanted it to buzz again.

She let her head rest against the wall and looked at the medal on the nightstand. Winning should have filled her up. It should have meant something tonight. Instead, it looked small in the dark, just a bright circle that meant nothing in this room.

Her father's voice drifted back into her mind.

It's never just a race.

Olivia closed her eyes. Sleep crept in around the edges, not gentle but slow and thick, like fog rolling over an empty road. No one was cheering now.

And the victory still felt thin.

Chapter Two

The Secret Meeting

Hollow Whispers

By the time the house settled into night, Hollow's Edge had gone still. The last traffic had thinned to a whisper from the highway. Somewhere down the block, a loose gutter tapped once, then stopped. Even the dark felt careful. Olivia lay flat on her bed and stared at the ceiling fan as it turned in slow, uneven circles, dragging thin shadows across the walls. The rhythm should have calmed her. It should have pulled her under. Instead, each lazy turn only made her more aware of time passing while sleep stayed just out of reach.

Her phone rested on her chest, screen dark now, Danny's last message still pressing at her like a hand she could not quite shake off. She had told herself she would ignore him. That she was done letting a few words pull her in. None of that helped.

Her father's snores rolled faintly through the wall, deep and steady, the sound of someone resting easy in a house the never let her do the same. Olivia turned her head and looked across her room. Old medals hung from a pushpin near the desk, dull in the dark except where the weak lamp light caught an edge. Everyone thought she ran because she loved it. Because she was built for it. Because winning meant something. Sometimes she wondered if she ran for one reason only. For a few minutes at a time, it felt like moving fast enough to leave.

She picked up the phone before she could talk herself out of it. The light washed her face pale in the dark. For a long time, she only stared at the empty message box, her thumb hovering, her pulse ticking higher with every second. Then she typed.

You know I can't leave.

The words sat there, small and bare and far too honest. She almost erased them. Instead, she pressed send and felt the regret hit almost at once. The reply came so quickly it made her stomach turn.

Danny: You always say that. Yeah, you can. I want to see you. Can you come to our spot?

Olivia read it twice, hearing his voice in the words without meaning to. Calm. Sure. Almost amused. Like he already knew what she would do. She should have put the phone down. She should have rolled over and force herself to sleep. But instead, she typed one word.

Okay.

The moment the message left her screen, the room felt different, thinner somehow, as if the walls already knew what she had decided. Olivia sat up slowly and listened.

The house stayed still. Her father's snores carried on through the wall, covering the quiet with that same heavy sound.

She slid from the bed and crossed the room with careful steps, wincing at every faint creak beneath her feet. She pulled on her track shorts, then bent to lace her shoes with hands that wouldn't stop trembling. When she was done, she stood at the window for a moment, her breath shallow, and listened again.

No footsteps in the hall. No shift in the floorboards.

She eased the window open, the frame giving a small sound that made her freeze, but nothing changed. A second later, she swung one leg over, then the other, and dropped into the grass below.

The night air felt cooler than she expected. She stayed close to the dark side of the house, clear of the porch light, and slipped toward the street with her heart pounding hard enough to make her lightheaded.

Then she was moving, quick and quiet, away from the house and deeper into the part of town that felt forgotten after dark.

The Tracks

The old train yard waited at the far edge of Hollow's Edge, where the rails split apart and disappeared into weeds. Rust had claimed almost everything left there. The steel looked tired in the moonlight, and the gravel underfoot shifted with a dry crunch that sounded too loud in the open quiet. A boxcar lay tilted on its side beyond the fence, its metal skin scarred with layers of graffiti. Names crossed over names. Threats faded into declarations of love. Old paint peeled around newer colors, and the whole place looked less abandoned than discarded, like the town had dragged its broken things there and stopped asking questions.

The air smelled of oil, rust, and wet metal. Somewhere deeper in the yard, a loose sheet of tin knocked softly against something else whenever the wind stirred. Danny stood near the tracks with his hands in his pockets, shoulders hunched against the cold. He looked up as soon as Olivia stepped into the yard, like he had been waiting for the exact sound of her shoes on the gravel. His clothes were the same as always, dark and worn. Black denim frayed at the cuffs. The collar of his jacket was held together in one spot by a safety pin. Nothing about him looked polished, but that was part of what made him seem so certain of himself. Even standing in a dead place under a weak moon, he looked like he belonged there.

"Didn't think you'd come," he said.

Olivia stopped a few feet away and kept her arms folded tight. "I almost didn't."

A quick smile touched his mouth, then vanished. "But you did."

She hated how easily he made that sound like proof of something. Danny jerked his chin toward the tipped boxcar and climbed first, moving with the kind of practice that said he had done it a dozen times before. Olivia followed, catching her hand once on the cold metal before finding a better grip. The steel bit into her palms and scraped at her skin, but she hauled herself up and sat beside him. From the top, the town looked farther off than it really was. The streetlights near the neighborhoods blinked in weak rows, and the houses beyond them looked flat and small. Distance didn't make Hollow's Edge beautiful. It just made it seem less real.

Danny pulled a flask from his pocket and twisted the cap off with a scrape of metal. He offered it to her without a word. Olivia shook her head. He took a swallow himself, then put it away, the smell of whiskey drifting toward her a second later. For a little while they sat without speaking, looking out over the edge of town. The wind worked its way through the broken seams of the boxcar and moved around them in thin, cold threads. Olivia pulled her sleeves lower over her hands and tried to settle her breathing.

Out here, Danny felt different than he did in messages, or in the stolen moments when he caught Olivia alone. Less careless. Less easy to dismiss. With the town spread out below them and the tracks disappearing into the dark, he seemed quieter now, harder to read. That should have made Olivia more careful. Instead, it made it easier to stay. The train yard felt cut off from everything waiting for her back home. No rules. No watchful silence. No T.V. murmuring from the next room like a warning. Just cold air, rust, and the dangerous comfort of being somewhere her father would hate.

She should not have felt calmer there. She knew that. But the farther she was from the house, the easier it became to pretend the rules waiting for her there were not real.

"You really want this to be your whole life?" Danny asked at last, his voice low enough that she almost missed it.

Olivia kept her eyes on the lights in the distance. "Not tonight."

He turned slightly toward her. "Then when?"

The question settled into her chest and stayed there. She didn't answer because she didn't have one. She could feel him waiting anyway. That was part of Danny's gift. He knew how to leave space in a way that felt less like patience and more like pressure. Like silence itself would eventually do the work for him.

Warnings

A train horn sounded somewhere far off, thin and lonely. The sound carried through the dark long after it should have faded. Olivia drew her knees up a little and rested her arms over them, trying to ignore how cold the metal had become beneath her. Danny stayed quiet for another few seconds, then said, "Your Dad talked to me." The words made her turn so fast her shoulder brushed his arm. He didn't move away.

"What?" she asked. "When?"

"Last week. At the gas station." Danny leaned back against the car and looked out over the yard instead of at her. "He saw me there and decided he had something to say."

Danny let out a short breath that was not quite a laugh. "That I should stay away from you. That I was trouble. That you were fragile."

He turned then, one brow lifting like the word still offended him. *"Fragile."*

A thin, shaky laugh slipped out of Olivia before she could stop it. It sounded wrong in the open air. "Right."

"You don't seem fragile to me," Danny said, and there was something soft in his voice that made the words land harder than they should have. Olivia looked away and pulled at the cuff of her sleeve, twisting the fabric between her fingers. She could hear Ethan's voice anyway, not the exact words, but the feeling behind them. The ownership of it. The certainty that he got to decide what she was.

Danny shifted closer, not enough to crowd her at first, just enough to let her feel the warmth coming off him in the cold night. Then he rested an arm across her shoulders. For a second she let herself lean into it. For a second it felt good to be held by someone who asked less of her. Or maybe that was not true. Maybe Danny just made what he wanted sound easier.

"Olivia," he said quietly, "I'm not trying to push you." He always said things like that before saying the things that pushed anyway. "But you need to see this for what it is. That isn't protection. Not really. He doesn't want to keep you safe. He wants to keep you."

Her throat tightened. "He's still my Dad."

The words came out smaller than she meant them to, and she hated that. Danny nodded once, slow, like he understood more than he let on. "Yeah," he said. "That's the problem."

Olivia looked down at the tracks below them and tried to sort through the mess those words stirred up. Ethan worked hard. He paid the bills. He cooked. He folded her clothes. He made sure the house stayed full and running and normal from the outside. But normal had edges in that house. It had rules that shifted. It had kindness that sometimes felt too tight around her ribs. She thought of the way he watched her when he thought she was changing too fast. The way his voice flattened when Riley's name came up. The way he touched everything in her life like it belonged to him. He was still her Dad. That had to mean something. It had to. But sitting there in the cold, with Danny's arm across her shoulders and the town stretched out below them, she could not stop herself from wondering what it meant if it was not enough.

Back Through the Shadows

The cold finally drove them down from the boxcar. By then Olivia's fingers had gone numb, and even Danny seemed less steady than before, though whether that was from the whiskey or the hour, she couldn't tell. They crossed the yard side by side, their shoes grinding over gravel, their breath rising pale and thin in front of them. The quiet around them felt heavier now, as if the night had drawn closer while they sat talking. Once they left the tracks behind and reached the streets again, the town looked more awake than it had from a distance. Porch windows glowed here and there. A T.V. flashed blue through a set of curtains. A porch chain knocked softly against metal in a backyard they passed. Small signs of life. Small reminders that every house held its own kind of silence.

Danny walked with his hands deep in his pockets and glanced at Olivia every few steps as if he were checking whether she might disappear. She kept her eyes ahead. The closer they got to her street, the tighter her chest became. Houses she knew by daylight looked different now, flatter and more secretive, each porch light casting weak little islands onto cracked walks and dry grass. She could feel the shape of home before she even saw her block. It was there in her body already, in the way her shoulders pulled in, and her steps lost some of their ease. Out by the tracks, Danny's words had made things sound simple, almost possible. Back in the neighborhood, nothing felt simple at all. The streets were familiar enough to know exactly how trapped she still was.

Neither of them spoke for a while. Olivia was glad for that. She didn't trust herself to talk without saying too much. Danny had a way of pulling words out of her, not by force, but by waiting just long enough for silence to start feeling unbearable. She could still hear him from the boxcar. He wants to keep you. The words stayed with her all the way down the block, rubbing against everything she had spent years trying to make sound normal in her own head.

Two blocks from her house, Danny stopped beneath a streetlight that flickered faintly before settling into a weak yellow glow. The light cut his face into shadow and gold, making him look older for a moment, or maybe just harder to read.

"You don't have to go back," he said.

Olivia gave a smile that didn't fully form. "I know."

"Then why do you?"

She looked past him toward the dark end of the street. From there she could almost picture the porch light, the weeds in the walk, the shape of the house waiting the same way it always did.

"Because I don't know what happens if I don't."

Danny stepped closer. Not much. Just enough to change the space between them. Then his fingers brushed her arm through the sleeve of her hoodie, light and warm and careful in a way that made her heart jump harder than it should have.

"Then maybe it's time you found out," he said.

Part of her wanted to believe that was all it would take. One choice. One night. One act of courage. Part of her wanted to lean into him and let that version of the world carry her somewhere else. But the rest of her stayed locked in place. Fear had sunk too deep for a moment like that to lift it. She could not answer. Above them, the streetlight buzzed once and held steady. Olivia stepped back first, and Danny let her. He watched her for one long second, his face unreadable again, then nodded toward the street.

"Text me when you're inside."

She nodded, though she didn't promise anything out loud.

The Glow of Windows

Olivia slipped back through her bedroom window and landed softly on the carpet, one hand braced on the sill until her balance settled. Her pulse still raced hard enough to make her feel sick. She stayed still and listened. The house answered with the same low rumble of her father's snoring from the other room. No movement in the hall. No floorboard groan. No hand on her doorknob. She lowered the window inch by inch until it sat closed again, careful not to let the latch click too loudly, then turned and faced the room.

Everything looked the same, and that almost made it worse. The stack of folded clothes still sat on the dresser where Ethan had left them earlier, neat and square and a little too careful. The room smelled faintly of laundry soap, old wood, and the trace of his cologne from whenever he had come in to set them there. He always called it helping. Olivia always thanked him because not thanking him felt dangerous in ways she could never explain cleanly. Tonight the smell turned her stomach. She sat on the edge of the bed and pressed both hands flat against the mattress until the shaking in them eased enough to notice.

Her phone buzzed in her pocket, startling her so badly she nearly dropped it. She pulled it out and looked at the screen.

I'm glad you came.

That was all. No heart. No plea to stay out longer. No demand for an answer. Somehow that made the message feel even more loaded. Olivia stared at it while too many replies crowded into her throat and mind at once. Some felt too honest. Some felt cruel. Some sounded like the kind of lies people told when they wanted to keep one foot in two different worlds. In the end, she typed nothing. She turned the phone face down on the blanket and lay back slowly, staring up at the fan again as it moved through the dark with the same slow, uneven rhythm.

Her breathing would not settle. Every few seconds she thought she heard something in the hall and went still to listen, only to realize it was the house itself, shifting and settling around her. Minutes passed like that. Maybe longer. Her eyes burned. Her body felt heavy. But her mind kept moving in circles. Danny's hand on her arm. Ethan's voice in the kitchen. Riley saying, *Be careful, Olivia.* The old train yard. The weak streetlight. The stack of folded clothes waiting on the dresser like proof that care and control could wear the same face. By the time exhaustion finally began to pull at her, it did not feel gentle. It felt like losing ground. Like hearing footsteps gaining behind her in a race she had already run too long. Olivia kept her eyes open until she could not anymore. Then sleep came over her all at once, and this time it reached the finish line first.

Chapter Three

Hollow's Edge High

The Golden Girl

Morning light cut sharp across the polished floors of Hollow's Edge High. It caught at odd angles in the waxed tile, making the halls look brighter than they should. Lockers gleamed. The floor held the kind of shine that suggested constant scrubbing. Everything smelled faintly of lemon disinfectant and old air.

Olivia walked through it as if she belonged there. Her backpack rested high on her shoulders, and her hair was pulled into a neat ponytail that looked effortless, though it never was.

Teachers nodded when she passed. A few smiled. Students moved aside without thinking, parting around her like water. Olivia was the kind of girl whose reputation arrived before she did. Star runner. Top student. Respectful daughter. The golden girl of Hollow's Edge.

On the outside, she carried herself like someone who had already won. Straight spine. Chin level. Eyes forward. Inside, she felt every mile of lost sleep dragging at her bones.

Her phone still weighed in her pocket, heavy in a way no object should. Danny's last message had already been answered, but it did not feel finished. Nothing ever really did. She kept her face smooth and her steps steady. The trick was making sure nobody looked too closely.

She slipped into Ms. Porter's English class and settled into her usual seat by the window. The glass rattled in its frame whenever students rushed past in the hallway. The room smelled like lavender hand cream, dust, and old paperbacks that had been handled too many times. It was warmer than the rest of the building, the heat trapped in a way that made the back of her neck damp.

Today's lesson was Sylvia Plath.

"What do you think she meant by 'The woman is perfected'?" Ms. Porter asked.

A silence followed. The fluorescent lights hummed overhead. Students shifted in their seats, flipped pages they were not reading, and glanced down at notebooks that stayed mostly blank. Eyes moved everywhere except toward the teacher.

Except Olivia's.

When Ms. Porter's gaze landed on her, Olivia twirled her pen once between her fingers. The answer slipped out before she could stop it.

"It's about control," she said. Her voice came out even, almost detached. "About deciding for yourself when it ends."

The room stilled.

A few heads turned. Some looked confused. Others looked curious.

Ms. Porter paused. Something sharper entered her expression, the kind of interest that did not feel entirely safe. Then she gave a small nod.

"Interesting," she said. "Dark, but thoughtful."

Olivia lowered her eyes and underlined a sentence in her notebook that had already been underlined twice.

The bell rang soon after. Chairs scraped. Backpacks zipped. The usual rush toward freedom filled the room. Olivia made it almost to the door before Ms. Porter spoke again.

"You've been quiet lately," she said.

Olivia turned.

Her teacher's tone was gentle, but there was something probing under it. "Everything all right at home?"

Olivia smiled too quickly, too neatly. It was the kind of smile adults liked because it gave them permission to stop asking questions.

"Of course."

Ms. Porter held her gaze for one second too long, then nodded and let her go.

And like most adults, she left it there.

Lunch at a Distance

By lunch, the cafeteria had settled into its usual chaos. Voices rose and fell in waves. Trays clattered against the counter. Chairs scraped over the floor in bursts that made the whole room sound restless. The smell of fried food and artificial cheese hung heavy in the air, cut by the sugary scent of spilled fruit juice drying somewhere nearby.

Olivia sat across from Riley at a table near the back doors. When someone forgot to shut them all the way, a breeze slipped in from outside, carrying the smell of cut grass and the faint metallic bite of the track.

Riley was halfway through a story, already laughing at her own disaster.

"So I'm trying to make brownies for me and my mom," she said, grinning as she talked with her hands. "Only problem is, I accidentally mixed up the salt and sugar. The whole pan came out looking perfect, smelled perfect, and I was standing there feeling proud of myself. Then my mom took the first bite."

Riley slapped the table.

"She spit it right back out and went, 'What did you do, season these like steak?'" Riley snorted. "I swear, I thought she was about to launch the whole pan at my head."

Olivia almost smiled.

Almost.

The corner of her mouth twitched, then faded. Her eyes drifted instead to the clock above the lunch line, where the second hand jerked forward with stubborn little clicks.

"Hey." Riley waved a hand in front of her face. "Earth to Olivia."

Olivia blinked and forced her attention back. "Sorry. Didn't sleep much."

She rubbed at one eye like it meant nothing.

Riley leaned back in her seat and studied her with the kind of frown that came from caring too much to pretend not to notice. "Sneak out again?"

Olivia did not answer.

That was answer enough.

Riley let out a breath through her nose. "I don't get it. You do everything right. You run, you study, you get the good grades, you smile for all the teachers. You're basically Hollow's Edge royalty. And your dad still acts like you're five."

"He's just overprotective," Olivia said softly.

"Yeah, well, so is a mother bear. Get too close to her cub and you're dead."

"Riley."

"I'm not saying he's some monster." Riley's voice softened a little. "I'm saying you look tired all the time. Like really tired. And every time somebody says his name, you go still." She paused. "You look trapped."

Olivia's breath caught. Her fingers tightened around the edge of her tray hard enough to make the plastic creak. Something sharp moved through her chest, fast enough to hurt. She looked away first and stared down at her food.

The mashed potatoes had gone gray around the edges. The corn looked wet and tired. She had not touched any of it.

Riley's tray was already half empty. Olivia found herself staring at it for a second too long. Riley ate when she was hungry. Laughed when something was funny. Slept without guilt. Moved through the world like it belonged to her too.

Olivia could not remember the last time anything felt that simple.

For her, everything came with rules.

Everything had to be earned.

Silence. Good grades. A calm face. The right answers. The right version of herself.

Riley tore open a ketchup packet and frowned. “You know you can tell me things, right?”

Olivia’s fingers stayed curled against the tray. For one second, she almost did.

Then the bell rang.

The sound cut through the room like a snapped wire.

Students pushed back their chairs. Conversations broke apart mid sentence. Riley groaned and grabbed her tray.

Olivia stood too, relieved and disappointed in the same breath.

“Practice after school?” Riley asked as they carried their trays toward the trash.

Olivia hesitated. “Maybe.”

Riley gave her a look that said she did not believe her, but she let it go. “Text me later.”

Olivia nodded, though they both knew she might not.

Lessons and Warnings

By afternoon, storm clouds had bruised the horizon. Their dark weight stretched shadows across the school grounds and dimmed the light in the halls. The air felt charged, as if static had settled over everything. Students moved faster between classes, unsettled in the way people often were before a storm, even when they could not explain why.

In history, Mr. Cole stood at the chalkboard with his sleeves rolled to the elbows. White dust clung to his fingers and the cuff of his shirt. He taught with the kind of restless energy that made it seem like the past was not over, just waiting for people to repeat it.

"Power, when abused, always collapses," he said, tapping the chalk once against the board. "The only question is what cracks first. The people or the pressure."

Olivia copied the line into her notebook word for word. Her pen pressed so hard against the page that her wrist began to ache.

"Ms. Harper."

Her head lifted.

Mr. Cole turned toward her. "What do you think? Is order the same as safety?"

Her throat tightened.

The answer came anyway.

"No," she said. "It only feels safer. Until it doesn't."

The room went quiet.

A few students glanced at her. One boy near the front gave her a strange look, like he was trying to decide whether she was being deep or just weird. Mr. Cole only tilted his head and considered her for a moment.

Then he gave a slow nod.

"Fair answer."

Olivia lowered her gaze again, but her heart beat harder than it should have. The rest of class blurred around her. Dates. Names. A map on the wall. The scratch of pencil on paper. None of it stayed with her. Her own words did.

It only feels safer.

Until it doesn't.

When the bell rang, she packed up slowly, still caught on the thought.

Most students rushed for the buses or the parking lot once the final period ended. Olivia drifted instead toward the gym, pulled by a restless energy that made home feel impossible. Practice had been canceled because of the storm rolling in, but she went anyway.

Coach Rowland's office sat just off the locker room. The walls were lined with faded posters about discipline, grit, and winning. The room smelled like old leather, sweat, and the stale coffee he always forgot to finish.

He looked up when she appeared in the doorway.

"Thought practice was canceled," he said.

"It was." Olivia stayed near the frame, one hand still curled around the strap of her backpack. "I just didn't feel like going home yet."

Something flickered across his face, quick enough to miss if she had not been looking for it.

He opened the binder on his desk and flipped through a few pages. "You broke your personal best again this week."

Olivia gave a small shrug.

"No," he said, more firmly. "Don't do that." He tapped the page. "This matters. College scouts would love numbers like these."

Her gaze dropped to the floor.

"My dad says college is too far," she said after a moment. "He doesn't think I'm ready."

Coach Rowland leaned back in his chair, jaw tight. "Well, I think you are."

She did not answer.

He folded his hands on the desk and kept his voice steady. "You've got talent, Olivia. Real talent. And talent like that deserves a future bigger than this town."

The words should have felt hopeful.

Instead, something in her chest tightened.

He must have seen it, because his tone softened. "If you ever need somebody in your corner, you've got me."

Olivia swallowed.

That was the problem, though. It was never about people standing in her corner. It was what happened after. What it cost. What it stirred up. What it made worse.

She looked down at her shoes. "That's not the problem."

Coach Rowland started to say something else, but Olivia straightened too fast, already stepping backward.

"Thanks, Coach," she said, putting on the same practiced smile she used for teachers and doctors and anyone who wanted reassurance. "I should get going."

He did not look convinced.

Still, he let her leave.

Familiar Roads

The walk home felt heavier than usual.

Storm clouds pressed low over Hollow's Edge, thick and gray, swallowing what little daylight remained. Wind pushed against Olivia as she followed the cracked sidewalk beside chain link fences and overgrown yards. Every step felt slower, as if the whole sky wanted to stop her from moving forward.

She adjusted her backpack higher on one shoulder and kept going.

She passed the same landmarks she always did. The crooked mailbox leaning toward the ditch. The dented stop sign scarred with an old scrape. The sagging fence where vines twisted through the gaps. They had all been there for years, ordinary and worn and easy to ignore.

Tonight they felt wrong.

Tilted somehow. Stretched.

Like the town had shifted half an inch while nobody was looking.

A lawn sprinkler clicked a few houses over, spraying water over dry grass that was about to be drowned anyway. The smell of wet earth rose on the breeze. Somewhere nearby, a screen door slammed.

Thunder rolled low in the distance.

Olivia pulled her hood up.

Her phone buzzed in her pocket.

She took it out and looked down.

Danny: Are you okay?

Her steps slowed.

The screen cast a pale glow over her fingers as she stared at the words. For a long moment, she only stood there with her thumb hovering over the keyboard.

She almost told the truth.

That she had not felt okay in a long time.

That everything she used to love felt like it was shrinking around her.

That every day she woke up and stepped into a version of herself built for other people. Good daughter. Good student. Good girl. Smile here. Nod there. Stay quiet. Stay easy. Stay grateful.

She wanted to tell him about the weight in her chest. How it followed her into every room. How even now, under the bruised sky and the rumble of thunder, she could still feel it pressing down.

Instead, she typed:

Yeah. Just tired.

She stared at the lie for a second, then hit send.

The message left with a soft buzz.

Then silence.

Lightning flashed far off, lighting the street for a single heartbeat. Houses stood still and empty. Blinds drawn. Driveways dark and slick with the first thin spit of rain. In the puddles gathering near the curb, Olivia could see pieces of her reflection, warped and trembling.

She kept walking.

Her shoes splashed softly against the pavement. The rhythm was steady, almost calming. With each step, she told herself to breathe. To keep her face blank. To make sure nothing showed if someone happened to look at her.

No one ever did.

Still, she prepared anyway.

At the corner by the old oak tree, she slowed without meaning to. Its roots had cracked the sidewalk years ago, lifting one section higher than the next. When she was little, she used to balance along that edge like it was a finish line. Her dad would stand in the yard and clap, calling her name like she had won something.

The memory came quick and clean.

Then it was gone.

Now the only sound was the wind moving through the branches, making a hollow whisper that almost sounded like her name before it thinned into nothing.

Another flash of lightning lit the road ahead. Wet pavement. Empty yards. One porch light flickering in the distance.

Then darkness again.

Rain began to fall for real. Fat drops at first, scattered and soft. Then more. Then enough to matter.

Olivia pulled her jacket tighter and quickened her pace.

Her phone buzzed again.

She did not look.

By the time her house came into view, damp strands of hair clung to her forehead and her sneakers squished at the heel with every step. The curtains were drawn, but the faint glow of the television flickered behind them.

She stopped at the end of the driveway.

For a moment, she only stood there, staring at the familiar shape of the house.

The roofline looked uneven against the dark sky. Paint had chipped off the porch railing in places her father had promised to fix months ago. A flowerpot sat crooked by the steps, half full of rainwater and dead leaves.

Lightning flashed again.

For one second, she thought she saw movement inside. A shape passing across the glow. A shadow where no shadow should have been.

Then it was gone.

Olivia's pulse quickened. She told herself it was nothing. The house had always been full of ordinary sounds. Pipes groaning in the walls. Floorboards settling. The television murmuring from room to room.

Still, her hand trembled when she reached for the doorknob.

Behind her, the storm finally broke.

Rain hammered down hard enough to sting. Wind rushed through the trees. Thunder cracked so close it seemed to shake the air itself.

Olivia took one last breath of the outside world.

Then she stepped inside.

Chapter Four

Behind Closed Doors

Stale Air

The house was quiet when Olivia stepped inside.

The blinds were drawn, shutting out most of the late afternoon sun. The air felt stale and heavy, thick with beer and the bitter smell of something burned in the kitchen. The TV hummed in the corner, its low glow cutting across Ethan's face.

He didn't look up when the door clicked shut.

His boots were planted wide. One arm rested along the side of the recliner. A half empty beer bottle sat on the table beside him, the label wet with condensation.

"You're late," he said.

Olivia slipped her backpack from her shoulder. When it hit the floor, the sound felt too loud.

"I stayed after for tutoring," she said. The lie came out quick and easy from practice.

That got his attention.

He turned his head slowly, pale eyes settling on her. "With who?"

"Ms. Porter," Olivia said. She willed her hands not to fidget. "She wanted to check my essay."

The silence stretched.

Only the soft hiss of the TV filled the room. After a moment, he turned back toward the screen.

"Uh huh."

Olivia moved toward the kitchen, each step careful. Her pulse beat hard inside her chest. She set her bag down without a sound. Every part of her wanted to move faster, but she knew better. Fast looked nervous. Nervous led to questions.

The counter was mostly clean. A plate with crumbs sat beside the sink near an empty can. She picked it up, rinsed it off, and kept her voice low.

"Do you want me to make you something?"

"No."

She still pulled out bread and mustard.

The knife tapped lightly against the plate. She spread the mustard in slow, even strokes, watching the yellow drag across the bread. It gave her something to focus on. Something small. Something safe.

Behind her, Ethan spoke again.

"That boy," he said. "Danny."

Her hand stopped.

"You seeing him?"

She swallowed. "He's just a friend."

The recliner creaked.

The sound slid over her skin. She kept her eyes on the sandwich as he stood. His footsteps crossed the room one heavy step at a time. The space around her felt smaller with each one.

"You don't need friends like that," he said.

Her jaw tightened. "Okay."

The word felt rough in her mouth.

He stopped behind her. She felt him there before he touched anything. His breath carried beer and something sour. Then his arm reached past her and pulled the refrigerator door open with a low groan.

His hand brushed her shoulder.

Light. Casual.

Not an accident.

He took out another beer and twisted off the cap. The sharp hiss cut through the quiet.

"You're better than this town," he said. His voice had gone softer now, almost gentle. "But not if you keep acting like trash."

Olivia stared at the sandwich on the plate. She didn't answer.

A few seconds later, the chair creaked again as he sat down. The TV swallowed the room once more.

She stood there until her eyes blurred. The sandwich no longer looked like food. It looked like something made by someone else's hands.

She took one slow breath.

Then another.

When she finally turned toward her room, her hands were shaking.

Locked Spaces

Her room was the only part of the house that felt like hers.

Even then, the safety was mostly pretend.

She closed the door slowly and pressed it shut until the latch clicked. Her fingers stayed on the lock for a second before she turned it. The small sound sent a tight ripple through her chest.

He hated when she locked the door.

If he noticed, she would pay for it later.

Still, sometimes she needed the barrier, no matter the cost.

The room was warm and still. It smelled faintly of fabric softener, old paper, and dust. Olivia dropped onto the bed and sat there without moving. After a long moment, she slid her hand beneath the mattress.

Her fingers found the worn spine of her journal.

She pulled it free and opened it on her lap. The pages bent where the mattress had pressed them flat. The smell of ink and paper rose around her like something private and fragile. Her last entry sprawled across the page, crooked and rushed.

She uncapped her pen and bent over the paper.

He knows. I can feel it in the way he looks at me.

He's watching me closer now.

Danny said I could leave, but what if I can't?

What if he won't let me?

The words came fast. Each line looked more jagged than the one before it.

She stopped with the pen still hovering.

Her thoughts kept going anyway.

What if running makes it worse?

What if he catches me before I get out?

What if nobody believes me when I try to explain?

Footsteps sounded in the hall.

She froze.

The steps slowed outside her door.

Her breath caught so hard it hurt. Her chest tightened as she sat there without moving, listening.

One second.

Then two.

The silence pressed against her from all sides.

At last, the footsteps moved again. They drifted farther down the hall and into another room.

The air left her lungs in a thin, shaky stream.

She lay back on the bed and pulled the blanket over herself without changing clothes. Her shoes stayed on. Her laces stayed tied. If she needed to move fast, she wanted to be ready.

Her eyes stayed on the strip of light beneath the door.

Once, a shadow passed over it.

Then nothing.

Sleep came in thin, brittle pieces. Every time she started to drift, her body jerked awake again. What little sleep she caught was restless and uneven, full of footsteps that always stopped outside her door.

Echoes Outside

Morning light slipped through the blinds in a weak gray wash.

The house was silent. Ethan was already gone.

Olivia stepped into the kitchen and stopped when she saw the note on the counter. A folded twenty sat beside it.

Buy yourself lunch. Love you, kiddo.

The handwriting looked neat and almost warm. The words were written in the same hand that had wrapped itself around every bad night in the house and called it care.

She stared at the note.

To anyone else, it would have looked normal. Thoughtful, even. A small kindness from a parent before work.

To Olivia, it felt like a leash.

A reminder.

A way of saying I can still be the good guy if I want to be.

Her stomach twisted. She grabbed the bill and shoved it into her pocket harder than she meant to. Then she crumpled the note in her fist and held it there for a second before tossing it into the trash.

Even after that, the words stayed with her.

At school, the halls buzzed with the usual morning noise. Locker doors slammed. Shoes scraped across the tile. Someone laughed too loud near the vending machines. The sound made Olivia flinch before she could stop herself.

She kept her head down and moved through the crowd like she was trying not to leave a mark.

In first period, Ms. Porter paused beside her desk while the rest of the class worked. Her perfume carried a soft lavender scent that felt too clean for the morning Olivia had already lived through.

"You've been quiet lately," she said.

Olivia kept her eyes on the worksheet in front of her. "Just tired."

Ms. Porter didn't move away.

"Is everything okay at home?"

The question landed so softly it almost hurt more.

Olivia looked up, startled. For half a second, something opened inside her. A thin crack. A dangerous one.

She could tell her.

She could say something simple. Something small. Enough to make Ms. Porter stop and really look at her.

Instead, she smiled.

The same smile she always used with adults. Polite. Easy. Empty.

"I'm okay," she said.

Ms. Porter studied her face for another second. Olivia could feel it, that quiet searching look adults got when they sensed something was off but didn't know if they were allowed to name it.

Then another student raised his hand from the back of the room.

Ms. Porter glanced away. "All right. If you need help with the essay, you can stay after class."

Olivia nodded. "Okay."

The thought came fast and sharp. Good. Now if Ethan asked again, the lie would not be a lie anymore. Even so, her chest stayed tight long after Ms. Porter moved on.

At lunch, she carried her tray to her usual table, though she had almost no appetite. The folded twenty sat in her pocket like it weighed five pounds. She could feel it every time she shifted in her seat.

Riley found her halfway through lunch and dropped into the chair across from her.

"You look awful," Riley said.

Olivia gave a dry little shrug. "Good afternoon to you too."

Riley didn't smile.

That alone made Olivia uneasy.

For a second, Riley just watched her. Then she leaned in a little. "What's going on?"

"Nothing."

"That answer is getting old."

Olivia picked at the edge of her sandwich. "I'm fine."

Riley let out a quiet breath through her nose, already annoyed. "Danny says you've been dodging him."

Olivia looked up too fast.

That caught her off guard. Riley barely tolerated Danny on a good day. The fact that they had talked at all made something cold shift in her stomach.

"You talked to Danny?"

Riley gave her a flat look. "Yeah. Because he's worried about you too."

Olivia dropped her gaze again. "He's dramatic."

"And you're a terrible liar."

Olivia's hand stilled.

The cafeteria noise seemed to fade around them. Not all the way. Just enough for Riley's words to land harder.

Riley's voice softened. "Olivia."

Olivia looked up.

Concern sat plain on Riley's face now. No teasing. No edge. Just worry.

"I'm not asking to be nosy," Riley said. "I'm asking because something's wrong."

For one dangerous second, Olivia felt her throat tighten. She almost said it. Not everything. Not even close. But maybe enough to stop holding it all alone.

Instead, she looked back down at her tray.

"I'm just tired," she said again.

Riley stared at her for another moment, then shook her head once.

"Okay," she said quietly. "But I'm here. Whether you talk or not, I'm here."

Olivia swallowed. "I know."

The words scraped coming out.

Riley reached across the table and squeezed her wrist once. Quick. Gentle.

Then she stood and left Olivia there with a half-eaten lunch and a chest full of things she could not say.

The rest of the school day dragged.

By the final bell, Olivia felt worn thin. Every sound seemed sharper than usual. Every sudden laugh or slammed door made her nerves jump. When she passed a classroom window and caught her own reflection, she barely recognized it.

She looked tired.

Not sleepy.

Used up.

No Reply

That night, the train yard stretched wide and empty beneath the dark. Rusted tracks cut through the ground like scars. Danny sat on the hood of his car under a broken floodlight that buzzed every few seconds and gave almost no light.

The place felt abandoned. Like the whole town had stepped back and left it to rot.

His phone glowed in his hand.

He opened Olivia's messages and stared at the blank screen for a long moment. Then he typed.

Are you okay?

He looked at it, his thumb hovering over send.

Then he deleted it.

Too small.

Too normal.

Like this was just another night and not something sharp and wrong pressing at the back of his mind.

He tried again.

If you need me, send one dot.

That one stayed on the screen longer.

He could picture her seeing it. Could picture the little crease between her brows. Could picture her smiling a little, or rolling her eyes, or just staring at the words without knowing what to say back. He hated that he could still imagine all of that and have no idea which version of her was real tonight.

He erased that too.

The night around him felt huge and hollow. Somewhere in the distance, a train clattered through the dark. The sound rolled over the empty lots and old tracks like distant thunder. It faded slowly, leaving the yard quieter than before.

Danny looked toward the path she usually took.

Nothing.

No movement. No footsteps. No shape cutting through the dark.

He rubbed a hand over his face and let out a slow breath. He was tired, frustrated, and trying not to let either feeling turn into fear.

He thought about driving by her house.

He thought about doing the exact kind of stupid thing that would only make everything worse if she was already dealing with something bad.

So he stayed where he was.

Waiting.

The floodlight buzzed overhead. A moth circled it once, twice, then vanished back into the dark. Danny checked his phone again, even though he already knew the screen would be empty.

Still nothing.

He leaned back on his hands and looked up at the washed-out slice of sky above him. The air had turned cooler. He barely noticed. All he could think about was the way Olivia had looked lately. Too quiet. Too far away. Like part of her was always listening for something no one else could hear.

His jaw tightened.

He typed one last message.

I'm here if you need me.

This time he hit send.

The message went through in seconds.

No reply came.

Danny stared at the screen until it dimmed. Then he locked the phone and let it rest in his lap. The train yard felt colder now. Bigger.

Like something had stepped between them that he couldn't see yet but could already feel.

He stayed a little longer anyway.

Long enough for the silence to start feeling personal.

At last, he slid off the hood and got into the car. He sat there for a second with both hands on the wheel, staring through the windshield at the dark tracks ahead.

Then he started the engine and pulled away.

The silence followed him all the way home.

Chapter Five

Pressure Points

The Wrong Answer

Morning did nothing to help.

Sleep had come in shallow scraps, never deep enough to feel real. Olivia had drifted off more than once, only to jolt awake at the smallest sound. By the time she stood in front of the bathroom mirror, her eyes looked dull and bruised with exhaustion. No amount of cold water could fix that.

She stared at herself for a second too long.

Then she grabbed her backpack and left for school.

At Hollow's Edge High, the halls felt louder than usual. Students moved past her in warm waves of perfume, laughter, and chatter. Locker doors slammed. Shoes squeaked across the tile. Someone called out a joke down the hall, and a burst of laughter followed.

Olivia walked through all of it like she was underwater.

She smiled when she had to. She nodded when someone spoke to her. She kept her answers short and her face calm. The harder she tried to look normal, the more exposed she felt, like the whole building had turned its head and noticed something she had worked hard to hide.

By homeroom, her nerves were stretched thin.

Mrs. Wilkes moved down the rows with a stack of papers and a cup of coffee balanced in one hand. When she reached Olivia's desk, she set down a folded slip of paper without a word.

Olivia looked at it.

Report to Guidance Office.

Her stomach dropped.

The guidance office sat near the front of the school, tucked between the nurse's station and the main office. The hallway outside always smelled faintly of lemon cleaner, but inside, the air changed. Peppermint tea. Old carpet. Dusty paper. A room built to feel safe, even when it wasn't.

The walls were lined with faded posters about stress, anxiety, and asking for help. Their corners curled away from the wall like they had given up trying to hold on.

Ms. Calhoun sat behind her desk in a pale sweater, a notebook open in front of her. Everything about her looked soft. Her smile. Her voice. Even the way she held her pen.

Still, Olivia felt cornered the second she stepped inside.

"Olivia," Ms. Calhoun said, glancing up with practiced warmth. "Thanks for coming."

Olivia shut the door behind her and sat down. "You sent for me."

A small smile touched Ms. Calhoun's mouth. "I did."

She folded her hands over the notebook. "How have things been lately?"

Olivia kept her face blank. "Fine."

"At school?"

"Fine."

Ms. Calhoun tilted her head a little. "At home?"

That one hit harder.

Olivia looked at a stain in the carpet near the desk and shrugged. "Also, fine."

The pen began to move. *Scratch. Scratch. Scratch.*

It was a quiet sound, but in the still room, it seemed too loud.

"I've noticed you've seemed distracted lately," Ms. Calhoun said. "A little more tired than usual too. That's not like you."

"I'm just not sleeping much."

"Any reason why?"

Olivia's mouth went dry.

For a moment, she thought about telling the truth. Not all of it. Just enough to make someone understand that home never felt calm anymore. Enough to explain why every question sounded like a trap. Enough to say she was tired of being afraid in her own house.

Then Ethan's face rose in her mind.

The way his eyes went cold when she pushed too far. The way his voice could soften and still feel like a threat. The way every act of concern came wrapped around control.

Her fingers curled tighter around her backpack.

Ms. Calhoun leaned forward just a little. "Olivia, if something is wrong, you can talk to me."

Olivia swallowed.

The truth pressed against her teeth.

Then she shook her head.

"No."

Ms. Calhoun watched her for a moment. Olivia could feel the weight of that look, gentle but searching. Like the woman already knew the answer and was waiting to see if Olivia would say it out loud.

"You know you're not alone," Ms. Calhoun said softly. "Whatever it is."

Olivia nodded because it was easier than speaking.

"I'm fine."

The lie came out smoother this time.

That seemed to hurt Ms. Calhoun more than Olivia expected. Just a flicker. A sad little shift in her expression before she looked back down and wrote one last note.

When she finally dismissed her, it was with a kind voice and a smile that felt too careful to be real.

Outside the office, the hallway hit her all at once.

Noise. Motion. Light.

It made her head swim.

She had barely taken three steps before she saw Riley leaning near the lockers, arms crossed tight over her chest. Her face looked set, but her eyes gave her away.

"You lied."

Olivia stopped.

Her pulse kicked hard once. "About what?"

Riley gave her a look. "Really?"

Olivia glanced toward the office door behind her. "You were listening?"

"I was outside waiting." Riley's voice sharpened. "And yeah, I heard enough."

Olivia shifted her backpack higher on her shoulder. "There's nothing to hear."

Riley let out a breath through her nose, frustrated. "You think I don't know when something's wrong with you?"

"I don't need people staring at me like I'm about to fall apart."

"I'm not staring." Riley's voice dropped. "I'm here. That's different."

The words landed somewhere deep.

For a second, Olivia wanted to let them.

She wanted to stop holding everything by herself. She wanted to believe Riley meant it. That being seen wouldn't make things worse. That handing someone even a small piece of the truth would not bring everything crashing down around her.

But belief meant trust.

And trust meant risk.

And risk always came home with her.

Olivia looked away first. "I need to get to class."

Riley didn't grab her arm. Didn't block her path. Didn't try to stop her.

That somehow felt worse.

When Olivia walked away, she could still feel Riley standing there, hurt and angry and trying not to show either one.

She didn't look back.

Friction at Home

By the time she got home, the sky had turned the pale gray of dirty dishwater.

The house was quiet in the wrong way.

Not peaceful. Waiting.

The TV flickered in the living room, washing the walls in weak color. Somewhere in the kitchen, the refrigerator hummed. The air smelled faintly of stale beer and something fried hours ago.

Ethan stood at the kitchen window with one hand braced on the counter. He didn't turn when she stepped inside. His shoulders stayed square, tense under his shirt. Two fingers tapped the edge of the counter in a slow, steady rhythm.

"Where were you?"

Olivia shut the door carefully behind her. "Studying."

"With who?"

She hated how fast the answer came.

"Riley."

That made him turn.

Not quickly. That would have been easier. He turned in stages, like he had all the time in the world. His face gave almost nothing away at first, but she saw the suspicion settle in piece by piece.

"You could've texted."

"My phone died."

Too fast again.

His eyes narrowed just enough to make her stomach knot.

For a second, neither of them spoke. The silence stretched thin and sharp between them.

Then Ethan took one slow step toward her.

"The world is full of monsters, Olivia."

His voice had gone low and smooth. That was always worse than yelling.

"Girls disappear all the time," he said. "You know that, right?"

Her throat tightened. "I'm not a little girl."

Something shifted in his face.

Not anger exactly. Something quieter. Colder.

He moved closer and stopped in front of her. "No," he said. "You're not."

Olivia stood still.

His voice softened even more. "I'm not the enemy here. I'm the only one making sure you get home safe."

"I didn't mean anything by it."

"I know." He reached up and brushed a piece of hair from her face. His fingers slid along her temple and lingered at her cheek. The touch was light. That made it worse. "But girls your age make bad choices when they think somebody else understands them."

His thumb traced once across her cheekbone.

"Friends like Riley don't know how to protect you," he said. "And boys like Danny definitely don't."

At Danny's name, her stomach turned hard.

Ethan saw it.

Of course he did.

"I do," he said.

The words fell heavy between them.

Olivia stared at the floor just past his shoulder. "Okay."

It came out thin.

His hand stayed on her face one second longer.

Then he smiled, small and satisfied. "Good girl."

The words slid under her skin.

He bent and pressed a kiss to her forehead. Soft. Familiar. Final. Like that ended it. Like the whole exchange had been about love instead of power.

Then he stepped back and turned toward the window again.

Conversation over.

Olivia stood frozen, trying to force air into her lungs. The room felt smaller now. The hum of the TV seemed louder. Somewhere behind her, rain ticked once against the window above the sink.

She picked up her bag and headed for the stairs.

Each step creaked under her feet.

In her room, she shut the door and leaned against it until the shaking in her legs eased enough to move. Downstairs, the TV kept muttering to itself. A bottle clinked softly against the counter.

Her desk lamp cast a weak pool of light across the room.

The journal lay open where she had left it, pages half-filled in her slanted handwriting. She crossed to the desk and sat down slowly. The pen felt too heavy in her hand.

For a while, she only stared.

Then, with fingers that would not stop trembling, she wrote two words.

I'm scared.

She looked at them for less than a second before scratching them out.

The pen tore through the paper.

Storm Warning

The next day dragged.

By afternoon, thick clouds had rolled over Hollow's Edge and turned the windows dark. The air outside smelled like rain and metal. Even inside the school, Olivia could feel the pressure building.

In English, Ms. Porter moved through the room with a stack of graded assignments against her chest. Desks scraped. Someone near the back coughed into their sleeve.

Olivia kept her eyes on the page in front of her.

When her paper landed on the desk, the bright red A at the top should have meant something.

It didn't.

A yellow sticky note clung to the corner.

Beautiful work. There's a
sadness here I didn't see
before. My door is always
open. – E.P

Olivia stared at the note until the words blurred.

Then she peeled it off, crushed it in her fist, and shoved it into her hoodie pocket.

She didn't want kindness.

Kindness came with questions.

Questions came with choices.

And choices came with consequences she couldn't control.

Across the room, Riley was watching her again.

This time, when Olivia looked up, Riley glanced down at her own paper too late to make it convincing.

The space between them felt bigger than the classroom.

At lunch, they sat at opposite ends of the same table.

Not because there was no room. Because neither one knew how to cross the distance without saying the wrong thing.

The cafeteria rang with noise. Trays slapped onto tables. Plastic forks snapped. Someone laughed too hard two rows over. The smell of pizza, fries, and bleach drifted through the air.

Olivia pushed food around her tray without eating much of it.

Riley barely touched hers either.

At one point, Riley stood up, carried her tray to the trash, and **passed** close enough to slide something folded onto the table near Olivia's elbow.

She kept walking.

Olivia waited.

Only when Riley had disappeared into the crowd did she slip the note into her pocket.

She didn't read it until later, alone in the girls' restroom between classes.

The fluorescent lights buzzed above her. One sink dripped in a slow, steady rhythm. The stall doors were scratched with old initials and peeling stickers. The room smelled like cheap soap and wet paper towels.

Olivia locked herself into the far stall and unfolded the note with careful fingers.

Whatever it is, you're not
alone.

My house is always open.

No questions asked.

Olivia read it twice.

Then a third time.

Her chest ached with something sharp and tangled, half gratitude, half fear. Riley had written fast. The pen strokes pressed deep into the paper in places, like she had been angry when she wrote it. Or scared.

Maybe both.

Olivia folded the note back along its creases and tucked it deep inside her bag.

She carried it with her all day.

By the time she got home, the storm had broken open.

Thunder rolled over Hollow's Edge in deep, shaking waves. Rain hit the roof hard enough to sound like thrown gravel. Tree branches bent and whipped outside her bedroom window.

She sat on her bed with her knees pulled to her chest and watched the storm move through the dark.

Lightning flashed white across the room.

A second later, thunder followed.

Downstairs, Ethan paced.

She could hear each step through the floorboards. Slow. Measured. Heavy. Sometimes the sound stopped long enough to make her hold her breath. Then it started again, one boot dragging slightly at the end of every turn like a metronome made for dread.

Her phone buzzed on the nightstand.

Danny.

Just his name on the screen made something in her chest pull tight.

For a long moment, she stared at it. The glow lit the edge of her blanket. She thought of his voice, easy and warm. The way he made things feel normal for a few stolen minutes at a time. The way normal had started to feel dangerous too.

Her hand twitched toward the phone.

Downstairs, Ethan stopped pacing.

Silence rushed up through the floor.

Then came the small twist of a beer bottle opening.

Olivia turned the phone facedown.

The room went dark again except for the next flash of lightning.

She pulled the blanket tighter around herself and rested her forehead against her knees.

Outside, the storm battered the house.

Inside, it waited.

She thought about Ms. Calhoun and her careful eyes. Ms. Porter and that sticky note. Riley and the message folded tight in her bag. Danny too, his missed call still sitting there like one more chance she was too scared to take. Four open doors. Four chances to step toward something better.

She couldn't bring herself to touch any of them.

Another flash lit the room.

Another rumble rolled through the walls, closer this time, so deep she felt it in her ribs.

The rain would pass.

It always did.

But the fear never did.

Olivia squeezed her eyes shut and whispered into the dark, so quietly the storm nearly swallowed it.

"Just let it stop."

Downstairs, Ethan's boots started moving again.

Chapter Six

Cracks Beneath the Surface

A House That Listens

The storm left the morning dim and colorless.

Rain still clung to the kitchen window in slow, crooked trails. The sky outside looked thin and bruised. From the living room, the TV filled the house with its usual low drone. Ethan hated silence, so the news was always on.

Olivia stood at the counter and poured cereal she didn't want. The flakes hit the bowl with a dry, empty sound. Milk followed. The spoon knocked against the rim once, then again.

On the TV, the anchor spoke in the smooth, practiced voice people used for tragedy when they had said it too many times.

"Closing arguments are expected this week in the trial of Dr. Leonard Caldwell, the former college professor accused of stalking a student through anonymous letters and escalating threats. Prosecutors say Caldwell's behavior grew more alarming over time, with repeated messages, surveillance, and attempts to isolate the victim from people around her."

Ethan reached for the remote and turned the volume up.

The screen flashed a pale light across his face. He listened for a moment, then let out a short, annoyed breath.

"Whole world's soft," he muttered. "People act like words are the same as harm."

Olivia kept her eyes on the bowl.

Words.

Messages.

Isolate.

The report should have meant nothing to her. It was some professor in some other town. A stranger on the morning news. But it left one word lodged in her chest anyway.

Obsession.

She thought of Riley's face yesterday, the way hurt had broken through before she hid it. She thought of Danny's name lighting up her phone in the dark. She thought of Ethan pacing downstairs while thunder swallowed every sound in the house.

"Bring me your phone."

His voice cut through her thoughts so fast it made her flinch.

She looked up. "Why?"

"Because you live in my house." He held out his hand. "You don't hide things from me."

Her fingers tightened around the spoon.

For one wild second, she thought about lying. Saying she left it in her room. Saying it died during the storm. Saying anything that might buy her a little time.

Instead, she set the spoon down and handed it over.

The silence stretched thin as he scrolled.

Recent calls. Messages. Settings. Weather alerts. He moved through everything with the same calm care he used on the rest of the house, as if each swipe belonged to him more than it belonged to her.

Her stomach rolled every time his thumb paused.

Watching him hold her phone felt like standing on the edge of something high, waiting for the ground to give way.

At last, he handed it back.

His voice softened in that careful, measured way that always made her feel worse, not better.

"You tell me where you are after school. No more guessing."

"I have practice."

"Then text me when it starts. Text me when you leave. Simple."

She nodded and looked down at the cereal.

The milk had already turned the flakes gray and lifeless.

On the TV, the news moved on to weather. Flooded roads. Fallen limbs. Cars stalled in water two towns over. Ethan muttered something about people who never planned ahead.

Olivia picked up her bowl, dumped it into the sink, and rinsed it until the water ran cold over her hands.

As she turned toward the hallway, the anchor said the professor's name again.

Dr. Leonard Caldwell.

Olivia paused for a moment, listening.

Not because she cared about the case.

Because the world outside this house had words for men like that.

Inside this kitchen, there were none.

She grabbed her backpack and headed for her room with the TV still humming behind her like a leash.

Small Leashes

Her room still smelled faintly of rain.

The damp air held dust, detergent, and the stale chill that always came after a storm. Olivia crouched beside the bed and slid her fingers under the mattress until they touched the edge of her journal.

She pulled it free and held it in both hands.

For a moment, she only stared at it.

Writing was the last thing that still felt like hers.

She opened to the most recent page. Her handwriting curved tight and nervous across the paper. The last entry ended in the middle of a thought, like even the words had been too afraid to finish themselves. She shut the journal and glanced toward the bed.

Usually, that was where she kept it. Under the mattress. Close enough to reach, easy enough to hide. But after this morning, it no longer felt safe.

She crossed to the floor vent and knelt beside it. The screws were stubborn at first. She worked one loose with shaking fingers, then another, until the grate lifted. She slid the journal into the dark space below and set the cover back in place.

Then she opened the front pocket of her backpack.

Riley's folded note was still there.

She touched it once, then stopped.

Next to it sat the yellow sticky note from Ms. Porter, a little wrinkled now from being opened and folded too many times. Olivia smoothed the paper flat with her thumb, then tucked it back into her planner. Not because she wanted to keep it. Just because she could not bring herself to throw it away.

Down the hall, a drawer opened.

Then another.

Silverware clicked in neat, measured sounds.

Ethan was in the kitchen again, straightening things that don't need straightening, watching the house in his own quiet way. Every sound he made felt deliberate. Every sound carried a warning.

Olivia checked her bag twice.

English binder. History notes. Track shoes.

She pulled on her jacket, then left her bedroom door cracked open the way she always did when Ethan was home. Closed doors made him suspicious. Open ones made him feel in control.

Outside, the air felt cool and clean. Puddles shimmered along the sidewalk, catching thin strips of pale sky. Her shoes splashed through shallow water as she walked faster than usual. The smell of wet concrete rose around her. A car passed with a soft hiss of tires over rain.

Her phone buzzed in her pocket.

She braced before she looked.

Riley: Ride today? I can swing by after last period.

Olivia stared at the screen for a second. Riley was trying again like yesterday had not ended the way it did. Like maybe Olivia would make it easy for both of them this time.

She typed back.

Olivia: I'm good. See you at lunch.

Three dots appeared.

Then disappeared.

Before anything else came through, the phone buzzed again from a different thread.

Danny: Still breathing?

Olivia stopped walking.

The breeze lifted damp hair at the back of her neck. Her thumbs hovered over the keyboard longer than they should have. Then she typed before she could change her mind.

Olivia: Long night. Storm messed with practice.

She hit send.

She didn't mention Ethan.

She didn't mention the phone check.

She didn't mention that sleep only came after her body got too tired to keep fighting.

Olivia locked the screen and shoved the phone back into her pocket.

The morning pressed against her from every side as she kept walking toward Hollow's Edge High.

Hairline Cracks

School smelled like wet paper and bleach.

Umbrellas dripped into plastic bins near the entrance. Students dragged damp shoes through the halls, leaving thin tracks on the tile. Voices bounced off lockers in tired waves. The whole building felt a little swollen from the rain, as if even the walls had slept badly.

Olivia moved through it with her usual steady face.

Near the front office, she spotted Ms. Calhoun feeding papers into the copier. Olivia lowered her head at once and kept walking. She could feel the counselor's gaze brush over her anyway. It was never the loud kind attention that hurt. It was the careful kind. The kind that waited.

By first period, the hallway noise had dulled into the soft hum of class.

Ms. Porter moved between desks with a stack of revised poems in her arms. When she reached Olivia's table, she set the paper down facedown and rested her hand on it.

"Strong revision," she said softly. "You cut away the safe parts."

Olivia looked up.

Ms. Porter's expression stayed gentle, but her eyes were sharper than before.

"My door is still open," she said quietly. "That didn't change overnight."

Then she moved on before Olivia had to answer.

Olivia stared at the paper for a second, then slid it into her binder without checking the grade. Even that small kindness sat too close to the surface. Too close to everything she was trying not to feel.

By lunch, the halls had warmed with chatter again. Riley spotted her near the drink cooler and waved her over. She slid into the seat across from Olivia with a grin that looked real for half a second before worry broke through.

"You look like the storm slept in your eyes," Riley said.

Olivia unwrapped half her sandwich. "I'm fine. Just tired."

Riley gave her a look that said she didn't believe a word of it.

"You know you don't always have to be fine, right?"

Olivia picked at the edge of the wrapper. "I know."

"Do you?"

The question landed softer than it should have, which somehow made it hurt more.

Riley leaned back in her chair. "My mom works late tonight. You could come over after practice. We could order food, watch something stupid, and ignore the world for a while."

"I can't today."

Riley's face changed. Not anger. Not yet. Just that quick flash of disappointment she tried and failed to hide.

"You can't," she said slowly, "or he will not let you?"

Olivia went still.

Her fingers tightened around her milk carton. "I said I can't."

Riley looked down at her tray. When she spoke again, her voice had gone quieter.

"I'm not trying to start a fight."

"Then don't."

Riley let out a breath through her nose. "That's not fair."

Olivia said nothing.

For a moment, the noise around them seemed to pull farther away. All Olivia could hear was the scrape of a chair two tables over, the crackle of chip bags, the soft strain in Riley's voice when she spoke again.

"I'm trying here," Riley said. "You keep acting like I'm the one making this hard."

Guilt pressed hot and ugly behind Olivia's ribs.

Riley's mouth tightened. "I know something's wrong."

"Nothing's wrong."

"Olivia."

There was too much in the way Riley said her name. Too much history. Too much fear. Too much care that Olivia didn't know what to do with anymore.

Riley looked at her for another second, then gave a small nod like she understood something she didn't want to understand.

"Okay," she said. "Offer still stands. No questions. No pressure."

She paused, then added, quieter, "Just don't shut me out."

The bell rang before Olivia could answer.

She stood too fast, dumped her tray, and let the crowd carry her into the hallway. Laughter snapped around her in small bursts. It all sounded too bright. Too far away.

In history, Mr. Cole wrote across the board in quick, clean strokes.

Control promises safety. Pressure makes cracks.

He launched into a lesson on governments, fear, and the people who mistook control for order. Olivia barely heard any of it. Her eyes stayed locked on the board.

She copied the line into her notebook and underlined the word cracks until the paper softened under her pen.

Running in Place

After the final bell, Coach Rowland waited just inside the gym doors.

Rain had stopped, but the damp still clung to the air. The gym smelled like floor polish, rubber soles, and the faint trapped heat of an old building.

"Indoor drills today," he said. "Track's still too slick."

Olivia shifted the strap of her bag higher on her shoulder. "I can stay."

He studied her face.

"You don't have to."

"I know."

He nodded once and jerked his head toward the locker room. "Ten lap warm up. Then intervals."

The team was smaller than usual. A few girls had gone straight home after the storm. The rest moved though drills with tired eyes, damp ponytails, and quiet complaints. Someone groaned during stretches. Another girl laughed under her breath and told her to stop being dramatic.

Olivia welcomed the burn.

Sprint. Turn. Breathe.

Sprint. Turn. Breathe.

The ache in her legs was clean in a way nothing else was. It didn't ask questions. It didn't watch her. It didn't wait for a wrong answer. For forty minutes, her body belonged only to motion.

When Coach Rowland blew the whistle, Olivia bent forward with her hands on her knees and dragged air into her lungs.

"You alright?" he asked as the others drifted toward the benches.

She straightened too fast. "Yeah."

His eyes narrowed, but he let it go.

"Good work," he said instead. "You run like you're trying to outrun a fire."

Olivia gave him a ghost of a smile. "Maybe I am."

Something flickered across his face. Concern, maybe. Maybe recognition. But before he could say more, her phone buzzed.

The sound yanked her straight back into herself.

Ethan.

Of course.

She stepped away from the others and typed what he wanted.

Olivia: Practice over. Heading home.

The reply came almost at once.

Just two words.

Ethan: Straight home.

They still made her chest go tight.

Olivia locked the screen and shoved the phone into her pocket hard enough to sting.

The Edge of the Map

She didn't go straight home.

She only took one extra block, but it was enough to feel like a choice.

The air had turned colder by then. Puddles reflected a dull gray sky, broken every time her shoes stepped through them. Streetlights were beginning to hum awake, one by one.

The old laundromat came into view.

So did the mural painted on the brick wall beside it.

A pair of blue wings stretched across the faded surface, their color worn down by years of sun and weather. Paint curled at the tips like peeling feathers. Olivia stopped in front of them.

When she was younger, her mother used to take pictures there. Olivia would spread her arms wide and grin, certain the wings made her look lighter.

Now they just looked too high.

Too far above her shoulders.

Her phone buzzed.

Danny: Meet later? Ten minutes. The tracks.

Her pulse gave a hard, ugly jump.

The tracks.

That was where they met when neither of them wanted to be seen.

Olivia stared at the message while the sky darkened around her. Then she typed back.

Olivia: Not tonight.

She hit send and waited.

Three dots appeared.

Then vanished.

No reply.

The silence made her skin prickle.

She slipped the phone into her pocket and started walking again, faster this time. A car hit a puddle somewhere behind her, spraying water against the curb. She flinched hard enough to hate herself for it.

Then the phone buzzed again.

She stopped under a flickering streetlight, pulled out her phone, and looked at it.

Danny: I was already on my way.

For a second, her mind went blank.

Already on his way.

She turned toward the corner behind her, half expecting to see headlights. A truck. A shape moving through the fading light.

Nothing.

The street looked empty. Quiet. Harmless.

Still, the air felt tighter.

She typed with shaking fingers.

Olivia: Please don't. I'm heading home.

This time, no dots appeared.

The screen stayed dark.

By the time she reached her street, the porch light was already on even though the sun had not fully gone down. The yellow glow stretched across the yard in a thin warning line.

Inside, the TV murmured.

She could hear Ethan too. Not the words. Just the rise and fall of his voice blending with the steady tone of the newscaster. Everything in that house sounded measured. Controlled. Like he believed a calm voice could force the whole world into shape.

A folded note waited on the kitchen counter beside an empty coffee mug.

Dinner is in the fridge. Be smart. Love you, kiddo.

Olivia stood over it without moving.

The word love sat at the bottom like a dare.

She opened the fridge just to hear a different sound. Something mechanical. Something that didn't want anything from her. Cold air washed over her face. A leftover casserole sat inside under foil, untouched.

The hum followed her down the hall.

Later, after the house had gone still and the TV finally clicked off, Olivia lay awake in the dark beneath the slow spin of the ceiling fan.

The blades sliced the shadows into long, uneven bars across the ceiling.

Outside, a car took a corner too fast.

The gutter still dripped from somewhere beyond her window, steady and thin.

Her phone glowed beside her pillow.

She unlocked it and stared at the screen, half hoping for another message and half dreading it.

Nothing new.

Still, she could not shake the image of Danny by the tracks. Waiting. Phone in hand. Rainwater soaking into the gravel. Reading her message over and over with that tight look he got when things didn't go his way.

Or maybe he hadn't waited at all.

Maybe he had kept driving.

She opened a blank message and began to type.

He is watching closer. I think he wants proof that I will stay.

Her thumb hovered over the screen.

The longer she looked at the words, the less sure she was about who she meant.

Ethan.

Danny.

Or someone else entirely.

She deleted the message, locked the phone, and slid it beneath her pillow.

Sleep came slowly.

It crept in from the edges like fog, soft and patient, until her thoughts lost shape and her body finally gave up the fight.

Somewhere far away, thunder rolled again.

Faint. Familiar.

By the time it faded, the house was silent.

Chapter Seven

Denial is Easier

Fractures with Riley

The next day had dragged from the moment Olivia walked into school, and by lunch her nerves felt rubbed raw.

Trays slammed onto tables. Chairs scraped across the floor. Someone near the lunch line laughed so hard it cracked through the whole room. The air smelled like fryer grease, pizza sauce, and bleach. It should have felt normal. School always sounded like this at lunch. Today every sound seemed sharper, as if Olivia's nerves had lost whatever skin covered them.

She sat across from Riley with her sandwich still wrapped and her water bottle sweating onto the table between them. She had already peeled the corner of the wrapper open, then folded it shut again. Open. Fold. Her fingers kept moving like they belonged to someone else.

Riley watched them for a second before she said, "You're shutting me out."

Olivia kept her eyes on the wrapper. "I'm not."

The lie came out too flat. Even she heard it.

Riley leaned back in her chair, but the motion didn't make her look relaxed. Her shoulders stayed tense. Her jaw stayed tight. "You are," she said. "And you've been doing it for days."

Olivia made herself look up. "I've just had a lot going on."

"Yeah." Riley gave a small nod. "I noticed."

There was no sarcasm in it. That somehow made it worse.

Around them, people kept eating and talking and living like the table in the corner wasn't slowly coming apart. A carton of milk tipped over a few tables down. Someone cursed. A group by the vending machine burst into laughter. Olivia wanted to disappear into all of it. She wanted the room to swallow her whole.

Instead, Riley stayed right there, looking at her.

"You lie to teachers," Riley said. "You lie to me. And every time I try to help, you act like I'm the one making things harder."

"I never said that."

"You don't have to."

Riley's voice didn't rise. It stayed quiet and steady, which made every word land harder. She studied Olivia's face with that same awful care she always had, like she could see too much when she wanted to.

"You've never been this quiet," Riley said. "Not with me. You used to tell me things."

Olivia forced a smile that felt thin and wrong on her face. "You're reading into it."

Riley let out a breath and looked down for a second, like she was trying very hard not to say the next part the wrong way. When she looked back up, the hurt was easier to see.

"You think I don't notice?" she asked. "You slip away after school. You flinch every time your phone goes off. You look tired all the time. Not normal tired. Scared tired."

Olivia's stomach twisted so hard it hurt. She glanced around the cafeteria, suddenly sure someone had heard. No one was looking. That did not help.

"What people say," Riley went on, lower now, "I hear that too."

Olivia's head tilted. "What people?"

"Danny, for one."

His name hit like cold water.

Riley watched her reaction too closely to miss it. "I heard he's been talking. Saying you've been meeting up. Saying you owe him a chance to explain. What does that even mean?"

Olivia felt heat rise into her face. "He didn't say that."

"Maybe not like that," Riley said. "But close enough."

"He's not like that."

The defense came too fast. She knew it as soon as it left her mouth.

Riley's expression changed. Not triumph. Just more hurt. "You're defending him now."

"I'm saying you don't know him."

"No," Riley said. "I don't. But I know you."

That landed deeper than everything else.

Riley leaned in a little, keeping her voice low enough that it almost got lost under the cafeteria noise. "And I know what you do when you're scared. You pretend it's not real. You tell yourself if you stay quiet long enough, maybe it'll pass. Maybe if you act normal hard enough, whatever's wrong will get embarrassed and leave."

Olivia's hands had started trembling under the table. She pressed them into her lap and willed them still. "You don't understand."

"Then help me."

Riley said it so softly, Olivia almost wished she had yelled instead.

"Because right now," Riley continued, "I'm watching my best friend disappear a little more every day, and I don't know how to reach her anymore."

Olivia looked at her then.

Really looked.

Riley's face was open in a way it almost never was. The frustration was there, yes. So was the anger. But underneath both of them was something heavier. Fear. Not for herself. For Olivia. That made the guilt worse than if Riley had just snapped.

"You don't have to lie to me," Riley said.

Olivia swallowed hard. Her throat felt raw. For one second, the truth pushed up so hard she thought it might actually come out. Not all of it. Just enough.

He checks my phone.

He watches everything.

I'm so tired.

Instead, she heard herself say, "I'm not lying."

Riley went still.

It was such a small change, but Olivia felt it like a door closing.

The bell rang before either of them could say anything else. The sound cut across the room and sent people shoving trays aside and grabbing backpacks. Riley stood slowly. She slid her tray away and looked at Olivia like she was waiting for her to stop this. To take it back. To say one honest thing.

Olivia didn't.

Riley gave a tight nod that looked more like surrender than agreement. "Okay," she said quietly.

Then she picked up her bag and walked away.

Olivia stayed where she was, staring at the wet ring her water bottle had left on the table.

The seat across from her felt colder with Riley gone.

Alone at Lunch

The next day, Olivia sat alone.

She chose a table half hidden by a wide support column near the back of the cafeteria, far enough from the center to feel separate, close enough not to look suspicious. The room was just as loud as yesterday, maybe louder. It felt harsher without Riley there to cut through it.

Every laugh sounded sharper. Every shout from the lunch line hit too hard. The smell of melted cheese, ketchup, and industrial cleaner sat thick in the air. Someone dropped a tray nearby, and the crash made her jump before she could stop herself. A few heads turned. None of them stayed on her long.

Her tray sat untouched.

The fries had already gone limp. The fruit cup looked wet and bright in that fake way cafeteria fruit always did. Her sandwich was still wrapped. She told herself she would eat in a minute. Then another minute passed. Then another.

Across the room, Riley laughed at something one of the girls from track said.

The sound was real enough to hurt.

Olivia looked up before she meant to. Riley was standing near another table, one hand tucked around her drink, smiling at something somebody else had said. For a second their eyes met.

Riley's smile faltered.

Only a little. Barely enough to call it that.

Then she looked away.

Olivia felt the shift in her chest like something coming loose. She dropped her gaze to the table and told herself it was fine. Riley needed space. Maybe that was better. Maybe this was easier on both of them.

The thought didn't help.

She pulled out her phone.

Riley's name sat at the top of her messages, their last exchange still there. No new text. No are you okay? No I'm sorry. No one last try.

Below it, Danny's thread waited.

Still alive?

He's not worth it, Olivia.

Meet me. Just ten minutes.

Olivia stared at the screen until the letters blurred.

Her thumb hovered over the keyboard, then drifted instead to older messages. There were too many of them. Too many nights where his words had sounded like relief. Like he understood the pressure in her chest without making her explain it.

You're the only one who gets it.

I can't stop thinking about you.

I just want you safe.

Back then, the words had felt warm. Protective. Necessary.

Now they sat differently.

Too close. Too sure. Too willing to make themselves the center of her breathing.

She locked the screen and set the phone face down beside her tray.

For a second, all she saw was her own reflection in the black glass. Her eyes looked tired enough to belong to somebody older. Red at the edges. Hollowed out by too many thin nights and too many mornings that began before she was ready for them.

She had been having the dream again.

Running and running and never reaching the finish line.

Sometimes Ethan's voice followed her. Sometimes Riley's. Lately Danny stood at the end of the track too, one hand out like he was offering help, his face blurred by shadow.

The dream never told her which one to fear first.

A burst of laughter snapped somewhere behind her. A boy shoved his friend. Somebody started singing badly. The room kept going, loud and careless and full of people who still belonged to themselves.

Olivia looked down at the sandwich she had not touched.

She was hungry. That was the stupid part. She could feel it. The emptiness in her stomach. The weakness in her hands. But eating felt like work, and work required energy, and she had already spent too much of that just holding her face together.

By the time the bell rang, she had not taken a bite.

She packed up quickly, head down, tray barely disturbed, and slipped into the crowd before anyone could notice she had been sitting there alone the whole time.

No one stopped her.

No one called her name.

By the time she reached the hallway, the whole lunch period already felt unreal, like something she had watched happen to another girl from a distance.

Home Inspections

That evening, the house felt smaller than usual.

The kitchen light was too bright. The TV murmured from the living room, some anchor talking in a calm voice about something Olivia didn't hear. Ethan's boots crossed the kitchen tile in slow, heavy passes while she sat at the table with a history book open in front of her.

She had read the same paragraph four times.

Not one word stayed.

Ethan set his coffee mug down harder than he needed to. The sound made her flinch.

"Let me see your phone."

Olivia looked up. "Why?"

He turned toward her fully then. Not angry. Not yet. That careful, level look instead. The one that made her feel like she had already made a mistake and just had not found out which one.

"Because I asked."

The words were quiet. Final.

Her fingers hesitated around the phone before she slid it across the table. Ethan picked it up and unlocked it with practiced ease. Watching him hold it always did something ugly to her insides. It looked too natural in his hand. Too familiar.

He scrolled in silence.

Recent calls. Messages. Settings.

His thumb moved slow and steady, never rushed, which somehow made it worse. If he had been angry, if he had grabbed and demanded and snapped, she could have hated it cleanly. But Ethan did everything like it was reasonable. Like this was what care looked like. Like a good father checked.

When Danny's name appeared, his thumb stopped.

Olivia stopped breathing with him.

"Still talking to him?"

"No." The lie came out thin but steady. "He texts. I don't answer."

Ethan glanced up. "You're sure about that?"

She looked down at her hands. "Yes."

A long second passed.

Then another.

He set the phone on the table but kept one finger resting on it, like even that mattered. "He's bad news, Olivia."

She said nothing.

"You think I don't know what kind of boy he is?" Ethan asked. "I've seen boys like him my whole life. Fighting. Skipping. Looking for girls who feel lonely enough to mistake attention for love."

Olivia's throat tightened. "You don't know him."

"I don't have to."

His voice stayed calm. That calm always pressed harder than yelling. It filled the room and left no space for anything else.

"Trouble sticks to people like him," Ethan said. "And then it spreads. I won't have him dragging you down with him."

Olivia stared at the edge of her textbook until the line doubled. "I'll block him."

"You'll show me."

He slid the phone back toward her.

The screen lit up between them. Danny's name still sat there. One tap would do it. One clean cut. Ethan waited, not moving, his hand flat against the table.

"I'm protecting you," he said. "Riley doesn't understand. Danny doesn't care. I'm the one who keeps you safe."

The room was so quiet Olivia could hear the refrigerator hum.

She picked up the phone. Her thumb hovered over the screen while Ethan watched. For one second, she thought he might make her do it right there with him standing over her. Instead, he only waited.

"I know," she said softly, because agreeing was easier. Because agreement ended things faster. Because it was the answer he wanted.

Some of the tension went out of his shoulders at once.

"There you go." His mouth softened into something that almost looked kind. "Good girl."

The words crawled under her skin.

He stepped behind her chair and rested a hand on her shoulder. The touch stayed too long. Not firm enough to bruise. Not light enough to ignore. Just long enough to remind her he could touch any part of her life and call it care.

Then he squeezed once and walked away.

His boots crossed the room. The recliner creaked when he sat back down. The TV swallowed him again.

Olivia sat frozen at the table, the phone still in her hand.

The contact screen stayed open.

Block this caller.

Her thumb moved toward it.

Stopped.

Moved away.

After a few seconds, she locked the phone and slid it into the front pocket of her backpack instead. Out of sight. Not gone. Not answered either. Just hidden. Another thing she didn't know how to let go of.

Her textbook blurred in front of her.

She stayed at the table until the words stopped looking like words at all.

Slipping Further

Later that night, Olivia stood by her window with the glass cool against her cheek.

Outside, the streetlights buzzed softly. Moths circled the yellow glow in loose, stupid loops. Everything looked still enough to be peaceful, but the stillness felt wrong. Too still. Too balanced. Like the whole street had learned how to stand perfectly still and watch.

Her phone buzzed once on the sill beside her.

Danny again.

Still breathing?

She stared at the message, then typed back.

Yes.

She deleted it.

Then she typed again.

Stop worrying.

Deleted that too.

The screen stayed open in her hand, waiting for whatever honest thing might come next. Nothing did.

After a moment, she locked the phone and set it face down on the windowsill.

For a while she only looked at her own reflection in the glass. The faint outline of her face mixed with the light outside until she barely looked solid. Just pale features floating in the dark. Eyes too tired. Mouth set too tight. A girl becoming harder to recognize even to herself.

Riley's voice drifted back through her head.

He twists things to sound like the hero.

Then Danny's.

I'm the only one who's really on your side.

The worst part was that neither voice sounded fully wrong anymore.

She shut her eyes.

Memory came too easily after that. The first time Danny had really talked to her after practice. Rain tapping the metal overhang. His jacket damp at the shoulders. The way he had leaned against the bleachers and looked at her like he already knew the shape of her loneliness. He had not pushed then. He had just listened. Said Ethan sounded too hard on her. Said Riley didn't understand what it was like to live inside other people's rules.

At the time, that had felt like being seen.

Now, standing in the dark with his messages piling up and Riley farther away than she had ever been, Olivia couldn't stop turning the memory over. Looking at the seams. Wondering what had been comfort and what had always been a hook.

The guilt sat thick in her chest.

Riley had tried.

That was the part she could not get around. Riley had tried over and over, even when Olivia made it hard, even when Olivia lied, even when every answer she gave sounded like a door shutting. And still Riley had stayed until Olivia finally made staying hurt too much.

Olivia pressed her forehead harder against the window.

The relief of silence still hurt less.

That was the ugliest truth of it.

Silence meant no questions to answer. No eyes trying to search past her face. No chance of saying the wrong thing and making everything worse. Silence didn't fix anything, but it bought a little room. A little numbness. A little delay.

Denial was easier.

She crawled into bed without turning off the lamp. The sheets felt cold in the heavy, deep way that never warmed right away. She pulled the blanket up and stared at the ceiling.

The fan turned in slow circles over her head.

She thought about unlocking the phone again. About reading Danny's messages one more time without answering them. About texting Riley something small and stupid and easy, just to prove the distance between them was not final yet.

Her hand twitched once on top of the blanket.

Then stayed still.

Because sending either message would mean choosing.

And Olivia didn't feel brave enough for choices tonight.

So she lay there and let the room stay exactly as it was. Lamp on. Phone dark. Window throwing a weak square of light across the floor. Her whole life narrowed down to the quiet space between one heartbeat and the next.

When sleep finally came, it didn't feel like rest.

It felt like giving something up.

And even as she drifted under, Olivia knew what it was.

Not Danny.

Not yet. Riley.

That hurt enough to keep her half awake for one last minute in the dark.

Chapter Eight

The Pull of Control

Lines in the Gravel

Morning came gray and slow.

Olivia told herself she would stay home. She told herself she would keep her head down, stay quiet, and let the day pass without making anything worse. But the hours dragged. By afternoon, the silence in the house felt too heavy to sit inside. Her father was gone, the TV was off, and every room seemed to wait for something.

She left before she could talk herself out of it.

The road to the tracks had become familiar in the worst way. It was the kind of path her body knew before her mind caught up. One turn. Then another. Then the broken stretch of gravel and weeds that led toward the yard.

The train yard smelled like wet metal and crushed stone. Water sat in shallow dips between the rails, each pool holding a dull gray patch of sky. Rust streaked the old boxcars. Somewhere beyond the fence, a train moved with a low distant rumble that seemed to press up through the ground.

Danny waited near a tilted boxcar with his arms folded.

Mist had dampened his hair and darkened the shoulders of his jacket. He looked like he had been standing there a while, watching the road she always took in.

For a moment, neither of them spoke.

Olivia kept her hood pulled close and stared at the space between them. Her breath came pale in the cold air. Even here, with nobody close enough to hear, she felt exposed.

Danny was the one who broke the silence.

"You went quiet again."

His voice was low. Careful.

"I had to," she said. "He checks everything now."

Something in Danny's face hardened. "That's insane."

Olivia gave a small shrug that held no real feeling behind it. "It doesn't matter if it is."

Danny pushed off the boxcar and came closer. Gravel crunched under his boots. He stopped a few feet away, close enough that she could smell damp air and the faint clean scent of soap on his jacket.

"Then leave," he said.

She looked up at him. "What?"

"Right now." His eyes stayed on hers. "I mean it. I've got cash. Gas. Blankets in the truck. If we have to sleep in the back for a night, we sleep in the back. If we find some cheap motel outside town, fine. Just one night somewhere he can't get to you."

The picture came too quickly.

Headlights on an empty road. A locked motel room with thin curtains and bad carpet. A bed she could sleep in without listening for footsteps on the stairs. A night where nobody asked where she had been or how long she had taken.

For one dangerous second, she could almost feel it.

Danny saw the hesitation in her face and stepped into it.

"You would not have to figure everything out tonight," he said gently. "You'd only have to get in the truck. I'd handle the rest."

The words should have comforted her.

Instead, something in her chest pulled tight.

Not because he sounded cruel. He didn't. He sounded certain. Warm. Ready.

That was what scared her.

"And then what?" she asked quietly.

"Then we keep going until this place is behind you."

Behind you.

Not behind us.

Olivia looked away from him and toward the rails. They stretched off in both directions, cold and straight and endless. For a second she imagined herself climbing into his truck and shutting the door before she could think too hard about it.

Then her father's voice rose in her head. Calm. Firm. Certain. Telling her that safety meant staying close. Staying home. Staying where he could protect her.

"I can't," she whispered.

Danny exhaled through his nose and turned away for a few steps. He paced once, then came back, trying to wear his frustration down before it showed too clearly.

"You keep waiting for the perfect moment," he said. "There is no perfect moment, Olivia. You know that, right? By the time you think you're ready, he's going to have every part of your life locked down."

His words hit because too much of them felt true.

She wanted to tell him he didn't understand. That leaving was not just leaving. It would mean aftermath. Questions. Anger. Consequences that would not stop at her.

But part of her had already leaned toward the truck.

That was the part she hated.

Danny came a little closer again. "You don't have to live like this," he said. "You don't need him making every choice for you." his voice softened even more, "And you don't need Riley filling your head with more fear either. You have me."

The words landed wrong.

Soft on the surface. Heavy underneath.

He was smiling, but his eyes stayed too still. Too fixed. There was no room in them for doubt. No room for anything except the answer he wanted.

Olivia took a small step back. "I should go home."

Danny's hand twitched at his side as if he almost reached for her and stopped himself. When he spoke again, his voice was calm.

"Okay."

But the word didn't sound like agreement. It sounded like patience.

Olivia turned before he could say anything else. She started down the gravel path, counting ties and broken stones beneath her shoes so she would not look back too soon.

She still did.

Danny had not moved.

He stood where she left him, watching her with that same unreadable stillness. His hands opened once, then closed again.

Then Olivia faced forward and kept walking.

Family Settings

By the time Olivia reached the house, the sky had dimmed to the color of iron.

Ethan's truck was already in the driveway, parked straight and close to the porch. The light above the door burned early, throwing yellow across the wet steps. Inside, the TV filled the silence with voices that never stopped talking.

Olivia paused at the door before going in.

The heaviness in her stomach had already started. The kind that warned her to keep her face blank, her answers short, and her movements quiet.

Ethan sat in his recliner with the remote in one hand. The blue glow of the TV washed his face pale.

"You're late."

"Coach kept us," she said. "Indoor drills."

His eyes moved to her then, cool and unreadable.

"For how long?"

She slipped her backpack from her shoulder and set it carefully by the wall. "A while."

He let the silence stretch just long enough for her to feel it.

Then he said, "You'll do your homework at the table."

Olivia nodded.

"And your door stays open upstairs."

"Okay."

He turned his attention back to the TV, but not fully. He never did. She could feel it in the way the room held her, as if even his silence had rules inside it.

She moved to the kitchen table and spread her books into neat rows, lining up the corners so her hands had something to do. The page in front of her blurred once, then steadied. She read the same sentence three times without keeping any of it.

Behind her, the news rolled into weather. A blue light flashed across the walls. Ethan barely moved.

Her phone sat beside her workbook, dark and silent.

Even that felt like a rule now.

Her pen hovered over the page without moving. She wanted to check the screen anyway. Wanted to see whether Riley had sent anything. Wanted to know whether the world outside this house still remembered she existed when she was not in front of it. Instead, she kept staring at the same unfinished sentence while Ethan sat behind her, quiet as a locked door.

Rooms Out of Place

Later, when the dishes were done and the house had settled into its late quiet, Olivia climbed the stairs.

Something felt wrong before she even reached her room.

The air upstairs had changed. It smelled stale, faintly sweet, like dust disturbed by movement and then left to settle again. She slowed at the doorway.

At first glance, everything looked normal.

That made it worse.

The lamp sat on the desk. The curtains were drawn. Her bed was still made.

But the lamp had been nudged slightly left. The curtain edge was tucked too neatly on one side and loose on the other. The top drawer of her desk sat open by less than an inch, like someone had shoved it closed too fast and walked away believing that was enough.

Olivia stepped inside without taking a full breath.

Her skin had already gone cold.

She crossed to the desk and pulled the drawer open. It caught halfway, then gave. Inside, her notebooks were stacked in the wrong order. The blue one should have been on top. It wasn't. The loose pens had been gathered near the corner instead of scattered the way she always left them.

Someone had gone through this.

The thought moved through her like ice water.

She looked toward the bed.

Then the vent.

Her heartbeat turned loud and uneven as she dropped to her knees on the floor and reached for the opening. The screws looked untouched. Tight. Exactly where they should be. Her fingers still shook as she slid two of them through the narrow slots.

Cool metal.

Then paper.

The hidden edge of the journal touched her finger.

Relief came so fast it almost hurt.

It was still there.

Still sealed in darkness. Still hers.

But the relief didn't last.

When she stood, something white on the desk caught her eye.

A single sheet of paper.

Blank except for the object resting in the center.

A house key.

Olivia stared at it without moving.

Then she stepped closer.

Her name had been scratched into the metal in deep ugly letters. O L I V I A. Not written. Carved. The grooves looked rough, as if whoever did it had pressed hard enough to enjoy the sound.

Her breath shortened at once.

The room seemed to tilt around the edges.

Whoever left it there had wanted her to find it. Not tomorrow. Not by accident. They had wanted her standing exactly where she was now, looking down at proof that even this room no longer belonged only to her.

She thought of Ethan first. His calm voice. His rules. The way he moved through her life as if every door, every choice, every silence should pass through him before it reached her.

Then Danny rose behind that thought, quieter but harder to shake. The way he had said. *'You have me'*. The certainty in his voice. The fixed look in his eyes when he talked about leaving, as if all roads should end with him.

Either one could call it protection.

Either one could mean ownership.

Olivia reached for the key and nearly missed it because her hand was shaking so badly. The metal felt colder than it should have. She turned it once between her fingers, then set it back down almost at once, like touching it too long might mean agreeing to something she didn't understand.

A tight sound slipped out of her throat.

Not quite a gasp. Not quite a sob.

She sat on the edge of the bed and stared at the desk until the letters in her name blurred. The room darkened by slow degrees around her. Shadows thickened in the corners. Somewhere downstairs, the TV kept talking in the same steady voice, unaware or pretending to be.

Olivia didn't cry.

She barely moved.

She only sat there with her hands locked together between her knees and breathed as quietly as she could, as if the room itself might still be listening.

The Word She Does Not Send

The house creaked as it cooled.

Pipes ticked inside the walls. The hallway floor gave one long sigh. Wind brushed against the siding in slow passes that sounded almost like fingers trailing over wood.

Olivia lay on top of the blanket with her phone glowing in her hands.

She opened the old thread anyway.

Danny's name still sat near the top; above the last message he had sent before everything tightened further around her. She stared at the empty space beneath it for a long time before her thumb finally moved.

No.

The word appeared on the screen.

Small. Bare. Too honest.

She looked at it until her throat tightened, then deleted it.

She tried again.

I'm fine.

That one looked even worse.

She erased it too.

Her thumb drifted down to Riley's name.

For a moment, she only stared.

Riley's face came back with painful clarity. The way she had leaned across the lunch table. The way hurt had shown so plainly when Olivia lied to her. The way she kept offering the same thing in different forms. A ride. A couch. A place to breathe. A chance to say something true.

Just don't shut me out.

Olivia could almost hear the words.

Her chest tightened hard enough to sting.

She locked the screen and set the phone face down on the bed beside her.

The silence that followed felt heavier than the words had.

She turned onto her side and stared at the far wall, but her body refused to settle. Every muscle held a little too much tension. Her mind kept circling the same things. Danny at the tracks. Ethan downstairs. The key on the desk. Riley's face.

Outside, the wind pressed once against the window. Somewhere under the floorboards, the house shifted.

She told herself it was only wood. Only pipes. Only old walls settling into night.

But the room no longer felt like a room.

It felt like a place something had entered and left changed behind it.

Exhaustion ached through her bones, yet sleep still held back. When it finally came, it didn't come gently.

She was running.

Bare feet on cold gravel. The train yard stretched around her, endless and silver beneath a sky with no color in it. Rails split apart and crossed and bent away in every direction, too many paths and none of them clear.

Someone was calling her name.

At first, it was Danny.

Then Ethan.

Then both of them at once.

Their voices layered over each other until they became one sound, low and close and impossible to place.

"Olivia."

She tried to answer.

Nothing came out but a thin whisper that the wind took immediately.

Ahead, a single light flickered. Faint and orange. Like a porch lamp. Like home from a distance. Like a trap when she looked at it too long.

She moved toward it anyway.

The gravel shifted beneath her feet. Then softened. Then dragged. Each step pulled harder than the last until it felt like she was running through wet earth. The voices behind her grew closer.

"Olivia."

"You're safe now."

The words wrapped around each other so completely she could no longer tell who was saying them.

She woke with her heart racing and her throat dry.

For a second she didn't know where she was.

Then the room came back. The ceiling. The weak line of hallway light slipping through the open door. The quiet hum of the house. The shape of her desk in the dark.

The key caught the light first.

It gleamed faintly from the paper where she had left it, small and sharp and waiting.

Olivia pulled the blanket to her chin and turned her face toward the wall, but she could still feel it there.

Not just the key. The message in it.

The house stayed still.

She didn't.

Chapter Nine

Tighter Circles

Morning Rules

The room was pale with early light when Olivia woke. For a moment she couldn't tell if the sound in her ears was rain or her own pulse. The train yard drifted through her mind in broken pieces. Gravel under her shoes. Danny's voice. The feel of cold metal pressed into her palm.

A key.

Her name carved into it.

She lay still for a second longer, staring at the ceiling while the memory settled over her skin. The letters had looked rough, cut by hand, not clean or careful. It should have felt small. Instead, it had stayed with her all night, as if the weight of it had outgrown the metal.

Downstairs, the house smelled of bitter coffee and wet earth. Ethan stood at the counter with a mug in one hand and his phone beside him. The morning news filled the kitchen with talk of flooding and traffic delays.

"The app is set," he said. "Family Safety. It shows me where you are."

"I need check ins," he continued. "Lunch. Practice. Home. No exceptions."

"Okay," she said. Her voice barely carried.

"Keys." He held out his hand.

She froze for half a beat before reaching into her pocket for the house key. The metal felt colder than it should have. She laid it in his palm and watched his fingers close around it.

He turned it over once, then again, like he was studying something more than a key. The little scrape near the teeth. The worn edge of the head. Ordinary marks. Proof it had passed through her hands, even if it had never really belonged to her.

"I'll make a copy," he said. "For safety."

She almost said he already had one. She almost said this one only opened the door because he allowed it to. But the words stayed where they were.

He set the key beside his phone.

For one brief second, the image split in her mind. Her plain house key on the counter. The other key from yesterday, the one with her name carved into it like a secret. One opened the door she was expected to return to. The other felt like something else entirely. Not freedom. Not safety. Just another hand reaching for her.

He picked up her phone and started checking settings one by one. "You keep this on. Answer when I call."

He spoke each rule as if placing bricks in a wall. "Phone stays on the kitchen charger at night. You ask to use it."

She nodded. "I have practice after school."

"Text when it starts. Text when you leave."

"Okay."

He leaned down, brushed her back, and kissed the top of her head. "Good girl."

The words clung to her skin. She grabbed her backpack and slipped into her hoodie. As she left, her eyes caught on the key still sitting by his phone.

It struck her then, hard and simple.

In this house, even the way in and out passed through his hand first.

She left without finishing breakfast. The drizzle outside was thin and cold. She didn't look back when the door closed behind her.

What Friends See

School lights always seemed too bright after a morning like that. The halls hummed with locker doors, sneakers, and voices that felt louder than they should have. Olivia moved through it all with her shoulders tight, as if one wrong look might split her open.

Ms. Porter paused beside her desk before class began.

"You look tired," she said softly. "If you need a quiet place, my door is always open."

"Thank you," Olivia answered, folding the words into herself like something fragile she didn't know how to use.

At lunch she sat at the edge of their usual table, tracing the damp ring her water bottle had left on the plastic. Riley slid her tray aside and leaned forward.

"Can we reset?" she asked. "You don't have to pretend with me."

"I'm fine."

The lie sat heavy in Olivia's mouth. Riley heard it anyway.

"Fine isn't the same as safe," she said. Her voice stayed calm, but her eyes didn't leave Olivia's face.

Olivia glanced toward the cafeteria doors, then back down.

Riley looked around once, making sure no one was paying attention. Then she reached into her pocket and placed a small brass key between them.

"My place," she said quietly. "Anytime. No questions."

Olivia stared at it.

It was such a simple thing. Small. Dull at the edges. Warm from Riley's pocket.

Not carved.

Not presented like a promise.

Not held over her like a rule.

Just offered.

Something in her chest tightened so fast it almost hurt. She curled her fingers around it and felt the solid little shape settle into her palm. Metal. Weight. Choice.

No one had handed her a key like that before.

Not to watch her. Not to test her. Not to make her prove where she had been.

This one asked nothing from her at all.

Her hand trembled as she slipped it into her pocket. For a second she thought of all three keys at once. The house key Ethan used to remind her where she belonged. The carved key she had found on her desk, her name cut into it with unsettling care. And now this one, plain and quiet in her pocket, which somehow felt the most dangerous of all because part of her wanted what it offered.

Outside, rain pressed against the windows in gray streaks. Through the glass she caught a shape she almost recognized, a dark truck parked near the library steps. She blinked, and it disappeared behind passing cars.

Riley followed her stare. "Isn't that Danny's truck?"

Olivia forced a smile. "He probably just had errands."

Riley didn't answer right away. Her expression softened into concern. "Just be careful."

The bell broke the moment. As they gathered their trays, Olivia's phone buzzed in her pocket.

Danny: Tracks after school. Ten minutes. Please.

She typed, erased, then typed again.

I can't today. He's watching closer now.

Three dots appeared, then vanished. No reply came. Still, when Olivia looked back toward the windows, the parking lot beyond the rain streaked glass seemed to be watching her anyway.

Out of Reach

After the last bell, her phone lit with a message from Ethan.

Stop by the shop. Need a hand. Then home.

The garage smelled of oil, rubber, and rain soaked concrete. Water tracked across the floor in dull streaks beneath the lifts. A fan hummed near the back wall, pushing air that carried grit against her shoes. Somewhere deeper in the bay, metal clinked against metal. The sound made her shoulders pull tight.

"Floor's filthy," Ethan said as soon as she stepped in. His eyes dropped to her backpack. "Give me that."

She hesitated only a second before slipping it off her shoulder.

He took it from her and walked it into the small office off the bay. Instead of setting it by the chair beside her, he placed it on top of the tall file cabinet near the back wall, higher than she could reach without dragging over a chair.

"I'll put it there," he said. "Keep it out of the dirt."

Olivia stood in the doorway for a beat longer than she meant to. He opened a thin binder on the desk and handed it to her.

"Read this while I check inventory."

The binder held order sheets and supplier lists. Page after page of numbers. Her eyes moved over them without taking anything in.

Roy, the older mechanic, rolled a tire past the doorway and nodded without speaking. The radio near the tool bench played low country music through a layer of static. Ethan moved through the shelves with the kind of neatness that never felt calm. Every bin lined up. Every label straight. Every drawer shut all the way.

She kept pretending to read.

From the office, she could hear him crossing back and forth between the shelves and bench. Once, she heard the soft scrape of the file cabinet behind her. Then she heard the light click of a zipper. So quiet she almost thought she imagined it.

When she glanced over her shoulder, Ethan was in the office with his back to her, one hand resting near the top of the cabinet where her backpack sat. He looked up at once.

"Stay focused," he said.

"Sorry."

He gave her a small smile that didn't reach his eyes and went back into the shop.

Olivia looked down at the binder again. The page blurred. She told herself it meant nothing. He had probably shifted the bag to make room. Maybe checked for her phone. Maybe nothing at all.

Still, she couldn't shake the feeling that he had touched it longer than he needed to.

When her phone lit on the desk a few minutes later, Ethan's head turned almost before the screen had fully brightened.

"You texted at lunch," he said. "Good girl. Keep that up."

Her throat tightened. "Do you need anything else?"

He wiped his hands on a rag. "Just your attention. Then go home."

By the time he finally handed her backpack back, his grip stayed on the strap a second too long before letting go. Then he gave it a casual pat, almost gentle.

"Homework at the table," he said. "Curfew still stands."

She slipped the strap over her shoulder. The bag felt the same.

Maybe.

Still, something about it sat wrong against her back, as if the shape had changed in a place she couldn't name.

She stepped into the evening air with the smell of the shop clinging to her clothes. Across the street, for one brief second, she thought she saw Danny's truck rolling past. Headlights washed over the curb and were gone.

Pins in the Map

The house was quiet that night. Only the ticking clock filled the space between Olivia's breaths. She spread her books across the kitchen table and pretended to read while Ethan moved through the house in slow, steady patterns. His footsteps passed down the hall. A cabinet opened. Closed. The TV murmured from the living room.

She reached into her backpack for a pen.

Her fingers caught on something they didn't recognize.

She stopped.

The inside lining felt wrong beneath her hand. Too stiff in one spot. Too flat. The shift was small, but once she felt it, she couldn't unfelt it.

A cold thread moved up her arm.

Very carefully, she pressed her thumb to the place again. There. Hidden between layers of fabric. Something thin and hard, tucked where it was never supposed to be.

The kitchen suddenly felt smaller.

She glanced toward the hall, listening. No footsteps. No voice.

Using the edge of her nail, she eased at the seam from the inside. The fabric gave just enough.

Something thin and square sat buried in the lining, smooth and flat, no larger than a coin.

For a second her mind emptied.

Then the feeling hit.

Not surprise. Not exactly.

Violation.

The kind that went deeper because it had been done quietly. Carefully. While she had been close enough to hear him breathing and still had not known.

Her stomach turned. She thought of the shop. The office. Her backpack set high on the file cabinet. The faint zipper sound. Ethan's hand resting near the top as if that were the most normal thing in the world.

Her mind reached for him first. It should have stopped there.

But it didn't.

Danny at the library steps. Danny waiting at the tracks. Danny showing up where she had never quite told him to be.

I'd find you anywhere.

The memory moved through her like dirty water.

She stared at the square until her vision blurred. It was small enough to hide. Small enough to forget about, if that was the point. Not a warning. Not something meant to be found. Something meant to stay close to her without her knowing.

Footsteps creaked in the hall.

Olivia pressed the lining flat at once and pulled her hand free. She straightened the open textbook just as Ethan appeared in the doorway.

"How's the work?" he asked.

"Good," she said.

He nodded, his face unreadable in the kitchen light. "Don't stay up."

Then he was gone again.

She sat very still until his steps faded up the stairs.

Only then did she slide the backpack off her lap and lower it carefully under the chair, as if it might react to rough hands. Her own skin felt unfamiliar. Touched in some place no one should have reached.

Her phone chimed once on the counter.

Riley: I'm home. Doors unlocked until midnight.

Olivia stared at the message.

In her mind, she felt the shape of Riley's key in her pocket. Warm from another hand. Freely given.

Then she looked down at the backpack under the table and thought of hidden things. Of doors. Of who got to come through without being invited.

She reached for the phone.

Stopped.

Then set it face down beside her books.

Upstairs, she left her bedroom door open a hand's width. Sleep didn't come easy. When it did, it pulled her under like a slow tide.

Library Steps

The next day brought a dull sky and wind that smelled of wet leaves. Practice ended early, the coach letting everyone go when the rain picked up again. Olivia waited until the rest of the team left the field before glancing at her phone.

4:25 p.m.

She knew practice was supposed to last until five. Ethan expected a message when it ended. If she timed it right, she could still walk home at the usual pace and be there when he thought she should be.

She typed a message.

Olivia: Practice wrapping up now. Heading home soon.

Then she slipped her phone into her pocket, heart beating quick but steady. It wasn't really lying. Just managing time.

The sidewalks shimmered with puddles as she passed the side of the library. She slowed when she saw him—Danny—leaning against his truck near the steps. His hands were buried in his jacket pockets, shoulders relaxed, eyes fixed on her as if he'd been waiting all along.

She hesitated. "Danny? What are you doing here?"

Her fingers brushed the key in her pocket before she even meant to move. Riley's, not his. The small shape steadied her for half a second, then did nothing more.

He smiled. "Was just driving by. Lucky timing."

"I didn't tell you I'd be here."

"I know." He shrugged. "Guess I got lucky twice."

Something about his tone made her stomach tighten. Still, she stepped closer, scanning the street for anyone she knew. A few students passed without looking their way.

He reached for her hand but stopped short. "You've been quiet. Everything okay?"

"Things are...complicated."

"I can tell. He's still keeping you on a leash, huh?" His eyes narrowed slightly. "That's what guys like him do. They make sure no one gets close."

Olivia folded her arms. "You don't know him."

"I know what I see." His voice softened again. "You don't have to hide when you're with me."

She glanced toward the school. "Someone could see us."

"Then don't tell anyone we met," he said. The words came smooth, gentle, but they left a chill behind. "They wouldn't understand."

Before she could answer, Riley's voice cut through the air. "Olivia!" Riley jogged up from the sidewalk, breath visible in the cold. Her eyes flicked to Danny, then back.

"Didn't know you were getting picked up," she said.

"I wasn't," Olivia replied too quickly.

Danny gave a polite nod. "Hey, Riley."

Riley returned the nod but didn't smile. "Well, see you later, Liv." Her look lingered a second longer, a silent question Olivia didn't know how to answer.

When Riley walked away, Danny exhaled slowly. "She doesn't like me much."

"She doesn't really know you."

"Maybe." He smiled again, small and almost sad. "I just don't want anyone keeping us apart."

Olivia shifted her bag on her shoulder. "I should get home."

"I'll walk you halfway," he said.

They moved down the sidewalk together, quiet except for their steps and the sound of wind pushing through trees. Near the corner where the houses began, he stopped.

"Message me when you get home," he said. "Promise?"

She nodded. "I will."

He reached up as if to brush a strand of hair from her face but let his hand fall. "Good. I like knowing you're safe."

Circles Closing

The house smelled faintly of soap and motor oil. Olivia slipped off her shoes by the door, careful not to track water inside. She had texted Ethan earlier: *Practice wrapping up now. Heading home soon.*

Still, his voice met her before she could take another step. "You're late."

Her stomach dropped. "Practice ran over," she said softly.

He didn't look at her. The glow from the TV painted his face in dull light. "You know the rules."

"I do."

Ethan nodded once, slow and deliberate, before turning back to the screen. The low hum of the newscaster filled the silence; words lost under the sound of her heartbeat.

Olivia set her backpack near the table and crossed to the counter. Her hands felt unsteady as she plugged her phone into the kitchen charger. The screen lit briefly, showing her own reflection.

She turned toward the window over the sink, parting the curtain with two fingers. The house key sat on the ring by the door. Riley's key rested in her hoodie pocket. One waited in plain sight. One stayed hidden against her side. Olivia wasn't sure which one felt safer anymore.

The street was empty except for the puddles shining under the porch light.

Her phone buzzed, making her jump.

Danny: I asked for you to message me when you got home.

Her throat dried. Through the narrow slit in the curtain, a faint red glow flickered—taillights easing away from the curb, slowing just before they turned the corner. Her breath caught.

"Something outside?" Ethan's voice came from behind her.

Olivia spun, heart hammering. "No," she said quickly.

He stood a few steps away, the blue light of the TV flickering over his face. His gaze moved from her to the window, then to the glowing phone on the counter.

"Lock up soon," he said.

"I will."

He lingered a beat longer, then turned toward the hallway. His footsteps creaked on the stairs until the sound faded.

Olivia's shoulders sagged. She watched the phone screen dim, the faint reflection of her face fading with it. The kitchen felt colder now, smaller somehow.

Outside, another car passed, its headlights sweeping across the window before vanishing down the street. She didn't look this time. Her eyes stayed on the dark glass, waiting for her heartbeat to slow, wondering which of them had drawn the tighter circle around her life tonight.

Part II

What's Left Behind

Chapter Ten

The Distance Between

What Riley Sees

Riley knew something was wrong before first period even started.

She saw Olivia halfway down the hall and straightened without meaning to. Olivia usually moved with purpose, even on tired days. This morning, every step looked measured, like she was checking where to place her feet before trusting the floor. She kept her eyes down and slipped past clusters of students without brushing against anyone.

A teacher called her name in passing.

Olivia glanced over and kept walking.

Riley stayed where she was for one more second, then followed.

At her locker, Olivia didn't stop. At the corner by the office, she almost turned too soon, corrected herself, and kept going. By the time they reached English, Riley already had that tight, helpless feeling in her chest she hated most, the one that came when you knew something was wrong and had no clean way to reach it.

She took the desk beside Olivia just before the bell.

Ms. Porter started class with a discussion on control. She talked about how people revealed themselves in quiet moments, not loud ones. How fear changed the choices a person thought they had. Most of the class looked half asleep. A few kids pretended to take notes. Olivia stared at her notebook and moved her pen in slow, distracted loops.

Riley leaned a little.

They were not notes.

Not words either.

Just circles. One inside another. Then another pressed over the first hard enough to darken the page.

When the bell rang, Olivia closed the notebook too fast and stood.

Riley caught up with her at the door. "Walk with me."

Olivia's eyes went straight to the clock. "I have class."

"You have five minutes."

Olivia looked ready to refuse. Riley saw it happen in her face, the instinct to pull away before anyone could ask too much. Then Olivia nodded once.

They took the longer route by the library and stopped near the stairwell window, where the passing traffic from the halls thinned out. Outside, students crossed the lot in twos and threes, backpacks swinging, voices carrying through the glass.

Riley turned to face her fully. "You still have my key?"

Olivia's fingers brushed her hoodie pocket before dropping away. "Yeah."

"That wasn't me just being nice for one second." Riley kept her voice steady. "I meant it. You can come over any time. Late. Early. Middle of the night. My mom will not ask any questions."

Olivia's mouth tightened. She looked out toward the parking lot instead of at Riley. "Okay."

Riley studied her for a beat, then asked the question she had been carrying for days.

"Are you safe at home?"

Olivia didn't answer right away. Her lips parted, closed, then pressed together. When she finally spoke, her voice sounded small and scraped thin.

"I have rules now."

Riley waited.

"I have to text when I get home. When I leave. If I stay somewhere too long." Olivia swallowed. "He tracks my phone."

Riley felt her whole body sharpen.

"He can see where you are?"

Olivia nodded.

"For real, not just checking messages?"

Another nod.

Riley looked down the empty stretch of hall and forced herself to think instead of reacting. "Leave it with me after school. Just for an hour. I'll keep it on. Same battery. Same place. Then I'll bring it back."

"I can't."

"He won't know if we're careful."

Olivia turned to her then, and Riley saw how close to the edge she really was. "He notices everything."

The words came out so flat they scared her more than tears would have.

Riley lifted a hand like she might touch Olivia's arm, then stopped. She didn't know what would feel like comfort anymore and what would feel like pressure.

"Then listen to me," she said quietly. "If something changes, if it gets worse, if you get even one chance, text me one word."

Olivia blinked at her. "What word?"

"Run."

For the first time that morning, something real moved across Olivia's face. Fear, yes. But also relief. Like hearing a door open somewhere you had forgotten there was a door at all.

The warning bell rang.

Students started pouring from classrooms nearby, voices swelling back into the space around them. Olivia stepped back at once, pulling herself shut.

Riley caught her wrist lightly before she could turn away. "I mean it."

Olivia looked at her, eyes bright. "I know."

Then she slipped into the crowd and was gone.

Riley stayed there a second longer, staring after her.

Run.

It had sounded simple when she said it.

Now it felt like a promise she had no idea how to keep.

Danny Refuses Quiet

The last bell had barely finished ringing when students spilled into the back lot.

Danny stood by the fence with his hands in his pockets and watched the doors. Someone shouted across the row of parked cars. A truck engine coughed twice before starting. A group of freshmen cut through the lot too fast, laughing at something on one of their phones.

Then Olivia came out.

She held her backpack close to her side and moved with the kind of focus that was really fear dressed up as control. Danny fell into step behind her, keeping enough distance not to draw attention.

When she reached the quieter end of the lot, he called her name.

She stopped, but only because pretending not to hear would have made things worse.

"Ten minutes at the tracks," he said when she turned. "You don't have to talk. You just need air."

"I can't."

"I'll drive you back."

"I still can't."

He took a step closer. "You can text from my truck. He'll never know."

That made something harden in her face.

"Please stop." She tightened her grip on the strap of her backpack. "I have to be home. I have to be seen."

Danny lifted his hands in surrender. "I'm trying to help."

"Then help by listening."

The answer hit clean and sharp. He went still for half a second.

A couple of students walked between them on their way to the far row of cars. Danny waited until they passed before speaking again. When he did, his tone had changed. Softer. Lower. More careful.

"You have my number and Riley's key." He watched her face closely. "That's two ways out. At some point, you have to choose one."

Olivia froze.

The phone in her hand suddenly felt too heavy. Riley's key. She had never said that out loud. Not to him. Not to anyone who might have repeated it back.

"How do you know about that?"

Danny gave a small shrug. "People notice things."

"What people?"

"The people who pay attention when someone starts disappearing in front of them."

It was the sort of answer that sounded meaningful until you looked at it too long. Then it turned slippery.

Olivia took a step back.

Danny saw it and softened his face at once. "I'm not trying to scare you."

"You already did."

For the first time, the hurt on his face looked thin enough for something uglier to show through beneath it. It vanished almost right away, but she caught it.

He breathed out and reset himself. "Olivia, I'm the one standing here telling you the truth."

"No." Her voice shook, but she held his eyes. "You're standing here telling me what I should do."

He stared at her for a moment, jaw tight.

Then he said quietly, "He's shrinking your world one rule at a time."

Her gaze dropped to her phone screen. The text window sat open. Her fingers hovered over it.

"I know," she said.

This time the words didn't sound defensive. They sounded tired. Defeated. Like she hated that he was right about any part of it.

She started typing her check in.

Danny watched the glow from the screen light her fingertips. "You don't have to keep doing this."

She hit send and locked the phone. "I have to go."

"Because he said so?"

She looked at him, and for a second, he thought she might answer. Instead, she shook her head once and turned away.

She crossed the lot quickly, not running, not looking back, moving with the careful control of someone who could feel eyes on her even after the distance should have made her safe.

Danny stayed where he was until she disappeared behind a row of cars.

Then he pulled out his phone and typed.

I'm here if you blink.

He sent it and stared at the screen, waiting for the reply bubbles.

Nothing.

Around him, the lot kept emptying. Doors slammed. Tires rolled over loose gravel. The noise thinned until all that was left was the fence at his back and the distant sound of a train horn carrying from somewhere beyond the trees.

He stayed there longer than he meant to.

When he finally walked away, it was not toward home.

Circles on a Map

The front door had barely clicked shut behind Olivia when Ethan looked up from his chair.

"You made good time."

The TV talked softly in the corner, some news anchor moving from one bad story to the next in the same flat voice. Olivia set her bag down carefully and nodded.

"Traffic was normal."

He studied her face for a second, then gave a small approving smile. "Good. Sit down. Start your homework."

She went to the table without arguing.

That was the part he liked most. Not silence exactly. Compliance.

She opened her binder and stared at the page in front of her long enough to make it look real. The worksheet lines blurred. The questions might as well have been written underwater. She uncapped her pen anyway.

Behind her, Ethan moved through the house.

Front window.

Kitchen.

Back door.

Hall.

He checked locks and curtains with calm, practiced hands, the same way some people cleaned up after dinner or folded laundry before bed. He didn't rush. He didn't need to. The point wasn't urgency. The point was habit.

When Olivia reached into her backpack for another pen, her fingers slid along the inner seam first.

The small square was still there.

Cold. Flat. Hidden.

She only touched it for a second, just enough to feel its edges. Then she pulled her hand away and found the pen she had pretended to need.

Her phone buzzed against the table.

Riley: Home?

Olivia flipped it facedown so fast it made a sharp plastic sound.

"Everything okay?" Ethan asked from the hallway.

She kept her eyes on the worksheet. "Yeah."

A pause.

Then his footsteps started moving again.

Dinner came on schedule. Ethan heated leftovers and asked two questions about school, then spent the rest of the meal talking about the shop. A late part. A customer who thought everything should be easy. A worker who cut corners because he assumed someone else would fix the mess.

He never raised his voice. He didn't have to.

Every sentence felt aimed at something larger than itself.

Olivia ate enough not to be noticed and answered when she had to. She kept her eyes on her plate and her breathing even.

When dinner ended, Ethan picked up her phone and carried it to the kitchen charger.

"Sleep better tonight," he said. "You were restless."

"I'll try."

Upstairs, Olivia closed her bedroom door and stood still until the floorboards outside settled. She listened to the house the way she listened at the start of races, waiting for the smallest shift. Nothing came except the usual sounds. Air moving through the vents. Pipes clicking inside the wall. The low murmur of the TV downstairs.

She reached into her pocket and pulled out Riley's key.

It sat in her palm, small and worn smooth from use. Not special looking. Not dramatic. Just real.

She crouched by the vent, lifted the grate, and pushed the key deep into the toe of one of her running shoes. Then she shoved the shoe back into the shadowed space behind it and lowered the grate into place.

Only then did her shoulders loosen a little.

She sat on the floor with her knees pulled up and traced shapes into the carpet with one finger.

School.

Home.

Table.

Charger.

Room.

The same stops. The same return. The same loop tightening until it barely felt like movement at all.

A map made of circles.

No road leading out.

When she finally climbed into bed, she lay there staring into the dark for a long time. She tried not to think about Riley waiting for a text. About Danny knowing things he should not know. About Ethan downstairs, calm and certain, already planning tomorrow like today had gone exactly the way it should.

Sleep came slowly.

Not gently.

Like something she gave in to because fighting it took more strength than she had left.

And somewhere in the room, hidden behind the vent, a key waited in the dark.

Chapter Eleven

Closer Watch

Morning Checkpoints

The kitchen felt colder than the weather outside.

Steam lifted from Ethan's cup in thin white strands. The TV murmured about traffic, rain, and slow moving roads. Olivia stood at the sink and rinsed her bowl, letting warm water run over her hands longer than she needed.

"New rule," Ethan said.

She didn't turn. "Okay."

"You call me at lunch now. No more texts."

"Okay."

"And right after last period. Before practice."

She set the bowl in the rack and dried her hands slowly. "Okay."

He took a sip of coffee and set the mug down with care. "And come straight home today. No extra blocks."

Her shoulders tightened. "What do you mean?"

He picked up the mug again and looked at her over the rim. Calm. Steady. Certain.

"You took the long way yesterday. Elm Street."

Olivia's mind jumped to the walk around the library, then to the map on her phone. Family Safety. Her chest tightened.

"I was with Riley. We were talking."

His expression hardened. "I didn't ask who you were with."

"You can talk here," he said. His voice stayed mild, which made it worse. "I like knowing your path."

He held out his hand for her phone.

She gave it to him.

He opened the location screen and scrolled through it with quiet patience. The map reflected faintly in the kitchen window. So did his face. Still. Focused. Patient in the worst way.

Her pulse slowed just enough to hurt.

He studied the time stamps, then set the phone back on the counter. "Good girl. Keep it simple. Keep it safe."

"I will come straight home," she said.

Her backpack sat open on the table. As she slid in her binder and planner, the zipper brushed her wrist. The yellow envelope in the larger pocket felt heavier than it should. She moved her hand away too fast and pulled on her jacket.

"Call me at lunch. I'll answer on the first ring," he said.

"I will."

He stepped close and kissed the top of her hair like everything in the room was soft and ordinary.

She smiled because that was part of it.

Then she stepped outside, and the gray morning air hit her face like a warning.

Open Door

Hollow's Edge smelled like wet paper and old wax.

Students moved through the halls in bursts of noise. Lockers slammed. Someone laughed too loud near the front office. Shoes squeaked on damp tile. Olivia kept her head down and walked through it all like she was trying not to leave a mark.

Ms. Porter stopped by her desk before class began.

"Writing lab is open after school," she said. "Quiet room. Open door. You can stay as long as you need to work."

Olivia looked up. Ms. Porter's voice was gentle, but the offer was not casual. It landed with care.

"Thank you," Olivia said.

Ms. Porter held her gaze for a second, then moved on.

At lunch, Riley found her near the back doors where a cool draft slipped through the frame. Students brushed past them on both sides, loud and careless, carrying trays and half finished conversations.

"Did he add more rules?"

Olivia nodded. "Calls now. Lunch and right after last bell."

Riley's mouth tightened. "He's shrinking your day."

"It already feels small."

"Then let school be your shield," Riley said. "Stay with me after last bell. We sit in Ms. Porter's room. He hears people in the hall. He hears a teacher nearby. It sounds normal."

Olivia pictured it before she meant to. An open door. Voices beyond it. A room that didn't belong to him.

Her throat tightened. "That could work."

"It will work," Riley said. Then softer, "At least for a while."

Olivia looked down at her hands.

Riley touched her sleeve once, then let go. "If it turns bad, text me the word *Run*. I'll meet you at the north steps."

"Okay."

"Do you still have the key?"

Olivia met her eyes. "Yes. I moved it."

"Good."

The bell rang.

At the same time, Olivia's phone buzzed in her pocket.

Her stomach clenched before she could even look at the screen. She pressed the phone to her ear and turned slightly away, keeping her face blank while the sound of the cafeteria moved around her like cover.

What She Cannot Keep

Danny waited near the bleachers after school.

The sky stayed pale and flat above the lot. A cold breeze moved through the chain link fence and carried the smell of wet concrete across the track.

Olivia kept her bag tight against her side.

"You need to let somebody help you," Danny said quietly.

She looked away. "I know."

The words barely sounded real once they left her mouth.

She pulled out a large yellow envelope with a flap folded down and sealed with strips of clear tape. The paper was worn at the corners, softened from being carried too often. Something small and square pressed faintly against the paper from inside, padded by fabric. The flap had been opened before. The tape did not sit flat anymore. She held it to her chest with both hands.

Danny looked at it, then at her face.

"What is it?" he asked quietly.

Her fingers tightened.

For one second, it looked like she was going to answer. For one second, it looked like she was going to hand it to him and let the whole thing leave her body.

Then her phone buzzed.

She flinched so hard the envelope crinkled under her grip.

Danny glanced at the screen in her hand. She didn't.

"I was going to ask you to keep it," she said, voice barely there. "Just for a while."

He stayed still.

Olivia looked down at the envelope, then shook her head once. Fast. Sharp. Like she hated herself for even thinking it.

"I can't."

"Olivia."

"If he notices it's gone, he'll know." Her breathing had gone shallow. "He'll go through everything. He'll ask questions. He'll watch harder."

Danny's face tightened. "Then let him. You need things out of that house."

"No." She pulled the envelope closer. "Not yet."

He studied her for a moment, then lowered his voice. "When you're ready, I'll take it. Sealed. I won't ask what's inside."

Her eyes lifted to his.

"Promise?" she asked before she meant to.

He nodded once. "I promise."

Something moved through her face then. Relief. Fear. Shame for needing any of it.

She slipped the envelope back into her bag with hands that would not stay steady.

"I have to call him."

Danny said nothing while she made the call. She kept her voice level and short, every word chosen before it left her mouth. By the time she hung up, she looked older than she had that morning.

"I have to go."

He stepped back enough to give her room. "Text me one word if you need me. Any word."

She nodded.

Then she turned and walked back toward the building while he stayed where she left him, watching her go with his hands deep in his jacket pockets.

Writing Lab

Olivia cut through the lobby and headed for Ms. Porter's room.

The hallway clock clicked one slow second at a time. By the time she reached the door, Riley was already inside with a book open in front of her and a second chair pulled close beside the desk.

"You made it," Riley said. "Sit. I'll work. You breathe."

Olivia set her binder down and sat.

The room smelled like dry markers, paper, and old books. The door stood open on a wedge. Voices moved in and out of the hall. Nothing in the room felt hidden. That was what made it bearable.

"Call him when you need to," Riley said. "I won't say a word."

Olivia nodded and pressed the phone to her ear just as the final bell rang.

"Homework first," she told Ethan. "Then home."

She tilted the phone slightly so he could hear the hall behind her. Students passing. Lockers shutting. A teacher laughing two rooms down.

He sounded pleased at once.

"That's good. Call me when you leave."

When she hung up, the room went quiet again.

Olivia stared at the page in front of her and wrote the date at the top. Then she underlined it once. Then again.

After a long moment, she looked at Riley.

"Danny told me you two have been talking about me."

Riley's pen stopped moving.

"He let that slip?" Riley asked.

Olivia's throat tightened. "So it's true?"

Riley closed her book and leaned back in the chair. "He came to me because he was worried."

"And that was enough?"

"No." Riley's voice stayed calm. "What was enough was watching you get quieter every week."

Olivia looked down at the paper.

"I still don't trust him fully," Riley said. "That isn't the point. He kept showing up scared for you, and I couldn't ignore that."

Olivia's fingers pressed harder around the pen. "So now both of you make plans behind my back."

"We make plans because you don't let anyone stand beside you long enough to make them with you."

The words landed hard.

Olivia said nothing.

Riley's voice softened a little. "You really think I wanted Danny involved?"

Olivia looked up.

Riley held her gaze. "I wanted you safe. That's not the same thing."

For a second Olivia couldn't answer. The room felt too open and too close at the same time.

"You think it's that bad?" she finally asked.

Riley didn't hesitate.

"I think you're trapped," she said. "And I think you're scared to say it out loud."

The words left a hollow ache behind them.

Olivia underlined the date again until the pen nearly tore the page.

They stayed like that for almost twenty minutes. Riley reading without turning a page. Olivia writing nothing after the date.

When Olivia finally stood, Riley stood too.

"I'll walk you down," she said.

The Surprise Pickup

The front doors opened onto damp air and fading light.

At the curb, a truck idled.

Olivia saw it and stopped so suddenly Riley almost walked into her.

Ethan leaned across the seat and waved through the open window. His smile looked warm from a distance. Up close, it always looked like something else.

"Surprise," he called. "I was nearby."

Olivia's stomach turned, but her face stayed even. "Hi."

Riley went still beside her.

Ethan's eyes moved to her at once. His smile didn't change.

"Riley Mercer," he said smoothly. "I know who you are."

Riley held his gaze. "She was with me."

"Is that so?" Ethan said.

Then he looked back at Olivia. "Bag in the back. Seat belt."

Olivia hesitated for half a second, then obeyed.

As she opened the back door, the yellow envelope in the larger pocket shifted against her leg, pressing against everything else she carried.

She slid into the seat and shut the door.

"Text me," Riley said quietly from the curb.

Ethan smiled wider. "She'll be busy tonight."

His voice stayed light. The warning inside it didn't.

He pulled away from the school in a slow, smooth line. The engine hummed low under the silence.

After a minute, he said, "I like this plan."

Olivia kept her eyes on the window. The mural with the chipped blue wings blurred as they passed.

"Writing lab is safe," he went on. "Teachers nearby. Other students around. A good use of time."

She knew what was coming before he said it.

"I can pick you up on days I'm free."

Her throat tightened. "Okay."

"You kept to your path today," he said. "Good girl."

She looked at her hands. "Thank you."

At home, he set her phone on the kitchen charger and turned the TV on low. He talked about late orders at the shop, customers who never paid, and people who made life harder than they had to be. His footsteps moved through the house like checkpoints.

Upstairs, Olivia pulled Riley's key from her running shoe and held it in her palm until the edges pressed a red shape into her skin.

She kept the shoe beside her and reached for the backpack instead. The yellow envelope came out creased and softer than it had looked at the field. She sat on the floor and peeled the flap open the rest of the way.

Inside, the journal pressed against the paper in a shape that no longer felt hidden enough. Her old track hoodie had been folded around it for padding. She pulled both free, stared at them for a second, then wrapped the journal tighter in the hoodie and shoved the empty envelope deep into the bottom drawer of her desk.

Only then did she slide the journal back behind the vent and push the shoe in after it.

Beyond the metal, hidden in the dark, the journal was still where she had left it. Wrapped tighter now. Untouched. Still hers.

That should have made her feel safer.

It didn't.

She sat on the floor with her back against the bed and listened.

The vents sighed. The porch light buzzed. A car passed once outside, then everything went still again.

School had felt like an open door for one short hour.

Now even that felt smaller.

Olivia closed her eyes and tried to picture a road that didn't bend back home.

Sleep came late.

It felt like a bargain she had never agreed to make.

Chapter Twelve

Tight Lines

The New Rules

Ethan was already at the table when Olivia came into the kitchen. His coffee sat untouched beside his phone.

"Same plan today," he said. "Call me at lunch. No text."

She nodded. "I know."

"And right after last period. Then again when you get home."

"I know."

Her own voice sounded small. She hated that he could do that to it without even raising his.

He set the mug down and reached for her phone. His thumb moved through settings with the ease of practice. He opened Family Safety and checked the screen. The blue dot sat at the house, right where it should.

"Good," he said. "Leave location on. If your battery drops below thirty, plug it in."

"I will."

He stood and held out a hand. "Bag."

She passed the backpack.

He checked the front pocket first, then the second. He slid two fingers into the mesh by the water bottle. His hand skimmed the lining, close enough to make her pulse jump.

Olivia kept her face still and made herself breathe slowly. She wasn't afraid he would find anything. She was afraid he would realize she already knew it was there.

He zipped the bag and handed it back. "You are doing well. Keep it simple. Keep it safe."

She slipped the straps on. "I come straight home after study hall."

"Good girl."

He kissed the top of her hair like he meant well. The kiss sat on her skin like a weight.

"Don't take Elm Street again," he said. "Side trips worry me."

She froze for half a second. "We were walking. The steps were crowded."

"You can walk Main where everyone can see you." His voice stayed flat. "No more long ways."

She looked at the floor. "Okay."

He checked the clock and picked up his keys. "I will be at the shop until six. If you need anything, you call me. Not Riley. Not Danny. Me."

"I know."

"Have a good day, kiddo."

Outside, the air felt damp and cool, like the sky had not finished raining. Olivia pulled her hood tighter and texted Riley while she walked down the front path.

Leaving now. Lunch call from school

She almost added a period at the end, then deleted it. It felt too deliberate. Too much like she was trying to say more than the words said.

The street still shone from last night's drizzle. The oak at the corner shook loose a few leaves. She moved faster than usual. The tighter she stayed to the route he expected, the less likely he was to stare at the maps and time stamps later.

At the end of the block, she checked the time. If she kept this pace, she would be early to first period. Early felt safe. Early meant fewer questions.

She crossed at the light and merged into the stream of students heading toward school. One boy laughed too loud about a game. Two girls compared quiz answers. Olivia walked in the middle and tried to disappear into normal.

Ms. Porter stood at the classroom door with a stack of papers tucked to her chest. "Good morning," she said. "You're early."

"Bus ran fast," Olivia said. She did not ride the bus.

Ms. Porter studied her face for a moment. Not long. Not invasive. Just long enough to count the shadows under her eyes.

"I'll be here after last bell," she said. "Door open. Quiet room. Good place to work."

"Thank you."

Ms. Porter let her pass and greeted the next student in the same steady tone. No question. Just cover. Olivia felt the shape of that and knew exactly what it was.

By midmorning, she moved on habit alone. Notes in history. Short answers in math. Small sips of water until her stomach felt cold.

At lunch, she stood by the windows where the signal stayed strong and called Ethan. He answered on the first ring.

"Good girl."

"I'll be in writing lab after school. Ms. Porter is staying."

"That's fine. Text me when you leave. Then come straight home."

"I will."

He hung up without saying goodbye.

Olivia stared at the dark screen for a second before slipping the phone back into her pocket. She had made it this far without slipping. The day felt like something thin stretched over a drop.

Her phone buzzed again as she turned toward the cafeteria.

Danny: You okay?

She typed, deleted, then tried again.

Olivia: In class. Talk later.

A few seconds passed.

Danny: Okay. Just checking.

She stared at the words. They should have felt harmless. They didn't. She locked the screen and kept walking.

Quiet Terms

They met behind the library after the last bell.

The brick wall cut some of the wind. The smell of cigarettes from the far corner drifted through the space and covered their voices. Riley got there first, hood up, hands deep in her pockets. Danny came from the lot at a quiet pace and stopped short when he saw her expression.

"No drama," she said. "We keep this useful."

He gave a short nod. "Fine."

They stood a few feet apart. The distance felt careful, not casual. Riley had never liked him. Danny had always looked at her like he knew it.

"She called him at lunch," Riley said. "I was near the hall. He made her check it."

Danny swore under his breath. "He treats her like property."

Riley's jaw tightened. "He treats her like obedience is the same as safety."

He leaned back against the wall and looked away for a second. "Yesterday he picked her up. Did she tell you?"

"Yes. He wanted to see who she was with. Wanted to watch her act normal."

Danny let out a bitter breath. "How did you handle it?"

"Polite. Boring. Harmless." Riley looked toward the door. "He liked it too much."

For a second neither of them spoke.

Then Danny said, "We need a plan."

"We need limits," Riley said. "For her. For you. For me."

That got his attention.

"You think I'm the problem?"

"I think you show up when you feel like it," she said. "That stops now."

He opened his mouth, then shut it.

Riley kept going. "Writing lab three days a week. Ms. Porter's room. Open door. People around. If Olivia needs cover, that's where she gets it."

Danny stared at the cracked brick at his shoulder. "And me?"

"You stop waiting by the gym. You stop texting when she can't answer. You stop making yourself one more thing she has to manage."

His face hardened at that, but he didn't argue.

"If she needs a fast ride," Riley said, "you stay near the north steps. Not the main lot. Not the front. And not unless she asks."

Danny looked back at her. "You think he's tracking the bag too?"

"I think she's scared of it," Riley said. "That's enough."

He scrubbed a hand over his mouth. "I hate standing back."

"Hating it is not strategy."

A humorless laugh slipped out of him. "You always sound like you're about to grade somebody."

Riley ignored that. "If she texts the word, I go first. You follow my lead. She doesn't get pulled in two directions."

That sat between them for a moment.

Then he nodded once. "Fine."

"One more thing," Riley said. "No late texts she can't explain."

He looked annoyed now. "I got it."

"Do you?"

He met her stare. "Yeah. I do."

Riley reached into her pocket and handed him a sheet of paper. Three numbers. Two addresses. Her writing sat in neat block letters.

"My cell. My mom's. Ms. Porter's room number. My place and my aunt's."

He looked at it, then folded it once and tucked it away. "You trust me this much?"

"No," Riley said. "I trust that you care enough to be dangerous if I don't give you boundaries."

That landed.

Around the corner, a bus coughed to life. Someone shouted for a ride. The flag rope knocked softly against the pole.

Riley tipped her head toward the doors. "Go. If she sees us standing here together, she'll feel watched."

Danny pushed off the wall. "Text me if anything shifts."

"I will."

He backed away, then turned toward the lot. Riley waited until he was gone before stepping into the flow of students, just another person moving in the right direction while carrying too much in silence.

Whispers in the Hall

The next day felt thinner from the start.

The sky stayed pale and blank. Hall lights hummed overhead with a low and steady buzz that settled behind Olivia's eyes. She walked the same route she always did, but the building felt flimsy somehow, like a place held together by schedules and fluorescent light.

In English, Ms. Porter wrote three words on the board.

Control. Witness. Consequence.

A few students offered examples. Olivia didn't. She stared at the words and thought about how each one already lived in her day.

After class, Ms. Porter paused beside her desk.

"You have lab again today," she said. "I'll be there after the bell."

"Yes. Thank you."

"You look pale. Do you need the nurse?"

"No. I'm just tired."

Ms. Porter watched her for a second longer, then nodded and moved on. She didn't push. She only left the door open.

At lunch, Olivia sat at the far end of a table away from the loud center of the room. She ate half her sandwich and counted the blue lines on the napkin. Riley didn't sit with her. They had agreed on less obvious contact. Less pattern. Fewer eyes.

Riley passed once with a tray and glanced toward the south exit. Olivia gave the smallest nod in return.

She went to the window and called Ethan.

"I'm checking in," she said. "I'll call again after last bell."

"Good girl," he said. "If you stay late, send a picture."

She hung up and watched the screen dim.

As she crossed back toward the cafeteria, whispers drifted past in scraps.

A girl with red nails said Olivia looked thinner.

A boy near the soda machine said she looked like a ghost.

Someone else, closer than that, said she had a boyfriend now. One of those older ones. The kind who kept girls on a leash.

The word leash closed her throat.

She dumped her trash and walked the hall until the bell.

Math came and went in straight rows of numbers that meant nothing. She copied them anyway. Copying felt safe. In history, Mr. Cole talked about governments, fear, and what happened when people confused order with control. Olivia wrote the date and kept one eye on the clock.

Her phone buzzed under the desk.

Danny: You left fast yesterday.

Her stomach tightened.

Olivia: I had to.

A reply came back at once.

Danny: I know. Still would've been nice to hear from you.

She looked at the screen for a moment, then typed back.

Olivia: Thank you for helping.

The answer came fast.

Danny: I keep showing up, Olivia. Don't shut me out too.

Olivia locked the screen and set the phone at the far edge of the desk.

Her hands wouldn't stop shaking. Mr. Cole's voice went on, steady and warm, but none of it reached her.

When the bell rang, she packed up and went straight to writing lab.

Borrowed Safety

Ms. Porter's room felt honest in a way most places no longer did.

The door stayed propped open. Sound from the hallway drifted in and kept the room from sinking into silence. Riley sat two rows back with a book open and a pen in hand. She didn't look up when Olivia came in. Ms. Porter arranged papers at her desk and let the room settle on its own.

Olivia sat in her usual seat and opened her binder. Her hands still shook, but less now. She could breathe here. Not deeply. Not all the way. But enough.

The after-school bell rang.

She called Ethan and put him on speaker, holding the phone low so the open door and hallway noise carried through.

"Lab again," she said. "Twenty minutes. Then home."

"Good girl. Send a picture of the room."

She took one quickly. Desk. Door. Hall. Nothing else.

His reply came at once.

Okay.

That single word should not have felt threatening. But it did.

When she stood to leave, a freshman near the door fumbled a binder. Papers slid across the floor in a messy white spill.

"Oh, crap."

Olivia bent without thinking and helped gather them. The kid looked embarrassed and too young for how red his face went.

"Thanks," he said.

"Be careful."

It felt like something from another life. A normal moment. A normal kindness. A world where helping somebody didn't leave a mark.

She and Riley walked into the hall with a little space between them.

"You okay?" Riley asked quietly.

"Fine."

The lie was weak enough that both of them heard it.

Riley kept her eyes ahead. "You don't sound fine."

"He wants pictures now," Olivia said. "Rooms. Doors. Proof."

Riley's mouth tightened. "Next time I'll stand in the frame."

They reached the front steps. Wind pushed at the glass doors behind them.

Olivia checked the time. If traffic stayed light, she could still make it home with minutes to spare.

Her phone buzzed.

Danny: Nice of you to help that freshman with the papers.

The cold that moved through her felt instant and total.

She stopped walking.

"What?" Riley asked.

Olivia didn't answer right away. She read the message again, then looked at the doorway, the windows, the parking lot beyond them.

She typed.

Olivia: Who told you that?

No answer.

Not right away. Not at all.

The silence felt worse than a reply would have.

Riley didn't ask again. She only looked at Olivia's face and understood enough.

"Text me when you get home," she said.

"I will."

They split at the walkway. Riley went right. Olivia went left. Their eyes caught once in the reflection of the glass and then were gone.

Halfway down the sidewalk, her phone buzzed again.

Danny: North steps. Two minutes. Just say Run.

Olivia didn't answer.

She kept walking.

The Weight of the Key

Night settled early, slow and gray.

The house smelled like supper, dish soap, and whatever Ethan had used to wipe down the counters. The TV glowed in the living room like a nightlight left on by mistake. Olivia did homework at the kitchen table while Ethan checked the locks. He liked to test each bolt with his hand. He liked to hear the click.

"Good work today," he said from the doorway. "I like this rhythm."

She kept her eyes on her notes. "I called when you asked."

"You did." He smiled a little. "Keep doing that."

He picked up her phone and set it face down on the counter and plugged it into the charger. His hand rested on the cord for a second as if even that belonged to him. Then he walked down the hall and left the TV to keep speaking into the room.

When she finished her work, she stacked her books, rinsed her plate, and wiped the table until it felt smooth beneath her palm. Then she went upstairs.

At her door, she stopped and listened.

The house breathed in all its usual ways. Porch light buzzing. TV low. Pipes ticking somewhere inside the walls.

Her room looked the same as always.

Bed made. Desk neat. Lamp off.

She shut the door to the width he allowed and knelt by the vent. Her fingers found the running shoe tucked behind the grate. She slid Riley's key from inside it and held it in her palm.

The brass was dull in the low light. Plain. Warm from her hand within seconds.

She pictured the route to Riley's house without meaning to.

Right at the corner. Past the church. Left at the little store with the broken ice machine. Porch light on. Chipped steps. A door that might open without asking anything first.

For one dangerous moment, the picture held.

Then Ethan crowded it out.

She saw him in his chair. She saw him look up and notice the charger without the phone. The empty bed. The cold space where she should have been. She saw him check the map. Call once. Then again. Then keep calling until the whole town felt too small to hide in.

The second picture swallowed the first.

Olivia closed her hand around the key until the edges bit into her skin.

She wanted to be brave in a way that didn't put Riley in the path of what came next.

Her phone buzzed on the desk.

She set the key on her knee and checked the screen.

Danny: You went quiet again.

She stared at the screen, then answered before she could overthink it.

Olivia: I'm tired.

Danny: Tired isn't the same as okay.

Olivia: Please stop texting tonight.

A long pause followed.

Danny: Then tell me you're okay and I will.

She stared at the words until they started to blur. Then she locked the phone and set it face down.

The house hummed around her.

After a while, she slid the key back into the shoe and pushed it behind the grate again. She checked the screws with her nail, one by one.

At the desk, her hand moved toward the drawer where she usually kept her journal. She stopped before she touched it. Even writing felt dangerous tonight. She pulled a plain notebook closer and wrote two words.

Not yet.

Then she turned off the lamp and lay on the bed with her eyes open.

The ceiling fan turned slowly above her. Time thickened around the room.

School. Lab. Home. Table. Charger. Door.

The route lived in her body now.

She tried to picture a day with no route at all. No check in. No watched screen. No voice at the other end of the line.

Sleep didn't come quickly.

It came like water rising.

The house settled. The charger light glowed on the desk. The door stayed open the width of a hand.

Then her phone lit the dark with a soft flash.

Family Safety: Location sharing paused.

Olivia stopped breathing.

The message vanished.

A second one appeared almost at once.

Family Safety: Location sharing resumed by Organizer.

She stared at the screen until it went dark again. Somewhere in the house, a floorboard clicked. A car passed outside and kept going.

Her phone buzzed one last time.

Danny: Saw you by the steps today. You looked tired. Get some rest.

She looked at the word rest under his name and felt nothing in it that sounded restful.

She turned the screen face down and lay still.

The key waited inside the shoe behind the grate.

The house waited too.

And the night around her felt like it was holding its breath.

Chapter Thirteen

Lines That Blur

Test and Traps

Olivia moved through the day as if the floor itself had rules now.

Call at lunch.

Call after last period.

Text when you get home.

Every check in brought the same reply.

Good girl.

The words used to feel safe. Now they felt like something fastened around her throat.

That evening, the house sat under its usual hush. The TV murmured from the living room. Ethan sat in his chair with the remote in one hand and a cup of coffee cooling beside him. He would not drink it. He liked the smell more than the taste.

When Olivia set her books on the table, he looked up and smiled.

"Homework first," he said. "Then you can relax."

She sat and opened her math notebook. Her fingers cramped around the pen before she even finished the date. Ethan stayed in the kitchen doorway with his arms folded, glancing now and then at the phone resting on its charger.

"Long day?" he asked.

"Yes."

"You sleep too late sometimes." He lifted the cup, then set it back down. "Not last night, though."

Her chest tightened. "I went to bed early."

"I know." His tone stayed easy. "I checked. Good girl."

She kept her eyes on the page, though the numbers had already started to swim. He clicked through channels without watching any of them for long. News. Sports. Weather. Then back again. The TV filled the room with voices that never said anything she needed.

She thought about the one time she forgot to text him after school.

Months ago, her phone had died in the bottom of her backpack. When she got home, Ethan had not raised his voice. He had only handed her the charger and said nothing at all.

The next morning, a folded note sat beside her phone.

No excuses again.

She had never missed another message.

Later, she climbed the stairs.

Her heart dropped the second she saw her bedroom door.

It stood open wider than she had left it that morning. Not much. An inch, maybe two. But enough.

Enough to tell her he had been inside.

She stepped into the room and closed the door carefully, matching the angle he preferred. Then she sat on the edge of the bed without moving. Her backpack leaned against the desk. The hidden square inside the lining felt heavier tonight, as if she could feel it through the fabric.

She wanted to rip the seam open.

She wanted to dig the thing out and throw it as far as she could.

Instead, she pictured Ethan finding the torn lining. She pictured the pause before the questions. The way he always sounded calmest when the answer mattered most.

So she stayed still until her pulse eased.

The she crawled under the blanket and turned toward the wall.

She thought of Riley's key hidden in her shoe.

A door she could open.

Just not yet.

Sleep came thin and uneven.

Fault Line

The next afternoon, Riley texted Danny the second the bell rang.

Riley: Library steps. Ten minutes.

She waited while students spilled outside in loud, careless waves. Backpacks knocked against legs. Car doors slammed. Someone shouted about food. Someone else laughed too hard. Riley kept her hood up and her hands wrapped tight around her straps.

Danny showed up a few minutes later.

He looked worn out. His jaw stayed tight. Dark shadows sat under his eyes. He dropped onto the step beside her, close enough to talk, not close enough to touch.

"You called me here," he said. "So, what's the move?"

Riley kept her gaze on the parking lot. "No move yet."

His mouth flattened. "That's not good enough."

"It has to be."

Danny leaned forward with his elbows on his knees. "She looks worse every day."

"I know."

He let out a sharp breath. "You know she's tired. That's not the same thing."

Riley turned to him. "Then say it."

He looked back toward the lot. "She looks like she's bracing all the time. Like every answer costs her something."

That part, Riley could not argue with.

"She needs cover," Riley said. "Patterns that look normal. Teachers who don't push too hard. Noise around her when she calls. That's how we keep her steady."

"Steady?" Danny snapped. "She's not steady, Riley. She's trapped."

A few students glanced over. Riley lowered her voice.

"I know that. But if you rush this, she pays for it."

He stood and started pacing in front of the steps. "Every hour in that house makes it worse."

"And what do you want me to do?" Riley asked. "Tell her to jump into your truck tonight and hope he doesn't follow the map?"

He stopped.

His face changed for a second. Not anger. Something rougher than that. Something desperate.

"You think I haven't thought about it?" he asked.

"You think that helps?"

He dragged a hand over his mouth and looked away.

Riley stood too. "You keep acting like the answer has to go through you."

His eyes narrowed. "You think I'd hurt her?"

"I think you want to be the one who gets her out," Riley said. "And right now, that makes you reckless."

That landed.

Danny looked down at the pavement. His hands shook once before he shoved them into his pockets.

Then he said, too quickly, "He checks her phone before bed, right?"

Riley went still.

She had never told him that.

Danny caught it a second too late. "She mentioned it," he said. "A while ago."

Riley watched him.

Maybe Olivia had said it. Maybe. But his answer came too fast, too polished, like he had already rehearsed it.

"You keep talking like you know things I don't," Riley said.

He looked up at her then. "Maybe you don't know everything."

The words hung there.

Riley felt something cold move through her chest. "That's exactly the problem."

For a second neither of them moved.

The parking lot noise rolled around them. Tires on wet pavement. A bus engine turning over. A whistle from the practice field.

Finally, Riley said, "We hold the line until she moves. When she does, we're ready."

Danny stared at her for a second, then gave one tight nod.

"Fine," he said. "Your way. For now."

"For now," Riley said.

He started toward the lot, then paused.

"If she reaches out," he said without turning back, "don't make her wait."

Riley watched him walk away.

He was hiding something. She felt sure of that now.

She just didn't know whether it made him more dangerous or more useful.

The Hallway Eyes

By Thursday, the whispers had gotten louder.

At her locker, two girls leaned close and let their whispers carry.

"She looks pale."

"She missed practice again."

A voice drifted from somewhere near the vending machines.

"He doesn't let her go anywhere now."

Olivia shut her locker and walked away without turning to see who had said it. Her hands felt cold and damp.

In English, Ms. Porter handed back essays and paused at Olivia's desk.

"This one's strong," she said quietly. "But you look exhausted. Want to step outside for a minute?"

Olivia forced a smile. "No. I'm fine."

Ms. Porter studied her face for a second.

"Fine isn't the same as okay," she said.

Then she moved on.

At lunch, Riley did not sit with her. They had agreed it was safer that way. Still, Riley passed close enough to murmur, "Call me later," without breaking stride.

Olivia kept her eyes on her tray. Her heart hammered hard enough to make her feel sick.

Danny's name lit up her screen twice that afternoon.

She did not answer.

If Ethan saw a call answered at the wrong time, he would ask why. He would ask when. He would ask how long. Every answer would open another question.

By the time the last bell rang, Olivia felt scraped raw.

She drifted into writing lab, called Ethan, and listened to him answer on the first ring.

Riley sat two rows away with her head bent over a notebook. Neither of them looked at the other. The silence between them had become its own kind of language. That hurt worse than the open fights had.

As Olivia packed up, she caught two freshmen near the door whispering to each other.

"That's her."

"The girl with the older guy?"

The words struck harder than they should have.

Danny's face flashed through her mind first.

Then Ethan's.

Both wrong for different reasons.

She left without looking back.

The Key in the Dark

That night, Olivia climbed the stairs slowly.

Ethan had checked her homework, checked the locks, and set her phone face down on the kitchen charger before telling her goodnight. He smiled when he said it, but his eyes stayed on her until she reached the top landing.

Her room felt smaller than it had that morning.

Dust hung in the air. The vent hummed low and steady. She closed the door to the exact width he liked and sat on the bed.

A floorboard creaked somewhere below.

She listened.

Nothing followed.

Slowly, she knelt by the vent and pulled the shoe free. Her fingers found the brass key tucked inside. It slid into her palm, cool and solid and real.

She wrapped her hand around it and pictured Riley's house.

The chipped steps.

The peeling blue door.

The crooked curtain in the front window.

For one second, the picture steadied her breathing. Riley waiting inside. Porch light on. No questions asked.

Then the next picture ruined it.

Ethan checking the map.

Ethan calling and calling until the sound chased her through every street in town.

Her hand trembled. She pressed the key into her skin until it hurt.

She wanted to move.

She wanted to run.

But running would not stop with her. It would spread. To Riley. To anyone who opened the door.

She slid the key back into the shoe and shoved it behind the vent grate.

Then she stood.

The hallway light flickered once outside her room. Downstairs, her phone buzzed once, then went quiet.

Her throat tightened. She stood there waiting for footsteps that never came.

At the desk, she stopped with one hand on the chair back. The urge to write rose in her chest, sharp and familiar, but even thinking about paper made her pulse kick. Anything written could be found. Anything found could be used.

So she whispered the words instead.

“Still here.”

The sound barely reached her own ears.

The Quiet Before

The last day before spring break carried a strange charge through the whole building.

Students moved through the halls with loud relief. Plans spilled from every corner. Sleepovers. Road trips. Movies. Late nights. Freedom.

Riley sat at her usual table in the cafeteria, scanning faces.

She waited for Olivia's glance. Just one. That small look that meant I'm here. I'm still here.

It never came.

Olivia carried her tray with both hands as if it weighed more than it should. She sat at the edge of a crowded table and stared at her food without eating. Her hair had fallen forward, hiding most of her face.

Riley wanted to get up, cross the room, grab Olivia's hand, and make he say something real.

She did not.

Patterns meant safety. Breaking them meant attention.

So she stayed where she was and pretended to smile at a joke she barely heard.

At dismissal, the whole school felt feverish. Lockers slammed. Shoes squeaked. Voices bounced off the walls and followed everyone outside. The air smelled like rain.

Riley came down the front steps with the last wave of students and stopped near the curb, far enough from Danny not to draw attention, close enough to keep an eye on him.

Danny waited by the library steps, watching the doors.

Olivia came out with the crowd.

She moved like she was underwater. Slow. Hollow eyed. One hand locked around her bag strap so tightly her knuckles looked white. Danny stood still, waiting for her to look his way. Waiting for some tiny sign.

She passed him without a glance.

His jaw tightened.

For one second, Riley thought he might call her name.

He did not.

Olivia kept walking.

A few minutes later, Riley crossed the lot and caught up to him near the curb.

"Nothing?" she asked.

"Nothing," he said. "She walked right past me."

"She didn't look at me either."

Danny kept staring toward the sidewalk where Olivia had disappeared. "She looked half gone on her feet."

Riley swallowed. "We hold steady."

He let out a hard breath. "I hate this."

"I know."

"She's slipping."

Riley watched the buses pull away one by one. "Then we stay ready."

Danny did not answer.

He just kept watching the crowd thin out, like he was trying to memorize every face that was not hers.

That night, they texted in short bursts.

Riley: Did she talk to you?

Danny: Not a word.

Riley: Same. Not even a look.

Danny: She looked gone.

Riley: We stick to the plan. She'll reach out when it's safe.

Danny stared at the thread for a long moment.

Just tell me you're still there.

He looked at it.

Then deleted it.

In the dark screen, his own face stared back at him, pale and worn out.

Across town, Riley lay on her bed scrolling through old group photos. She stopped on one where Olivia was laughing in full sunlight, head tipped back, mouth open, looking like nothing in the world was pressing down on her.

Riley touched the screen with her thumb.

"Come back," she whispered.

Then she locked her phone.

Spring break passed in a gray blur.

Morning after morning, Riley checked her messages.

Nothing.

Night after night, Danny stared at his screen until sleep took him.

Nothing.

No texts. No read receipts. No accidental likes. No breadcrumb. No sign she was even holding her own phone.

On the last night before classes resumed, Riley sent one more message.

Riley: See you tomorrow?

She watched the screen, waiting for the word *Read* to appear under the message.

It never appeared.

Danny sent one too.

Danny: I'll be at the steps. Just show up.

The clock kept moving.

Neither screen changed.

Across town, Olivia sat in Ethan's truck at a stoplight.

Streetlamp glow slid across her cheek, then disappeared, then found her again at the next light. She kept her face turned toward the window, watching reflections drift past. Houses. Trees. The school sign half hidden behind branches.

She did not look at Ethan.

She did not look at the road behind them either.

She looked farther out than that, toward something no one else in the truck could see.

Rain started again, soft at first.

Then steadier.

By morning, it would feel like more than weather.

Chapter Fourteen

Gone

Olivia's Empty Seat

The first bell rang on the first morning back from Spring Break, sharp enough to make Riley flinch.

She slid into her usual seat in English and dropped her bag beside the desk. Around her, the room filled the way it always did after a week off. Half awake laughter. Backpacks thudding to the floor. Somebody complaining that teachers should not be allowed to assign anything the day after break. Ms. Porter's room smelled like old paper, dry markers, and the burnt edge of coffee from the mug on her desk.

Riley kept looking at the door anyway.

Olivia always came in quiet. Not late. Not loud. Just there, slipping into her seat like she had learned how to take up less space than everyone else. Riley waited for the soft scrape of her chair.

It never came.

Students kept filing in. The bell finished ringing. Ms. Porter stepped in and shut the door.

Riley looked up again, even then.

Nothing.

At first, she told herself it was nothing. Ethan could have made Olivia late. Olivia could have overslept. Olivia could have gotten sick. There were a hundred small reasons a person missed first period.

But the empty desk beside hers felt wrong fast.

Ms. Porter started roll call. Her voice moved down the list with its usual steady rhythm until she reached Olivia's name.

She paused.

"Absent."

The word landed softly, but it still seemed to echo. Ms. Porter's eyes lifted for a second and found Riley before moving on.

The rest of the period dragged.

Riley stared at her notebook without seeing it. The projector hummed. Pages turned. Somebody coughed near the windows. Every few minutes she glanced at Olivia's chair again, half expecting to find her there after all, head down, cheeks pale, apology already on her face.

By second period, Riley was no longer pretending it did not bother her.

She cut past Olivia's locker between classes and slowed down without meaning to. The metal door stayed shut. No books shifting hands. No quick glance over a shoulder. No pen tucked behind one ear. Students streamed past in clumps, loud and careless, while Riley stood there pretending to search through her own bag.

Nothing.

By lunch, the knot in her stomach had hardened.

She carried her tray to their usual table near the vending machines and sat alone. Sunlight slanted through the high cafeteria windows and streaked across the floor. Every time the doors swung open, she looked up.

Not Olivia.

A girl at the next table leaned close to her friend and whispered something that was not meant to carry.

"She's still not here."

"Maybe her dad kept her home."

A shrug.

"Wouldn't shock me."

Riley's fork stopped halfway to her mouth. The food had already gone dry and cold. She set the fork down and pushed the tray a few inches away.

By last period, she stopped making excuses for it.

She moved slower through the halls, scanning corners she had no reason to scan, as if Olivia might be tucked into one of them somehow. She checked the locker again. Walked past the office. Looked through the library doors.

Nothing.

When the final bell rang, the building emptied around her in a rush of voices and footsteps. Riley stayed behind in English a moment longer, staring at the empty chair beside hers until Ms. Porter clicked off the projector and the room dimmed.

That was when it stopped feeling like a weird morning.

That was when it started feeling wrong.

Silence on the Line

Danny was already at the library steps when the last bell rang.

He had been there early on purpose. He told himself it was because he did not want to miss her coming out. The truth was uglier than that. He had not trusted the silence over break, and he trusted it even less now.

Students poured through the doors in waves. Laughter. Shouting. Slamming car doors from the lot. He watched every face that came down the steps.

No Olivia.

He stayed where he was.

She could still be inside. Talking to a teacher. Getting held back. Avoiding him for some reason that would make sense once he saw her face.

The crowd thinned. The noise dropped.

Still no Olivia.

He pulled out his phone and typed before he could think too hard about how desperate it looked.

At the steps. Where are you?

Nothing.

A minute later he tried again.

Olivia. Ten minutes. Please.

Still nothing.

His jaw locked. He hit call and listened to it ring. Once. Twice. Three times. Voicemail.

He hung up and called again.

Voicemail.

Danny stood and started pacing the edge of the steps. Late sun caught the library windows and threw glare across the courtyard hard enough to sting his eyes. He scrubbed a hand down his face and told himself to breathe.

"She's fine," he muttered. "She's grounded. That's all."

The words sounded thin the second they left him.

What stayed with him was Friday. The last time he saw her at school. The way every answer had sounded like it cost her something. The way she looked worn down and too careful all at once. The way she moved like she was already braced for the next thing.

She had been scared.

Not dramatic. Not loud. Scared in that smaller, worse way. Quiet. Controlled. Already half hiding it.

Danny slammed the side of his fist against the stone step.

Pain shot up his arm. He hissed and pulled his hand back. A smear of blood marked the rough edge where his skin split.

Someone passing across the courtyard glanced over, then kept walking faster.

He did not care.

He looked back at the screen and typed one last message.

Please. Just one word. Anything.

It sent.

The screen went dark and turned into a black mirror, throwing his own face back at him.

Nothing came back.

Unread

Riley did not sleep that night.

She lay in bed with her phone lighting the dark above her blanket and reopened the same thread over and over.

The last message still sat there unanswered. See you tomorrow?

No reply. Not even marked read.

She typed *Are you okay? then deleted it.*

A minute later she typed *Call me.*

She deleted that too.

Anything she wrote felt wrong. Too loud. Too late. Too much like panic.

Across town, Danny sat in his truck at the edge of the train yard with the engine off and his phone in his hand. The yard stretched dark beyond the windshield, all rust and shadow and dead quiet.

He sent another message.

Say anything. Just one word. Please.

It went through.

No read notification. No reply.

He gripped the steering wheel until his hands hurt. The passenger seat looked too empty. He pictured Olivia there anyway, knees pulled up, eyes on the window, silent but there.

The picture died when he blinked.

He stared past the windshield toward the broken fence. Rain from earlier in the week had left the ground uneven in places. Near the fence line, one patch looked darker than the rest, raw and turned over. He looked at it for a second too long, then looked away.

Half the yard looked torn up. It meant nothing.

He hit the wheel once with the heel of his hand and leaned back hard against the seat, breathing through the anger because anger was easier than fear and still did nothing.

A little after midnight, Riley opened Danny's thread.

Danny: Heard anything?

Riley: No. Nothing. You?

Danny: Same. Not even a read.

Riley: She always leaves something.

Danny: I can't sit still.

Riley: Don't do anything stupid.

A long pause.

Danny: Too late for stupid. She's gone quiet.

Riley stared at the last line until her vision blurred.

Gone quiet.

It sounded like him trying to make the silence smaller than it was. Like if he named it right, maybe it would stay manageable.

She set the phone down. Picked it back up. Checked Olivia's thread again. Nothing had changed.

By morning, both of them had checked their screens more times than they could count.

No message.

No missed call.

No breadcrumb.

Just more silence.

What the Hallways Say

The second day was worse.

By then, the school had started talking for her.

The hallways buzzed from first period on, louder than usual, sharper somehow. Lockers slammed. Shoes squeaked on tile. Conversations cut off when Riley got too close, then started again just behind her shoulder.

"She's out again?"

"Maybe her dad pulled her."

"No, she ran off."

"With Danny?"

A laugh.

"Wouldn't shock me."

Riley kept walking, but each whisper landed anyway.

At lunch, she sat at the edge of a crowded table because being alone again would look like too much. The cafeteria smelled like pizza grease, fries, and cleaning spray strong enough to sting the back of her throat. A girl from band leaned toward another girl and said, too casually, "She probably ditched everybody."

Riley's fork hit the tray with a hard clatter.

"She didn't ditch anyone," she said.

The girls looked up, startled.

Riley could feel half the table go still around her, but she kept going anyway. "Something's wrong. It's not that."

No one answered.

A few exchanged glances. One girl looked down at her food. Another reached for her drink like she had somewhere else to be.

Riley stood, grabbed her tray, and walked out before her face gave away too much.

After last period, Ms. Porter caught her near the door.

"Stay a moment, please."

Riley stopped. "Yes, ma'am."

The room emptied out around them until it was just the two of them and the late afternoon light stretching across the floor.

Ms. Porter set her papers down slowly. "Olivia's seemed off lately," she said. "And now she's not coming at all."

Riley said nothing.

"You two are close." Ms. Porter's voice stayed careful, but there was more weight in it now. "If you know where she is, you need to tell me."

Riley tightened her grip on her bag strap. "I don't."

That part, at least, was true.

Ms. Porter studied her face for a long second. "If she reaches out to you, you come to me. Immediately. Promise me."

Riley swallowed. "I promise."

When she stepped back into the hallway, her fingers slipped into her pocket without thinking and brushed the key to her house. The metal edge pressed into her palm.

Warm from her body.

Useless all the same.

The Name Between Them

Danny was waiting at the library steps again when Riley reached them.

He looked like hell. Same clothes as yesterday. Same phone in his hand. Same tight look around the mouth, only worse now because it had been a whole day and still nothing had broken.

He straightened when he saw her.

"Well?"

His voice came out rough enough to scrape.

Riley shook her head. "Nothing. Not in class. Not at lunch. Not anywhere."

Danny dragged a hand through his hair. "So that's it? She just vanishes and everybody shrugs?"

"They're not shrugging." Riley stopped a few feet from him. "They're talking."

His face hardened. "About what?"

She hesitated. "That she ran off. That maybe she left with you."

Danny gave a short, humorless laugh. "Of course."

"They're scared," Riley said. "And scared people make up the version they can live with."

He turned away from her and stared out toward the parking lot. "It's him."

Riley did not answer fast enough.

Danny looked back at once. "You know it is."

"You don't know that," she said.

His eyes flashed. "Come on, Riley."

"I'm serious." Her voice tightened. "You do not get to decide what happened because it fits what you already believe."

"What I believe?" he shot back. "He tracks her. He checks her phone. He runs her whole life like a schedule."

"And you think that makes you the only one who sees clearly?" Riley took one step closer. "Because you don't."

Danny's hand closed hard around his phone. "Then what do you think happened?"

Riley opened her mouth.

Nothing came out right away.

That was the worst part. She had spent all day telling herself not to go there. Not to let her mind turn the fear into something solid before there was proof.

But fear had shape now. It had Olivia's empty seat. Olivia's unread messages. Olivia gone two days straight without a word.

Her voice dropped when she finally spoke.

"I think something is wrong."

Danny stared at her.

Riley held his gaze, even with her pulse kicking hard. "I think she didn't just decide to disappear. I think if she could answer, she would."

Something in his face shifted then. The anger stayed, but panic showed through it.

"She's gone," he said, quieter now. "Not hiding. Gone."

Riley hated how true it sounded.

They stood there with the late light thinning around them and neither one knowing what to do with the truth once it had been said out loud.

Danny looked down at the thread on his phone. Olivia's name at the top. Messages underneath it, unanswered and piling up.

"If she calls," he said, almost to himself, "I'll know what to do."

Riley looked at him sharply.

He did not seem to notice. Or maybe he did and did not care.

That was the part that chilled her. Danny looked scared. He also looked ready. Like part of him had been waiting for the moment when fear turned into action and he could finally move.

Riley was not sure which part of that scared her more.

A phone pinged.

Both of them jerked toward the sound.

Danny looked at the screen.

Not Olivia.

Just some useless update from the school app.

He let out a breath that did not sound like relief. Riley looked away, suddenly too tired to stand there another second.

The sun dropped lower. The stone steps gave back the cold they had been holding all day.

For the first time, Olivia's silence stopped feeling temporary.

It felt like something closing.

Part III

Shadows of Doubt

Chapter Fifteen

What He Kept

Their Spot

The night after Olivia vanished, Danny could not keep his mind on the library steps.

Every time the doors opened and someone else came out, memory dragged him backward again. Back to the train yard. Back to the last time Olivia looked him in the eyes and asked him for something he should have refused.

The yard had been quiet that afternoon. Rust touched every edge. Old boxcars sat along the tracks like tired animals. Wind moved loose dirt across the gravel in thin little sweeps. Danny stood near the broken fence with his hands shoved deep into his jacket and watched the road.

He had gotten there too early again.

He always did when it was her.

Waiting felt easier than being late. Waiting meant he could breathe for a few minutes without worrying he had missed her.

A crow cried from a power pole above him. The sound cut hard through the stillness. He hated it. He liked it too. It made the place feel less dead.

He checked his phone for the fifth time, even though he already knew there was nothing new on the screen. Her name sat at the top of the thread. Short replies. Long gaps. Too much silence doing half the talking.

Then he saw her.

Olivia stepped through the gap in the fence like she expected someone to be watching. Her eyes moved first, quick along the edges of the yard before they found him. Her hair was tied back in a loose knot. Her backpack hung from one shoulder. She kept that side lifted a little, careful without wanting it to show.

Her face hit him harder than he expected.

She looked thinner. Paler. The shadows under her eyes had gone darker since the last time he saw her. She was still Olivia. Still careful. Still holding herself together. But it looked like it cost her now.

"You scared me," Danny said.

He meant it as a joke. It came out strained.

"I know," she said. "I couldn't get away sooner."

He wanted to ask what had delayed her. He wanted to ask what happened this time. He kept it in. The answer was always some version of the same thing.

They walked toward the old flatbed car where they usually sat. The wood planks had gone gray with weather. Someone had carved initials into the far corner years ago. Most of them had faded into shallow scars.

Olivia climbed up first and tucked her legs under herself. Danny sat beside her, close enough to feel her there, not close enough to touch.

"I'm glad you came," he said.

She did not answer right away.

Instead, she looked out across the yard, past the rails, past the weeds, as if something out there might still change her mind.

Then she said, "I needed to."

The way she said it made his chest tighten.

"There's something I have to give you."

What She Carried

Olivia set the backpack in her lap and unzipped it with slow, careful fingers.

Her hands were shaking.

Danny watched her face. She would not look at him. She kept her eyes on the zipper, on the flap, on anything but him.

"Promise me something first," she said.

"What?"

"Promise me you won't interrupt. Just let me finish."

He frowned. "I don't even know what it is yet."

"Promise first."

The last two words came out thinner than the rest. Almost cracked.

Danny felt the air pull tight around them.

"Okay," he said. "I won't interrupt."

She reached into the bag and pulled out a bundle wrapped in her faded blue track hoodie.

His stomach dropped a little at the sight of it. He knew that hoodie. Everyone did. Olivia wore it to practice, to study hall, to cold meets when she wanted to disappear inside something familiar.

She held the bundle against her chest for a moment, like letting go of it hurt.

Then she passed it to him.

It felt heavier than it should have.

He looked down at the journal folded inside the hoodie.

Danny looked up at her. "This is what you almost gave me before."

She did not answer right away. Then she nodded once.

"I was trying to."

The simple way she said it landed harder than a longer answer would have.

He stared at the bundle another second. "Your journal?"

She nodded again.

"Why this?"

"Because I can't keep it there anymore."

The words came out flat with fatigue, not drama.

"Why me?" he asked.

That made her look at him.

For a second he saw how tired she really was.

"Because Riley would do something now," Olivia said. "She would try to help right away. She would go to Ms. Porter. She would make noise."

"And I wouldn't?"

"You would keep your mouth shut if I asked you to."

Danny hated how quickly he answered.

"Yeah," he said. "I would."

She nodded once, like that settled something.

"You keep it hidden," she said. "You keep it shut. Even if people ask questions. Even if it makes you look bad."

"That is a hell of a thing to ask."

"I know."

He turned the bundle once in his hands. "What is in it?"

Her face changed before she spoke. Not fear exactly. Something more tired than that. Like she had already spent too long deciding how much to say.

"Enough," she said.

"That isn't an answer."

"It's the only one I have."

He watched her.

After a moment, she added, "Rules. Dates. Things that sound small until you live under them. Things that stop sounding small once you put them all in one place."

His jaw tightened.

"Are you in danger right now?"

"I think he knows I'm slipping."

The yard seemed to go quieter around them.

Danny looked back down at the journal. "Then let me read it."

He started to pull the hoodie back.

Her hand clamped around his wrist so fast it surprised both of them.

"No."

The word came out sharp enough to cut.

Danny held still.

Her fingers eased, but she did not let go right away.

"Not now," she said, softer this time. "If you open it now, then it becomes yours too."

He stared at her. "Isn't that the point?"

"No." She swallowed. "The point is you keep it shut until it matters."

He let the hoodie fall closed again.

"What about Riley?"

Olivia looked away.

"If Riley knows too much now, she'll wear it on her face. She'll try to save me tonight. He'll see it. He always does."

Danny felt something cold slide through him.

"So I lie to her."

"I'm asking you to protect me."

The answer sat there between them.

Not clean. Not fair. Not something he could carry without feeling it.

Still, after a long second, he nodded.

"Okay," he said quietly. "I'll keep it shut."

Only then did she pull her hand away.

When the Line Breaks

For a while neither of them said anything.

The wind moved through the yard in small cold threads. Somewhere down the line, metal knocked softly against metal. The crow cried again and then went quiet.

Danny stared at the bundle in his lap.

Then he looked at Olivia and said the thing he had already been thinking.

"We should tell Ms. Porter."

Olivia gave a tired little shake of her head.

"She sees you," he said. "She isn't stupid."

"She is kind," Olivia said. "Kindness makes noise."

"That isn't always bad."

"It is if it gets back to him first."

Danny looked at her face again and felt anger rise in him so fast it made his hands go hot.

"You can't keep doing this," he said. "You look like you haven't slept in weeks."

"I haven't slept in weeks."

He pushed off the flatbed and stood, then sat back down again a second later because the yard suddenly felt too exposed and he did not want to tower over her.

"Then come with me tonight."

She did not answer.

"Olivia."

He leaned closer. "I mean it. Tonight. My truck is close. I've got cash. We go. We keep driving."

That got her attention, but not the way he wanted.

She went very still.

"He would follow the map," she said.

"Then leave the phone."

"He notices battery drops. He notices routes. He notices time."

"Then let him notice. Let me handle the rest."

The second it left his mouth, he saw it land wrong.

Her shoulders tightened. Her eyes moved to his face, searching it for something that made her chest pull in.

"That is the problem," she said quietly. "Everybody wants to handle the rest."

He sat back a little.

The shame came fast. So did frustration.

"You're waiting for a clean break," he said. "There isn't one."

"No." Her voice stayed low. "I'm waiting for a moment that doesn't burn everybody around me."

That shut him up.

For a second, all he could hear was the wind and the weak hum in the rails beneath them.

Then he said, softer, "And if that moment never comes?"

Olivia looked down at the gravel below the flatbed.

"When the line breaks," she said. "That is when."

Danny frowned. "What line?"

She gave the smallest shrug.

"The one I keep pretending is still straight."

He hated that answer because he understood it.

He hated it more because part of him wanted to ignore it, take her hand, walk her to the truck, and make the choice for her.

The thought flashed through him hard and ugly.

He did not move.

Olivia rubbed at her lower arm through the sleeve of her hoodie. It looked like a habit now. Or a place that hurt.

Danny looked away before he asked the wrong question and made her shut down again.

“I’m scared,” he said.

She gave a thin breath that might have been the start of a laugh in some other life.

“I know,” she whispered. “I am too.”

Keep Both

The light had started to thin by the time they climbed down.

The yard looked flatter now. Colder. Every shape sharper at the edges.

Danny tucked the hoodie bundle under his jacket. The square weight pressed against his ribs.

"He checks my phone more now," Olivia said. "If I go quiet, do not push."

"I will want to."

"I know." She looked at him then. "But do not make me manage that too."

The words hit. Not cruel. Just tired enough to tell the truth.

Danny nodded once.

"I'll be at the steps," he said. "If you need out."

"I know."

"Tell Riley something. Anything."

"That I'm okay."

"That will be a lie."

"She needs the lie more than the panic."

Danny hated that she was right.

He watched her pull the backpack higher on her shoulder. Watched her glance toward the road the way people glanced toward weather they did not trust.

"Come with me," he said one last time.

This time it came out quiet.

No plan in it. No push. Just want.

Olivia stepped closer instead of back.

For one second, two at most, she touched two fingers to his sleeve.

The contact was so light he almost thought he imagined it.

"Not yet," she said.

His throat tightened.

He tapped the bundle hidden under his jacket. "Then I keep this."

"And the promise."

He gave a tired, humorless breath. "Keep both?"

Her eyes lifted to his.

"Keep both," she said. "Even if it hurts you."

"That isn't fair."

"I know," she said. "But it keeps me alive a little longer."

Her words hit him like a punch.

Then she stepped away and moved toward the gap in the fence.

Danny followed a few paces behind and stopped there.

She slipped through first. On the other side, she turned back.

Wind lifted loose strands of her hair across her face. For one second she looked like she might say something else. Something bigger. Something that would change the whole shape of the night.

She did not.

She only looked at him with fear in her eyes and something smaller buried under it. Hope maybe. Or regret.

Then she turned and started toward the road.

Danny stood there until she was swallowed by scrub and darkening light.

Under the Seat

He stayed in the yard longer than he should have.

By the time he made it back to the truck, the cold had pushed through his jacket and settled in his hands. He got behind the wheel and did not start the engine.

The hoodie bundle sat in his lap now.

He stared at it.

He could feel the square corners of the journal through the faded blue fabric. He could also feel something worse.

The shameful little flicker underneath all the fear.

She had chosen him.

Not Riley.

The thought made him sick the second he had it.

He pressed a hand over his face and sat there breathing through the smell of old upholstery, dirt, and cold metal.

Then he leaned down and shoved the wrapped journal under the driver's seat.

He pushed it back until his knuckles scraped metal.

There.

Hidden.

Untouched.

He told himself it was temporary. One night. Maybe two. Just until he found somewhere safer.

But even then, with the engine still off and the dark thickening around the truck, he knew the truth.

He had already started building a secret around it.

Danny finally started the engine and drove with both hands locked on the wheel. He did not look at the seat again. He did not reach for the bundle. He did not unwrap it.

At the first stop sign, he said the words out loud anyway.

"I promise."

The memory broke there.

Danny blinked hard and found himself back at the library steps, hands raw from gripping cold stone too hard. The courtyard had gone mostly empty. Light drained off the windows in thin gray strips. Somewhere beyond the lot, a train horn carried over town.

Under the driver's seat of his truck, where he had shoved it that night and never found a safer place, Olivia's journal was still wrapped in the faded blue hoodie.

Still hidden.

Still untouched.

And the promise was still there with it.

Chapter Sixteen

Under the Seat

Questions by the Truck

The last bell spilled through the halls and into the parking lot in a rush of noise.

Students poured outside in groups, backpacks bouncing against their sides, voices stretching across the cracked asphalt. Some laughed. Some argued. Some talked too loudly about weekend plans. The air smelled like hot pavement and old exhaust. A breeze rolled paper cups along the curb and shoved dust through the rows of cars.

Riley lingered near the library steps with both straps of her backpack locked in her fists. She watched the crowd scatter, but her mind stayed somewhere else. Olivia had been gone too long now. Every hour without a message felt heavier than the last.

As she scanned the lot, something caught her eye.

Two men stood near the far edge by the teacher spaces. Uniforms. Clean boots. Steady posture. Their faces gave away almost nothing, but their attention moved over the lot with practiced patience.

Officers.

Riley's chest tightened at once.

She shifted closer to the railing and pretended to dig through her bag for a notebook she did not need. From there she could see Danny's truck in the third row. He sat hunched behind the wheel with his hood up, phone in hand, trying too hard to look like a person with nothing to worry about.

He had never been good at disappearing.

His nerves showed in the little things. The tap of his foot. The rigid grip on the wheel. The way he kept staring forward as if refusing to look might save him.

One of the officers crossed the lot and tapped the window.

Danny flinched hard, then rolled it down with slow fingers.

"Danny Holt?" the taller officer asked. His voice carried cleanly in the open air. "Mind if we ask a few questions?"

Danny swallowed. "About Olivia?" He tried to sound bored. He failed.

The officer traded a quick look with his partner. "That's right."

Riley edged a little closer, lowering her head as if she were still searching her bag. Her heart had already started pounding too fast.

Danny kept both hands on the wheel. His thumbs dug into a worn groove in the leather. "What about her?"

"When's the last time you saw her?" the officer asked, pulling out a small notebook.

Danny hesitated. His jaw shifted like he was grinding down a thought. "Couple days before break," he said. "She seemed tired."

The officer wrote that down.

"Did she ever talk about running away? Meeting anyone outside school?"

"No. Never," Danny said too quickly.

Riley winced.

The answer came fast enough to feel wrong. Whether it was true or not, it sounded like the kind of lie people told when they were trying to protect something bigger than themselves. She knew exactly how that would sound to the police.

"You sure about that?" the second officer asked, leaning in a little.

Danny's knuckles went white on the wheel. "I'm sure."

The officers let the silence do some of the work for them.

Students had started noticing by then. A few slowed on their way to the buses. A couple of boys pointed toward the truck. Somebody whispered behind a raised hand. Riley felt her stomach turn.

After a long moment, the taller officer stepped back.

"We may need to follow up," he said.

Danny nodded stiffly and stared straight ahead, refusing to meet either of their eyes.

The officers walked away.

The whispers stayed.

Riley could almost hear them crawl across the parking lot and latch on. This was how stories started in Hollow's Edge. Not from facts. From shape. From tone. From whatever version made people feel like they understood something before they really did.

She took one step toward Danny's truck, wanting to tell him he looked cornered. Wanting to tell him to breathe.

But the words stayed trapped behind her teeth.

Ethan's Shadow

By the time Riley reached the sidewalk by the exit, Ethan was already there.

He stood beside his truck speaking to the same officers who had just questioned Danny. His arms were folded. His voice sounded calm and controlled, almost gentle. It was the kind of voice adults used when they wanted trust to rise in the room before doubt had the chance to speak.

His posture showed no panic. No visible fear. Just readiness.

Riley stopped behind a cluster of students and stayed close enough to hear.

"She'd been pulling back before break," Ethan said. "These messages worry me."

He held out a set of folded printouts. The pages looked too neat. Too crisp. Not grabbed in panic. Prepared.

One officer unfolded them with care. "You're certain these came from her phone?"

"Same phone she always uses," Ethan said. "She keeps it on the kitchen charger every night. I check it before bed."

Riley's stomach dropped.

That part was true. Olivia had told her that. Riley had once thought it was strict parenting. Annoying, maybe. Overbearing. Now, hearing him say it out loud to the police, it sounded like something else. Something colder. Something that had been hiding in plain sight.

"And these are to Danny?" the officer asked.

Ethan's mouth twitched. It almost passed for sadness.

"Yes," he said. "I did not want to believe it either. But he's been pushing her. You can see that for yourself."

The officers read in silence.

Riley could not see the pages, but she did not need to. She could feel the shift. The way judgment settled. Quiet. Immediate. Clean.

"Thank you, Mr. Harper," the taller officer said.

Ethan dipped his head politely.

He looked calm. Composed. Helpful.

Very helpful.

Then his gaze slid past the officers and landed on Riley.

Their eyes met for half a second.

His expression did not change, but something in the air around him did. His stare held nothing warm. Nothing frightened either. Only patience. A careful sort of patience that made Riley's skin prickle.

She backed away slowly and let herself blend into the flow of students.

She wanted to scream. She wanted to run. She wanted to grab one of those officers and tell them they were looking in the wrong direction.

Instead, she stayed quiet.

Just like Olivia had.

The Weight of Whispers

By the next morning, the whispers had sharpened.

They slipped through classrooms and down hallways. They moved from locker to locker and changed shape every time they were repeated.

"Cops talked to Danny again."

"They pulled messages from her phone."

"She wanted space."

"He wouldn't leave her alone."

Riley shoved through the hall between first and second period, trying not to react. Every voice felt like a sting. Every rumor twisted the truth a little harder. The walls felt closer than usual, like the whole building was shrinking around one version of the story.

Near her locker, two teachers stood by a bulletin board talking in low careful tones. One looked up when Riley approached, then lowered her voice even more.

Heat rushed into Riley's face.

She slammed her locker harder than she meant to. Both teachers flinched.

She knew what they were thinking. They wondered how much she knew. They wondered if Danny had dragged her into trouble too.

By lunch, Danny finally showed up near the library steps.

His shoulders were pulled tight. He looked thinner than he had the week before. His face had lost color. The hood was up, but it did nothing to hide the fear in his posture.

Riley pushed through a cluster of students to reach him.

"They're twisting everything," she hissed.

"I didn't do anything," Danny snapped.

His voice cracked on the last word and came out too loud. Several heads turned.

Riley stepped closer. "Then why won't you say what you're not telling them?"

Danny's eyes flashed with panic and anger at once. "Because I promised."

Riley froze.

The word hit harder than she expected. It closed around her throat. She wanted to shake him. Wanted to demand he stop choosing the kind of silence that only made him look worse.

"So you're sticking to that?" she whispered. "Even now?"

Danny looked away. His own voice dropped with his eyes. "I gave her my word."

People nearby had already started slowing.

Riley saw the looks. The raised brows. The little smirks. The way the rumor mill leaned closer the second it smelled blood.

Someone whispered, "That's him."

Another voice answered, "Knew it."

Riley's chest tightened. Danny yanked his hood lower.

She wanted to tell them all to shut up. She wanted to stand in front of him and block the whole scene with her body. But his silence wrapped around everything like a locked door. She could not open it without breaking whatever Olivia had trusted him with.

Danny looked like he might come apart right there on the steps.

Riley placed her hand on his arm, steady and gentle.

"You can't face this alone," she said.

He gave a small, empty laugh that barely sounded human. "I already am."

Her heart ached.

Standard Procedure

After the final bell, the parking lot filled again with voices and slammed doors.

The afternoon sun had dipped low enough to throw long shadows between the cars. Riley crossed toward the steps and saw Danny heading for his truck. His hands shook when he reached for the door. He tried to hide it by shoving them into his pockets first, then thought better of it.

She started toward him.

Then she saw the officers.

The same two from the day before stood waiting near the edge of the lot, eyes fixed on his truck.

Riley stopped cold.

Danny climbed inside and shut the door fast. He leaned forward and dropped his head against the wheel. His shoulders rose and fell in quick breaths.

The officers approached with slow, steady steps.

Students nearby hushed and drifted toward the edges of the lot, pretending not to watch while watching everything.

One officer leaned down to the open window.

"Mr. Holt," he said. "We need to take a closer look. Standard procedure."

Danny gripped the wheel again and lifted his head. "Fine," he said. "Search it."

His voice shook on the last word.

The officers exchanged a glance and stepped back from the window.

Riley forced her legs to move. She reached the truck just as Danny pressed his forehead to the wheel again.

"They already think it's me," he muttered. "Ethan's feeding them lies, and they're eating it up."

Riley swallowed.

She wanted to tell him she believed him, but belief felt shaky now too. Not because she thought he had hurt Olivia. Because his silence kept turning every true thing into something that looked false.

She looked across the lot.

Ethan stood near his truck with one hand in his pocket, watching the scene unfold.

He did not smile.

He did not frown.

He simply watched.

Riley felt something cold slide through her.

"He doesn't even have to fight," she said quietly. "He just waits for us to fall in."

Danny closed his eyes.

Riley stood beside the truck and felt the noose of suspicion tighten around both of them as the sun dipped lower.

The day did not feel finished.

It felt like something worse had only just begun.

The Search

The first officer leaned into the truck with a flashlight.

The beam cut a clean stripe across the floor mats. Dust floated through the light in soft drifting specks. He moved with maddening patience, lifting loose papers from the console, checking cup holders, glove box, side pockets. One place after another came up empty.

Danny stood by the front tire with his hands on his hips, but Riley saw the twitch in his fingers. He curled them into fists to hide it. His jaw looked locked so tight it might crack.

Students edged closer in careful half steps.

Some leaned against nearby cars. Others slipped out of the bus line and stopped by the walkway. Phones started showing up in hands. Riley hated the sight of them. She wanted to knock every one of them to the pavement.

The officer crouched lower and angled the flashlight beneath the driver's seat.

Riley felt her heart slam once against her ribs.

Danny's breathing changed. Only a little. A small inhale that did not come back out right away.

The officer reached under the seat. His fingers brushed something. He caught a dusty corner of faded blue fabric and pulled.

The cloth snagged on the metal frame, then slid free.

Time slowed.

The blue shape unfolded in his hand and sagged toward the pavement.

Olivia's old track hoodie.

Dust streaked one sleeve. The cuff hung limp.

Riley's stomach turned. She knew that hoodie. Everyone did. Olivia wore it constantly. Seeing it in the officer's hands made the whole lot seem to drop a few degrees.

Then something slipped partway out of the folds.

Something small. Square. Brown at the corners.

Olivia's journal.

It looked closed tight. The cover was worn but unbent. The pages sat pressed together, too neat for something that had been read through in secret.

Riley's breath caught.

She had never touched the journal, but she had seen Olivia writing in it during study periods and after school. It was private. Important. Not the kind of thing Olivia would lose by accident.

The officer stood.

He held the hoodie and journal together as one bundle and looked at Danny.

"Sir," he said. "We found something."

Danny stepped forward too fast.

The second officer raised a hand and stopped him before he reached the truck.

"I can explain," Danny said. His voice shook. "It isn't what you think."

The taller officer turned the bundle slightly in his hands. "Belong to Olivia?"

Danny swallowed hard. "Yeah."

"You recognize it?"

"Yeah," he said again. His face had gone pale. "But I didn't take it from her. And I didn't hurt her."

The officer did not blink. "Then why is it under your seat?"

Danny opened his mouth.

Nothing came out.

His throat bobbed once. A hard silence filled the space around him.

Riley watched his face closely.

His eyes moved from the hoodie to the journal, then back to the officer. Fear was there, but something heavier sat under it too. Something that looked less like guilt and more like being trapped inside a promise he could not break without making everything worse.

Riley's mind raced.

Olivia could have given it to him. Riley knew that much. But if that were true, why hide it? Why not say one thing now that could stop this from collapsing in on him?

Riley leaned closer and lowered her voice.

"Danny," she said. "Just tell them. Please."

His eyes snapped to hers. His mouth parted like he was about to speak.

Then he stopped.

His gaze dropped to the pavement, like he had stepped to the edge of something and could not make himself cross it.

Riley felt the air leave her lungs.

His silence wasn't an answer.

But it felt like one.

Something closer to fear.

What the Lot Saw

The hoodie and journal sat in the officer's hands like a signal flare.

That was all it took.

Students stopped pretending not to watch.

A wave of voices moved through the lot.

"They found something."

"That's hers."

"Told you."

A boy near the buses muttered, "I knew it. He always acted weird around her."

"That's not true," Riley snapped.

Her voice came out louder than she meant it to. Heads turned at once. A few students stared at her like she had just stepped into the center of the story with him.

Danny glanced up at her. His eyes looked glassy, like he was holding something back with both hands.

A girl near the curb whispered, "She's defending him."

Another answered, "Maybe she knows more than she's saying."

Riley's skin went hot.

She wanted to cry. She wanted to scream. She wanted to grab the hoodie from the officer and tell the whole lot they were seeing the wrong thing the wrong way.

Mr. Cole took a step forward from the sidewalk.

"That's enough," he called.

Some students shifted away.

Not far.

The phones stayed up. The whispers kept moving, softer now but sharper.

Riley looked at the hoodie again. The dust on the sleeve. The way the journal sagged against the fabric.

It felt wrong.

Part of her still believed Danny.

It did nothing to change what the whole lot had just seen.

Danny stood stiff beside the truck like someone caught in headlights.

Riley wanted to grab his arm and pull him out of the lot. She wanted to tell him she believed him.

But doubt kept brushing against her mind like cold fingers.

Not because she thought he had hurt Olivia.

Because she could not explain any of this.

And the crowd would not wait for an explanation.

Taken Away

One officer slid the hoodie and journal into a clear evidence bag.

The plastic crackled in the quiet.

Riley flinched before she could stop herself.

The officers sealed the bag with tape. One slow pull. One firm press. The journal shifted inside the plastic, still closed, still tight, still giving nothing away.

Danny watched every second of it.

His breathing had gone shallow enough to hear. The brown cover showed through the plastic for a moment, then turned out of sight.

"Danny," the taller officer said. His tone stayed calm, almost gentle. "We need you to come by the station tomorrow. We've got more questions."

Danny nodded once. The motion looked stiff. "Am I under arrest?"

"No," the officer said. "Not right now."

Those last three words landed heavier than anything else.

Danny rubbed his hands together, noticed them shaking, then shoved them into his pockets. "Fine," he muttered.

The officers carried the bag toward their car. One of them opened the back door and placed it inside. For half a second, the journal pressed flat against the window.

Then the door shut.

The sound echoed across the lot.

Danny sank onto the curb like his legs had given out. He leaned forward with his elbows on his knees and both fists pressed against his temples. His shoulders rose and fell in short, uneven breaths.

Riley took a step toward him.

Then another.

She stopped when the voices started again.

"That looks bad."

"I always knew something was off about him."

"He snapped all the time."

The words wrapped around her ankles like chains.

A hand touched her shoulder.

Ms. Porter.

Her grip was light but firm.

"Riley," she said softly. "Let them handle it."

Riley nodded, but the motion felt wrong. Nothing about this felt handled.

Danny lifted his head.

His eyes were red, glassy, but dry. He looked straight at Riley.

For one moment, neither of them spoke.

She waited for him to explain. She waited for him to say one sentence that could shift the shape of everything.

Danny opened his mouth.

Then closed it again.

His jaw tightened. He shook his head once, slow and small.

Riley felt something cave in behind her ribs.

Not because she thought he was guilty.

Because he was still choosing silence, and she did not know why.

The officers climbed into their car. The engine turned over. The cruiser rolled out toward the gate with Olivia's things locked in the back.

Riley tracked it until it disappeared.

When she looked back, Danny was still on the curb. Smaller somehow. Folded inward.

The lot had started emptying. Buses pulled out one by one. Cars followed. The attention thinned, but the damage stayed behind.

Danny got to his feet slowly and brushed dust from his jeans with hands that still shook.

He did not look at Riley again.

She wanted to stop him. Wanted to tell him she believed him. Wanted to say she was sorry. Wanted to demand the truth.

Nothing came out.

He walked to the truck and opened the door. Paused with one hand on the frame.

For one split second, Riley thought he might turn back.

He didn't.

The door shut. The engine started. The truck pulled away, leaving a dark patch on the pavement where it had been parked.

Riley stood alone in the quiet lot and watched the last of the light slide across the asphalt.

In her mind, the moment kept replaying.

The hoodie.

The journal.

Danny's silence.

It did not feel like guilt.

It felt like protection.

And that scared her almost as much.

She tightened her grip on her backpack and turned toward the school.

Tomorrow, everyone would talk.

Tomorrow, the questions would come.

Tonight, one question refused to leave her alone.

What promise was worth letting this destroy him?

Chapter Seventeen

What the Lot Left Behind

After the Lot

Riley stood there long after the cruiser disappeared.

The parking lot had started emptying in slow waves. Buses pulled out first, heavy and loud, rattling toward the road. Then came the cars, one by one, headlights cutting across the fading light. Students still lingered near the curb and the walkway, but not because they had anywhere to be. They stayed because something had happened, and Hollow's Edge never let go of a thing once it smelled like a story.

Danny's truck was gone.

The dark patch where it had been parked still showed against the pavement.

Riley kept staring at it anyway.

The hoodie.

The journal.

Danny's face when the officers held them up.

She could still hear the rough scrape in his voice when he said it was not what they thought. She could still see the way his mouth had opened and then shut again when the officer asked why Olivia's things were under his seat. It had looked less like guilt than panic. Less like a lie than a person standing too close to something he didn't know how to say out loud.

Ms. Porter stayed close beside her as the lot emptied.

Riley let herself be guided back toward the building, though her eyes kept dragging to the dark patch where Danny's truck had been.

Riley looked over at Ms. Porter. Her face had gone pale under the late afternoon light. Her hands were folded tight in front of her, like she needed something to hold onto too.

"Come inside for a minute," she said. "You don't need to stand out here."

Riley glanced toward the lot again. A cluster of boys near the buses were already talking too fast, heads bent close. One of them looked over, saw Riley watching, and lowered his voice. A girl near the curb held up her phone and turned it toward her friend, replaying something on the screen.

The filming had not stopped.

The lot had only changed shape around it.

Riley swallowed hard and followed Ms. Porter toward the doors.

Inside, the hallway felt too bright. Voices bounced off the tile in sharp bursts. A locker slammed somewhere down the hall and made her shoulders jump.

Ms. Porter stopped near the front office and turned to face her. "Do you have a ride home?"

Riley nodded. "Yeah."

"Good."

The word came out careful. Too careful.

Riley knew that tone. Adults used it when they wanted to sound steady in front of kids, even when they were not steady at all.

Ms. Porter glanced toward the glass doors. "If anyone asks you questions tonight, you do not owe them answers."

Riley let out a short breath through her nose. "That's not really how this town works."

No smile touched Ms. Porter's face.

"No," she said quietly. "It isn't."

Officer Miller stepped in from the hall before either of them could move on.

"Riley Mercer?"

She turned too fast. "Yeah?"

His expression stayed calm. Not cold. Not accusing. Just steady.

"We'd like you to come by the station tomorrow after school and answer a few questions."

Riley stared at him. "Am I in trouble?"

"No," Miller said at once. "You're not in trouble. You're not under arrest. We just need help filling in a few gaps."

He held out a card.

Riley took it and looked down at the printed number and address.

"Do I need to bring my mom?"

"Only if you want to," Miller said. "That's up to you. This is voluntary. We just need clarity."

Riley nodded, though her fingers had already tightened around the card. She slipped in into her hoodie pocket before she could read the address again.

"We'll be there until early evening," he said. "After school is fine."

Then he stepped back and let the silence settle again.

For one second Riley thought Ms. Porter might say more. About Danny. About Olivia. About what the school had started to feel like all week. Instead, she only reached out and squeezed Riley's arm once.

"Go home," she said. "Try to rest."

Riley almost laughed.

Rest.

The word sounded like something people said when they had run out of useful things.

She nodded anyway, because there was nothing else to do, and made herself walk toward the exit with her head down and her backpack digging into both shoulders.

The voices followed.

Not loud. Not bold.

Just low enough to spread.

"They found her stuff."

"In his truck."

"I saw it."

Riley kept walking.

By the time she reached the sidewalk, she could already feel the story slipping out of the lot and into the town.

Not because anyone knew the truth.

Because they thought they had seen enough.

No Good Answer

Riley barely remembered the walk home.

The town passed in dull pieces. Side roads. Mailboxes. Sagging fences. A dog tearing across a yard and barking at nothing. Her phone buzzed once in her pocket. Then again.

She didn't check it until she was inside her room with the door shut.

One message was from a girl on the track team.

They found Olivia's stuff in his truck. Is that true?

The second came from a classmate Riley barely talked to.

My mom said the cops took her journal. Riley, what happened?

Riley stared at both messages without answering.

What was she supposed to say?

Yes, they found Olivia's hoodie and journal in his truck, but it still felt wrong.

Yes, Danny looked terrified, but not in the way people wanted.

Yes, the officers took everything, and no, none of it made sense.

She locked the screen and tossed the phone onto the bed.

Then she reached into her hoodie pocket, pulled out Officer Miller's card, and set it on the nightstand beside the lamp.

Downstairs, she could hear cabinet doors opening and closing in the kitchen. Her mom moved through the house in a familiar rhythm, unaware that something had shifted so badly Riley could still feel it in her chest.

A minute later, her mom called up the stairs. "You want to eat?"

Riley looked at the door without moving. "Not hungry."

A pause.

Then, "You okay?"

No.

"Just tired."

That answer was weak enough to sound false even to her, but no more questions came.

She had not told her mom about the card in her pocket.

She had not said that the police wanted her at the station the next day after school.

She had only said she was tired.

A second later, the TV came on downstairs, low and steady, filling the house with the kind of background noise people trusted too easily.

Riley sat on the edge of the bed and finally opened Danny's thread.

The last few texts sat there untouched. Small, ordinary things from before everything had gone sharp. A question. A quick check in. A line that now looked heavier than it had when he sent it.

Her thumbs moved before she decided what to say.

I know you didn't do this.

She stared at the words.

Then deleted them.

She tried again.

Why won't you tell them the truth?

Deleted that too.

Neither version got close enough.

She dropped the phone beside her and pressed both hands over her face. The darkness behind her eyes only made the lot come back sharper.

The clear evidence bag.

The journal pressed flat inside it.

Danny's silence.

That was the part that wouldn't settle right.

If he had done something to Olivia, why had he looked like that?

Why had the fear in his face looked so tangled up with shame and helplessness?

Why had Ethan already had those printouts ready for the officers, neat and folded like he had been waiting for the right moment to hand them over?

Riley lowered her hands slowly and stared at the floor.

She laid the pieces out in her head again.

Ethan had messages.

Danny had Olivia's journal.

The police had what looked like proof.

And still none of it fit together cleanly.

It should have.

That was what scared her.

Before Morning

By the time night settled in, Riley had done none of her homework.

Her books lay open across the bed in a messy spread of pages, highlighters, and loose papers she had not touched in over an hour. The house had gone quiet around her. A faucet clicked off downstairs. The TV murmured once, then went silent. Her mom's footsteps crossed the hall and faded into the bedroom at the other end.

Riley sat against the headboard with her knees pulled up and her phone in both hands.

Tomorrow.

Officer Miller's card still sat on her nightstand where she had left it. His words kept coming back anyway.

We need you to come by the station tomorrow after school.

Tomorrow, Danny had to go in.

Tomorrow, the questions would get worse.

She kept thinking about what would happen if he stayed quiet in that room the way he had stayed quiet in the parking lot. The police would press. He would lock up. His silence would look like guilt all over again.

And Olivia would still be missing.

Riley opened his thread one more time.

She typed:

Please don't shut down tomorrow.

That was true.

She erased it anyway.

Then typed:

I'm still with you.

Too weak.

Deleted.

Then she just stared, thumb hovering, until the screen dimmed and her own reflection showed faintly over it.

She thought of Olivia looking across the cafeteria like she wanted to say something and couldn't.

She thought of Danny by the truck, looking at Riley as if she were the last person still willing to see him as something other than the version hardening around his name.

She thought of Ethan's careful voice and those pages in his hand.

Riley unlocked the screen again.

This time she didn't type.

She pressed call.

The ringing started at once, thin and distant in the dark room.

Once.

Twice.

Three times.

Riley held her breath and listened.

No answer.

The ringing went on.

She nearly hung up, then stopped herself. Let it keep going one more ring. Then another.

Finally the call cut off.

Riley lowered the phone slowly and stared at the screen until it went dark in her hand.

The room stayed still around her.

Tomorrow was coming whether any of them were ready for it or not.

And somewhere out there, Danny was still alone with whatever silence had cost him the lot.

Chapter Eighteen

Screenshots

Empty Space

The lot outside the station smelled like wet pavement and old heat.

Danny sat in the truck with both hands on his thighs, his mind circling the space beneath the driver's seat.

Empty.

The shallow place where Olivia's faded blue hoodie had sat wrapped around the journal. Hidden. Sealed. Untouched.

Gone now.

He could still see the officer lifting the bundle free. The hoodie sagging at the sleeves. The journal pressing against the fabric inside the clear evidence bag.

His throat tightened.

He had not opened it.

That part mattered. It should have mattered more than it did.

His phone buzzed in his pocket. He ignored it once. Then it buzzed again, harder this time, and he pulled it out.

Riley.

He stared at her name until the screen dimmed, then locked it without answering.

His mind dragged backward anyway. Not to the whole afternoon. Just fragments.

The weight of the hoodie bundle in his hands.

Olivia's voice, tired and thin.

Keep both.

The promise.

The fear in her face when she made him say it.

He had kept both.

Now the police had one, and the other was choking him.

A knock on the window made him flinch.

Officer Miller stood outside the truck, calm as ever.

"We're ready for you, Mr. Holt."

Danny nodded once, shoved the phone back into his pocket, and opened the door.

The cold hit his face hard enough to wake up the part of him that still wanted to run.

He shut the door and looked once more at the empty space beneath the seat through the open cab.

Then he followed Miller inside.

Confrontation

They put Danny in a room that felt used up.

The walls were pale and bare. A scratched metal table filled the center. Two chairs faced each other beneath a clock that ticked loud enough to make the room feel smaller.

Danny kept his hands together on the table so he wouldn't clench them into fists.

Miller set a folder between them. Reyes stood near the wall with a notebook already open.

"This is not an arrest," Miller said. "We just need answers."

Danny nodded. "Okay."

Miller opened the folder and slid printed pages across the table.

Green message bubbles stared back at him.

His stomach turned before he even started reading.

"These screenshots were provided by Olivia's father," Miller said. "He says they were taken from her phone."

Danny leaned forward despite himself.

Olivia: I don't know if I should.

Olivia: He'll notice if I'm gone too long.

Danny: You always say that, but yeah, you can.

Danny: I'm waiting at our spot. Just sneak out for a little while.

Danny: He won't know. You just need to try harder.

The room pulled in around him.

“That's not the whole thing,” Danny said. His voice stayed low. “That's not how it went.”

Miller watched him. “Then how did it go?”

Danny dragged his phone from his pocket and unlocked it. His thumb shook hard enough to make him miss the thread the first time. He backed out, searched again, opened the messages.

Nothing.

He froze.

He backed out again and searched her name, then her number.

Still nothing.

"No," he whispered.

Miller's face did not change. "What is it?"

"They're gone." Danny looked up too fast. "The whole thread. All of it."

"Texts can be deleted," Miller said.

"I didn't delete anything." The answer came out sharper than Danny meant. He forced himself to slow down. "I didn't. I swear."

Miller nodded once, like he had heard that word all morning. "Her father gave us these screenshots. You're saying they're fake. Your phone doesn't have the thread."

"That doesn't mean I erased it."

"What does it mean?"

Danny pressed both palms flat against the table. "It means he had access to her phone before any of you did. He checked it all the time. He could make anything look real."

Reyes's pen scratched across the page.

Miller tapped one of the printed lines. "You called it 'our spot.'"

"Yeah," Danny said. "We said that sometimes. It was just a place."

"A place to meet in secret?"

"A place to talk."

Miller didn't blink. "Did you tell her to meet you there the day she disappeared?"

Danny looked at the folder, then back at Miller. "We met. But not the way those messages make it sound."

"She says she's scared. You tell her to stop stalling. To try harder. That reads like pressure."

"She was scared of him," Danny shot back. "Not me."

Miller watched him carefully. "Then why does this sound like you?"

Danny shut his eyes for one second, then opened them again. "Because some of it could. I sent one bad text once. Weeks ago. I sounded pushy. I hated it the second I sent it. If somebody saw that, they had enough to build the rest."

That made Miller pause.

"You admit some of the language is yours."

"Some of it. Not this thread."

Miller glanced down at the papers again. "And the hoodie and journal under your seat."

Danny stared at the folder.

He could tell them the truth halfway and still hand Olivia over.

Or he could keep doing what he had done from the second the officers pulled that bundle free.

He chose silence again.

"I didn't steal it from her," he said at last.

Miller leaned back slightly. "Then why was it under your seat?"

Danny's mouth opened.

Nothing came out.

The clock kept ticking.

Reyes kept writing.

Miller's voice stayed steady. "Right now, the evidence points at you."

The words landed hard.

Danny pressed both hands against his face. His voice came out muffled. "I'm not the one you should be afraid of."

When he lowered his hands again, the papers were still there. So was the version of him they had already started believing.

He had never felt so trapped in his life.

Riley's Turn

Riley had not told her mom she was going to the station.

She had told her she was studying late.

Now she sat in a room almost identical to Danny's. Same pale walls. Same metal table. Same clock ticking too loud. A box of tissues sat near the center of the table, untouched.

Miller came in first. Reyes followed with his notebook.

"Thank you for coming in, Riley," Miller said. "We just need some clarity."

She nodded. Her hands stayed flat on the table.

Miller opened the folder and slid the pages toward her.

Green message bubbles stared back at her.

"These screenshots were provided by Olivia's father," Miller said. "He says they were taken from her phone."

The first line hit her.

Olivia: I don't know if I should.

Olivia: He'll notice if I'm gone too long.

Danny: You always say that, but yeah, you can.

Danny: I'm waiting at our spot. Just sneak out for a little while.

Danny: He won't know. You just need to try harder.

Her chest tightened.

"That looks like Danny," Miller said gently. "Would you agree?"

Riley hesitated.

It did look like him. That was the problem. Not fully. Not cleanly. But enough to hurt.

"He said something like that once," she said. "A while ago. One line. He knew it sounded bad."

"So these messages are possible."

"They're possible to build too."

Miller watched her closely. "Did Olivia ever say she felt unsafe around him?"

"No." The answer came fast. Riley softened it a second later. "Never."

"Unsafe at home?"

Riley froze.

"She never said that," Riley said. "Not like that."

"How did she say it?"

Riley looked down at the green bubbles instead of his face. "She got tired. Worn down. But she never told me she was afraid of Danny."

Miller tapped one of the lines. "Did she ever mention a meeting place? A spot?"

"She never told me where that was."

That part was true.

"Did she ever say Danny pressured her to sneak out?"

"No." Riley swallowed. "Not like this."

"Not like what?"

"Not like she was scared of him. She was scared of getting caught."

"By who?"

Riley's heartbeat thudded in her ears.

The image of Ethan flashed through her mind. His flat voice. Olivia's phone buzzing. The way Olivia would go still before she even looked at the screen.

"She did not like conflict," Riley said carefully.

"That is not what I asked."

Riley lifted her eyes. "She never said she was afraid of Danny."

Miller held her gaze for a long second.

"He says the messages on his phone are gone."

Riley blinked. "Gone?"

"Deleted," Reyes said.

"That doesn't make any sense."

"It raises questions," Miller said.

Riley looked down at the screenshots again.

They were too neat.

That was what bothered her most. Too neat. Too straight. Too perfectly shaped to say one thing and one thing only.

Like someone had cut away everything that did not fit.

"Did Olivia ever mention someone checking her phone?" Miller asked.

Riley swallowed. "Yes."

"Who?"

"She did not always say."

"That was not the question."

Riley felt the room shift around her.

He wanted Ethan's name. Wanted it clean and direct. Something they could write down and build outward from.

But Olivia was missing. Danny was already drowning in something that looked too much like proof. Riley had no clean proof of her own. Only patterns. Silences. Fear that never came in one clear sentence.

"She never said she was afraid of Danny," Riley repeated. "That is what I know."

Miller closed the folder.

"We may have more questions later."

Riley nodded, though her head felt light.

As she stood, she glanced once more at the green bubbles before Miller slid them out of sight.

They looked like proof.

They also looked built.

She did not know which part scared her more.

Shaken Faith

The air outside the station felt damp and cold.

Riley stepped onto the concrete steps and stopped when she saw him. Danny sat two steps down with his elbows on his knees, staring at the pavement like it might give him something if he looked hard enough.

His phone rested beside him, dark.

He glanced up when the door shut behind her. "They showed you."

It was not a question.

Riley nodded. "They did."

Cars passed on the street. Tires hissed over wet pavement.

"It's fake," Danny said. His voice was low and tight. "You know that, right?"

Riley lowered herself onto the step beside him, leaving a little space between them. "I know some of it could be built from something real."

He let out a bitter breath. "That's what he does. Takes something real and bends it."

"They said your messages were gone."

"They were there last night."

"And now they're not."

Danny turned toward her. "You think I deleted them?"

She hesitated. "No." Then, because the whole day had rubbed honesty raw, "I don't know."

The words hung there.

Danny looked away. His jaw tightened.

"I didn't delete anything," he said. "Not after everything."

Riley rubbed her hands together against the chill. "Those words do sound like you."

"That's the point."

She swallowed. "Did you ever text her like that? Before. Not that night."

He did not answer right away.

"Once," he admitted. "Weeks ago. One bad line. I hated it the second I sent it."

Riley closed her eyes for a second. That matched what she remembered.

"They used that."

"Yeah."

She looked at him fully now. "Why didn't you tell them everything?"

His expression shifted.

"Tell them what?"

"Everything," Riley said. "About her. About what she was scared of."

Danny stared down at his hands. "I told them she was scared of him."

"That's not everything."

He stiffened. "You think I'm hiding something."

"I think you're protecting something."

He met her eyes at that.

"And you think that makes me guilty?"

She did not answer.

Because she did not know.

Danny leaned back and stared up at the gray sky. "She trusted me."

Riley's throat tightened. "I know."

"But you don't know with what."

The sentence sat heavy between them.

Cars kept passing. The sky darkened another shade.

Finally Riley said, "I'm not giving up on you."

Danny let out a breath that sounded almost like a laugh, but not quite. "That's not the same as believing me."

Riley did not have an answer for that either.

They sat there in silence, the space between them wider than it had ever been.

Neither of them moved closer.

The Rumor Mill

By nightfall, the town had chosen its version.

Nobody had the full story. That did not stop anyone from building one.

Group chats buzzed with clipped details and sharp guesses. Someone said the police had Olivia's messages. Someone else swore they came straight from her phone. A parent said Danny had been called into the station. Another said that only happened when police already knew enough.

They have texts.

That's enough for me.

No one posted proof. No one needed to.

Details changed every time they were repeated. One parent said he pressured her. Another said he pushed her to lie. By the third retelling, nobody was talking about screenshots anymore. They were talking about intent.

At Hollow's Edge High, even the adults leaned closer.

Near the copy room, one teacher lowered her voice and said, "They questioned him again."

Another answered, "If the police are that focused, there must be something there."

Nobody said maybe not.

Danny sat in his truck outside his house with the engine off and the lights dark. His phone kept lighting with new notifications. He did not open any of them.

He stared at the passenger seat this time.

The journal was gone.

The thread was gone.

And his name was spreading faster than he could answer it.

Across town, Ethan sat at the kitchen table with a mug of tea cooling between his hands. The television hummed softly in the background. His phone rested face up beside the mug.

It buzzed once.

Then again.

We're praying for Olivia.

If you need anything, we're here.

Ethan typed back slowly.

Thank you. I just want the truth.

He set the phone down and folded both hands around the mug.

The messages kept coming.

All over Hollow's Edge, the story kept moving.

It slipped through kitchens, across couches, and into bedrooms where people thought they were only asking questions.

In her room, Riley sat on the edge of her bed with her phone in one hand and the station card still on the nightstand beside her lamp.

Her phone lit again.

The first message came from a number she didn't know.

I have a daughter at Hollow's Edge too. If you know something, you need to say it.

Riley stared at the screen.

Before she could decide whether to answer, another message came through from a number she didn't know.

This is one of the track moms. Were you at the station because of Danny?

Her stomach dropped.

Then a third followed from another unknown number.

People are saying you were there too. Why?

Riley stared at the screen.

That was new.

Not just Danny now. Not just Olivia. The story was widening. Pulling in anyone close enough to touch it.

Her thumb moved toward the keyboard.

You don't know what you saw.

She stopped.

Then deleted it.

She set the phone down beside her and pressed the heels of her hands into her eyes until color flashed in the dark behind them.

Across the room, her track bag leaned against the dresser. One strap hung half twisted. Her spikes still stuck out of the side pocket. Everything looked the same.

Nothing was.

She lay back and stared at the ceiling fan as it turned in slow circles above her.

"I'm not giving up," she whispered into the dark.

But now it was not just Danny being swallowed by the wrong story.

It was everyone standing too close to him.

Outside, the wind picked up and rattled the loose branches against rooftops.

The story had started with fragments.

Now it was moving on assumptions.

And it was only getting louder.

Chapter Nineteen

Fractures

Whispers in the Halls

By Saturday morning, the local news had one update.

A reporter stood outside the station with a tight voice and tired eyes. The camera stayed back, like it didn't want to get too close.

This is still an active investigation. Police are searching for sixteen-year-old Hollow's Edge High student Olivia Harper.

She paused, letting the name settle.

Olivia was reported missing late Thursday night. Detectives have confirmed they are reviewing electronic communications connected to the case. No other details can be released at this time.

That was all.

It didn't matter.

The town did what it always did. It took one thin fact and filled in the rest.

By Saturday afternoon, people were repeating the phrase like it meant more than it did. Electronic communications.

By Sunday, the word messages had a face.

Danny's.

Half the town had already seen his truck outside the station. Someone said he walked in with his head down. Someone else said he looked angry. Another swore he looked guilty.

Nobody agreed on what they saw.

Everybody agreed on what it meant.

By Monday morning, the rumors had stopped sounding like guesses. They sounded like warnings.

Riley felt it the second she stepped into Hollow's Edge High.

The building looked the same. The air didn't.

It had always been loud there. Today the noise felt sharp. Lockers slammed. Shoes squeaked. Voices stayed low, but they still carried.

Riley kept her head down and walked fast. Her backpack pulled at her shoulders. Her chest felt tight, like she couldn't get a full breath.

She heard her name once.

Not spoken to her.

Spoken about her.

"Riley was at the station too."

Her stomach dropped.

Near the water fountain, a group of students leaned close together, voices quick and excited.

"My mom said the cops have messages," a boy said.

A girl beside him shook her head. "They didn't say that."

"They said electronic communications on the news," he argued. "That means texts."

Another kid snorted. "It means somebody screwed up."

Riley walked past them with her eyes forward. She didn't stop. If she stopped, she might explode.

She rounded the corner by the trophy case. Olivia's missing flyer was taped to the glass.

The photo was one Riley had taken. Olivia was squinting into the sun and smiling too big.

Someone had drawn a heart near her name.

Someone else had scratched through it.

The paper tore along Olivia's cheek.

Riley stared for a second, then forced herself to keep moving.

More voices followed her.

"My aunt saw Danny's truck at the station."

"My dad said they printed out the texts."

"If they're looking at his phone, it's him."

Riley's fingers curled hard around her bag strap. Her knuckles ached.

She reached her locker and spun the dial once.

Wrong numbers.

Her hands shook. She hated that they shook.

She tried again, slower this time, breathing through her nose and keeping her eyes on the lock.

Down the row, two girls whispered. Not softly. Just quiet enough to pretend.

"My mom said Olivia's dad told the police everything."

"My mom said the screenshots came from Olivia's phone," the other girl said.

Riley's head snapped up. "You don't know that."

Her voice came out louder than she meant it to. Heads turned.

The girls blinked, then traded a look.

"We're just saying what everybody else is saying," one of them said.

Riley felt her throat burn. "Everybody's guessing. That isn't proof."

The other girl shrugged. "Guessing feels true when a kid is missing."

Riley slammed her locker shut. The sound cracked down the hall.

The girls flinched and walked off, still whispering. Their words trailed behind them like smoke.

Riley stood there breathing too hard, eyes stinging, jaw tight enough to ache.

She turned and walked away before she did something stupid.

Even the adults weren't quiet.

As she passed the staff lounge, she heard voices near the doorway. Mr. Cole and Ms. Porter.

"They said it on the news," Mr. Cole murmured. "Communications."

Ms. Porter sighed. "That could mean anything."

"It means they have something."

"Or it means they want people to think that."

Riley's shoe scuffed the floor.

Both of them looked out at once. Their faces changed too fast.

"Morning, Riley," Mr. Cole said, forcing a smile.

Ms. Porter's smile came slower. "Hey, honey."

Neither one felt real.

Riley gave the smallest nod and kept walking.

The library was quieter, but it was not safer. Quiet only gave her thoughts more room.

She slid into a chair near the back and stared at her hands on the table. Her nails were bitten raw. She had not noticed herself doing it.

She tried to focus on anything else. A book title. A poster on the wall. The hum of the lights.

It didn't work.

All she could hear was the line from the news.

Electronic communications.

She could hear the way people repeated it. Like it was proof. Like it was a verdict.

Riley leaned forward and pressed her forehead into her hands.

One thought kept pushing through the noise.

Danny was falling.

And if he fell, Olivia disappeared with him.

What He Hides

The bell rang, and the library came back to life.

Chairs scraped. Books shut. Feet rushed for the doors. Riley stood slowly, like her legs did not belong to her.

She moved with the crowd, but she felt outside it. Every laugh sounded too loud. Every joke felt wrong.

At the end of the hall, the side doors waited.

Danny stood outside, just beyond the walkway. Not on school grounds, but close enough to make people look. His shoulders hunched forward, like he was braced for a hit. He kept glancing toward the building, then back at the street.

His truck sat around the corner, parked crooked by the curb. Dust streaked the hood like old fingerprints.

When he saw Riley, relief hit his face first.

Then anger.

"Finally."

Riley stopped a few feet away. "I was in the library."

"I know. I saw you go in." He dragged a hand down his face. "I could not just stand there."

Riley looked at him then. Really looked.

His eyes were red. His jaw was tight. His shirt looked slept in.

"Do you hear what they're saying?" he asked.

Riley nodded once. "Yes."

Danny let out a breath that sounded more like a growl.

"They're using the news now. Electronic communications. Like that means my name."

"People heard it and filled in the rest."

"They did not even wait."

"They saw your truck at the station," Riley said. "They saw you go in."

His eyes flashed. "So a parking lot is proof now?"

He stepped closer, then checked himself. He glanced at the hallway window behind her.

"You know what hurts?" he asked, voice low. "They do not even ask. They just decide."

Riley swallowed. "I tried to shut it down."

Danny gave a short, bitter laugh. "You cannot shut down a town."

Riley shifted her weight. "Did the police call you again after Friday?"

He hesitated. "No. Not yet."

"Then why do you look like you have not slept?"

His mouth twisted. "Because I found something."

Riley's stomach dropped. "What?"

Danny pulled out his phone and unlocked it. "Look."

He held the screen toward her.

Threads.

Dates.

Time stamps.

Then gaps.

Not a normal scroll. Not a clean run of days. Whole stretches looked scraped out, like someone had reached in and lifted pieces away.

Riley frowned. "That is not right."

"No," Danny said. "It isn't."

He tapped a date.

"That Friday morning. I texted you before first period. You answered. It should be here."

It was not.

He opened his call history next. Same problem. Missing space where there should have been ordinary things. A call. A reply. A routine.

Riley felt cold move through her. “Did your phone reset?”

He looked at her. “I did not reset it.”

“That is not what I asked.”

His jaw tightened. “It restarted during the night. I know because it made me use my passcode in the morning. That only happens after a restart.”

Riley stared at the screen again. “When?”

“A little after three.”

“In the morning?”

He nodded. “I was asleep.”

The words settled between them.

Riley kept her voice low. “Was it charging?”

“No.”

Her stomach tightened harder.

He locked the phone and shoved it back into his pocket. "Either somebody had it, or somebody made it look that way. Either way, it feeds the same story."

Riley looked up at him. “You need to show that to the police.”

“And say what?” His laugh was bitter. “Hey, maybe my phone erased the wrong parts of my life by itself?”

“Say exactly what happened.”

“The truth does not matter right now,” he said. “They already have their version.”

Riley took a slow breath. “Danny, if somebody got into your phone, they could shape whatever comes next.”

His eyes sharpened. “That is exactly what I’m saying.”

He lowered his voice.

"He's doing it."

Riley's stomach sank. "Ethan."

"Who else? He controls her phone. He controls her story. Now my messages start disappearing?"

Riley wanted to argue. Not because she trusted Ethan. Because she needed the world to make more sense than that.

"How would he even do it?"

Danny shook his head. "I do not know. I just know what I see."

Riley stared at him for a second, then said, "There is more, isn't there?"

His face changed too fast. "What?"

"You are not just scared about the phone."

He looked away.

Riley stepped closer, keeping her voice low. "Why didn't you tell them everything?"

That landed.

Danny's shoulders went tight. "I told them she was scared of him."

"That is not everything."

He looked down at his hands. For a second, he seemed younger. More tired.

"You think I'm hiding something."

He met her eyes then.

"And you think that makes me guilty?"

Riley did not answer.

Because she did not know.

Cars passed on the street behind them. A laugh spilled inside the building, sudden and bright and wrong.

Danny looked toward the glass again. "She trusted me."

Riley's throat tightened. "I know."

"But you do not know with what."

The words sat between them, heavy and ugly.

Riley heard herself say it before she decided to.

"The journal."

Danny went still.

He did not answer.

He did not need to.

Riley felt dizzy. "They took it from your truck."

His voice came out rough. "Yes."

"Why did you have it?"

"Because she gave it to me." Pain flashed across his face. "Before all of this."

Riley stared at him. "Why didn't she tell me?"

He looked down. "Because she told me not to tell anyone. Not even you."

That hit harder than she expected.

"Why?"

"Because she was scared."

"Of him?"

Danny nodded once.

Riley leaned in. "Then say that. Out loud. To everybody."

He flinched, like the building itself might have heard her.

"I tried."

"Then try again. They're burying you."

His eyes went wet. He did not wipe them.

"If I say the wrong thing, it buries her too."

"She is already missing."

The word hit him hard. She saw it.

Riley softened before she meant to. "I am not trying to hurt you. I am trying to save what is left."

Danny stared at her for a long moment.

Then he shook his head, slow and miserable. “I can’t break it. Not the way she asked.”

Riley’s throat burned. “And what about the truth?”

His voice cracked. “The truth will come. I just need time.”

“Time is what they’re using against you.”

A silhouette crossed the hallway glass behind her. Someone slowed, like they were looking out.

Danny’s shoulders tightened.

“I can’t stay here.”

Riley looked at the window too. “Let me help.”

For one second, he looked like he might let her.

Then the wall went back up.

“Do not let them turn you,” he said quietly.

“Danny.”

He stepped back toward the side street, not the doors.

Riley spoke fast, forcing fear into words. “If they take you, Olivia goes with you. And Ethan wins.”

Danny held still.

Then he gave one small, grim nod.

“I know.”

He turned and walked away with his head down.

Riley watched until he disappeared around the corner, then went back inside. The air felt colder when he was gone, and the hallway behind the glass kept moving like nothing had changed.

A Quiet Performance

By the end of the day, Riley's head felt full of noise.

Every class had been normal on paper. Every teacher had tried to act calm. None of it worked.

She kept seeing Danny's phone screen. Gaps where days should have been. Missing pieces dressed up as nothing.

Her own phone stayed heavy in her pocket. She did not check it.

When the last bell rang, the hallways surged.

Lockers slammed. Voices rose. Shoes squeaked. The sound felt too bright, too careless.

Riley moved with the crowd, but she felt hollow. Every laugh sounded like it belonged to another world.

Outside, the air was cool and thin. The sky was pale, clouds stretched flat and lifeless. She wished for rain anyway.

Rain always made whispers quieter.

Parents gathered near the front steps and curb. Some held coffee. A few stood close together with their voices low and urgent.

Riley's ride would not be there for a few minutes. She stayed near the steps and kept her eyes down, counting cracks in the sidewalk to stay steady.

"Riley."

Her stomach flipped before she even turned.

Ethan stood a few feet away, close enough to reach her. His shirt was pressed. His hair was neat. He looked tired in a careful way.

He held a stack of missing flyers under one arm. The top one showed Olivia's smiling photo.

It made Riley's throat tighten.

"I wanted to check on you," he said.

His voice was gentle. Warm. The kind adults used when they wanted trust.

Riley kept her face still. "I'm fine."

Ethan nodded like he believed her. His eyes stayed on hers, studying.

"I know you and Olivia were close. This has to be hard."

Riley's fingers curled around her bag strap. She nodded once, mostly to end the line.

Ethan shifted the flyers and stepped a little closer. Not enough to touch her. Enough to crowd the air.

"I saw the news update," he said softly. "The part about electronic communications."

Riley felt her stomach tighten again. "Yeah."

"People will run with that. They always do."

He glanced toward the curb where parents were already watching.

Then he looked back at her.

"But sometimes," he said, lowering his voice, "people run because they're right."

Cold slid through her.

She kept her tone flat. "What are you saying?"

He sighed like the question hurt him.

"I'm saying she was under pressure. I should have seen it sooner."

"Pressure from who?"

He did not answer right away. He let the silence work.

Then he said, quiet and careful, "Danny."

Riley's heartbeat thudded in her ears.

"That is not true."

His face did not change. His eyes stayed soft, the way adults looked when they were humoring someone younger.

"I am not accusing him," he said. "I am trying to understand what happened."

Riley's nails dug into her palm. "She never said she was scared of Danny."

His gaze flicked down and back up. Small, but she caught it.

Like he had been waiting for that answer.

"No," he said. "She would not say it like that. Olivia did not like conflict."

Riley's mouth went dry.

He leaned in a little more.

"You were her best friend. She must have told you something."

The trap closed around the sentence.

If Riley defended Danny too hard, it looked suspicious.

If she agreed at all, it became proof.

"She did not."

Ethan smiled then, gentle and empty.

"Okay. Then let me ask it another way."

Riley's throat tightened.

"Did she ever talk about sneaking out? Meeting someone? Being pressured?"

A parent a few feet away shifted closer without pretending anymore.

Riley felt every set of eyes at the curb start to lean.

"I'm not trying to put you on the spot," Ethan said. "I just want her home."

That was what made it worse. He knew exactly how to say it.

Riley forced a slow breath. "She talked about getting caught. That is all."

Ethan nodded like he had expected that too.

"Getting caught by who?"

Riley's stomach turned.

She saw Olivia in flashes. Going quiet when her phone lit up. Tensing when Ethan stepped into a room. Looking over her shoulder at things that should have felt ordinary.

Riley kept her face blank. "I do not know."

Ethan's eyes stayed kind.

"I understand," he said. "This is confusing for everybody."

He turned his body slightly, opening the scene to the parents around them. His voice rose just enough to carry.

"If anyone remembers anything, even something small, please tell the police."

Several parents nodded. One mother pressed a hand to her mouth.

Then he turned back to Riley and softened again.

"If you know something that could help, you can tell me."

The words sounded helpful.

They felt like a leash.

Riley stared at him. "I'm not talking to you. I'll talk to the police if I have to."

He blinked, then smiled like he respected that.

"Of course," he said. "That's smart. I'm glad you're thinking clearly."

Heat rose in Riley's face.

His tone stayed smooth.

"I just worry that people get scared and protect the wrong person."

Riley's chest tightened. "I'm not protecting anyone."

He nodded again. "Good. Then we agree. We both want the truth."

A woman stepped close and touched his arm. "Ethan, I'm so sorry."

His grief slid into place so fast it made Riley want to be sick.

"Thank you," he said softly. "I'm trying."

He looked down like he was fighting tears.

Then he looked up again, eyes shining.

Riley watched the exact pause. The exact breath. The exact sad little smile.

It was practiced.

He turned back to her, still gentle.

"You're doing okay. You do not have to carry this alone."

Riley almost laughed. The sound caught in her throat.

"I have to go."

He stepped back like he was being polite. "Of course. Be safe."

Riley started down the steps.

As she moved, she felt eyes on her. Parents watched her like she was a clue. Like she was a loose thread.

Someone whispered, "That's her."

Another voice answered, "She knows something."

Riley kept walking anyway.

Behind her, Ethan spoke to the parents in a calm, steady voice. He handed out flyers and accepted sympathy. He nodded at the right moments.

A quiet performance for a crowd that wanted one.

Riley reached the curb and waited there with her arms wrapped tight around herself.

As cars rolled past the school, she looked back once.

Ethan still stood on the steps with the flyers in his arm. He smiled at a grieving mother. He nodded at a father.

Then his eyes found Riley across the lot.

His face did not change.

But his gaze held her for one long second.

Like a reminder.

Riley turned away, heart pounding.

By the time her ride pulled up, the air around her felt colder than it should have.

What Starts to Break

That night, Riley tried to do homework.

She opened her laptop, stared at the screen, and realized she had no idea what the assignment even was.

She shut it again.

Her room felt too quiet. Even the fan sounded loud.

Her phone lay face down on the bed beside her, like it was something alive. She had not checked it in over an hour. She told herself it was better that way.

Then her hand reached for it anyway.

The screen lit up.

She opened her thread with Olivia.

The first thing she saw was a selfie from two weeks ago. Olivia was making a dumb face, cheeks puffed, eyes wide. Riley stared at it until her throat tightened.

She scrolled.

Silly pictures. Lunch complaints. Plans for the weekend. A voice memo of Olivia laughing so hard she could not finish her sentence.

Normal.

Safe.

Riley kept scrolling until her thumb ached.

Then she searched.

Ethan.

Dad.

Scared.

Help.

Nothing.

No warning. No message that said I can't do this anymore. No line that sounded like goodbye.

Her eyes stung.

She went back to the top and scrolled again, slower this time, like she might find something she had missed. A hidden crack. A coded phrase. Anything.

Still nothing.

Riley dropped the phone onto the bed and pressed her palms into her eyes.

"Did I miss it?" she whispered. "Did I not see it?"

Her voice broke on the last word.

She rolled onto her back and stared at the ceiling.

The fan turned in slow circles. The shadows of the blades chopped the dim light into pieces.

Her mind kept replaying small moments.

Olivia looking tired in class.

Olivia's eyes flicking to her bag when Danny asked questions.

Olivia walking faster when Ethan appeared near the doorway.

Riley had noticed those things.

She just had not named them.

Or had not wanted to.

Danny's phone flashed through her head again. Missing messages. Missing days. Gaps that felt handled instead of accidental.

Then the screenshots.

Green bubbles. Danny's name. A line that looked like him because maybe once, a long time ago, it had been.

You just need to try harder.

Riley's stomach turned.

Not because it proved everything.

Because it did not.

One bad line could be enough for a town that wanted a villain.

That was the part she hated.

She believed him.

She thought she did.

But belief was starting to feel like something she had to grip with both hands instead of something solid she could stand on.

Her phone buzzed once.

Riley looked at it and already knew whose name would be there before she turned it over.

Danny.

Don't let them turn you.

She stared at the message without opening the thread.

For a second, all she could see was him outside the side doors, eyes red, voice rough, trying to hold on to the truth without burying her with it.

Then Ethan on the school steps, soft voiced and steady, feeding the same crowd exactly what it wanted.

Two men.

Two versions.

Two people asking to be believed.

Riley's thumb moved toward the screen.

Stopped.

Then drifted away.

She set the phone beside her and pressed the heels of her hands into her eyes until color flashed behind them.

Across the room, her track bag leaned against the dresser. One strap hung twisted. Her spikes still stuck out of the side pocket.

Everything looked the same.

Nothing was.

She lay back and stared at the ceiling fan as it turned in slow circles above her.

"I'm not giving up," she whispered into the dark.

But the words did not feel as solid as they should have.

Because belief had started to change shape.

It was no longer something steady she could stand on.

It was something she had to keep choosing.

And tonight, for the first time, that choice felt heavier than it should have.

CHAPTER TWENTY

The Train Yard

The Discovery

Word moved fast. It leaped from phone to phone, then spilled into the halls. Someone said they found something at the old train yard. Someone else said they found her.

Riley did not think. She ran. She cut through the lot, past the buses, past the rusted fence that marked the end of town. Sirens pulsed in the distance. The air smelled like wet steel.

Police tape cut a bright line across the broken fence. Yellow against weeds and gravel. Officers moved in slow, careful paths, eyes on the ground. Miller stood near the opening with a small notebook. Reyes spoke to two rail workers who kept wringing their caps.

A white van idled by the tracks. The back doors were open. A stretcher waited inside, empty for now.

Riley stopped short. Her legs shook. Every sound felt far away.

Danny's truck swung into the dirt pullout and stopped hard. He jumped out and stumbled toward the tape. "Olivia!" His voice cracked on her name. "Tell me she's not here."

Miller raised a hand. "Danny. You need to stay back."

"Tell me," Danny said. He tried to duck under the tape. Reyes caught his arm. Danny jerked free, then saw the way Reyes looked at him. The fight left his body. He fell to his knees in the gravel and pressed both hands to the ground. "Please."

Riley could not make her feet move. Her mouth had gone dry. She watched Miller speak into his radio. She watched two officers carry a long black bag from beyond the fence. Not a bundle. Not a shape she could pretend away. A body.

They set it on the stretcher and zipped it higher. One corner of a white sneaker showed, streaked with dirt, laces loose. Riley knew that brand. She had watched Olivia tie those laces in a hundred different hallways.

A sound tore out of Danny before he could stop it. He shoved his fist into his mouth and failed. He tried to stand and could not. Reyes stepped in front of him again. "You don't want to see, son."

"She was alive," Danny said. He looked at the tape, then at the tracks, then at the officers. "She was alive."

Miller's eyes were tired. "I'm sorry."

They loaded the stretcher into the van. The doors closed with a soft thud that made Riley flinch. The engine hummed. No one spoke for a long breath.

Riley hugged herself and stared at the place where the bag had been. The weeds bent in a thin line toward the fence. A few black feathers clung to the wire. The whole world felt narrow and cold.

Danny finally stood. He wiped his face with the heel of his hand and took a step toward the tape, then stopped himself. His voice dropped to a ragged whisper. "He did this."

Miller did not answer. Reyes looked at the ground. The van pulled away.

Whispers and Silence

By afternoon, school tried to hold itself together. The principal gathered them in the gym. Teachers brought students in by homeroom. The bleachers filled with faces that did not know where to look. Phones glowed and then went dark when staff walked by.

Ms. Porter stood at the center line with a paper in her hand. She did not read from it. "Some of you knew Olivia well. Some of you only knew her smile in the hall. She mattered to this school. Please be kind to each other." Her voice shook. She paused and found Riley near the top row. Their eyes met. Ms. Porter's lips pressed together like she was holding back everything else she wanted to say.

Coach Rowland, still in his windbreaker, stepped up. He swallowed hard. "She ran even when it rained. She showed up tired and still beat the clock. That is the girl I knew." He looked at his shoes. "I should have asked more questions." He tried again. "I should have seen." The last word broke. He covered his face with one hand and nodded thanks when Ms. Porter touched his shoulder.

Whispers rolled across the rows.

"They found her by the fence."

"They said Danny was there last week."

"My aunt says the cops have those texts."

"He told her to sneak out. That was the last straw."

Riley stared at the wooden rail in front of her until the grain blurred. Mr. Cole stood near the exit, arms folded, eyes hard. When two boys snickered, he cut them off with a look. Ms. Porter moved along the lower row, leaning in to speak softly to anyone with wet eyes.

A girl from track climbed up to Riley and sat without asking. She twisted the strap of her bag. "She kept saying she was fine," the girl whispered. “I believed her.” She wiped her cheek. “Now I hate that word.”

Riley nodded. Her throat was too tight to trust her voice.

The principal spoke about counselors and phone hotlines. He asked for a moment of silence. It was not silent. Someone sobbed behind the scoreboard. The old heater clicked. Someone’s phone buzzed three times in a row. Riley closed her eyes and tried to count her breaths.

When he dismissed them, no one stood right away. The room felt like a held breath that could not be released.

The Mask of Grief

Riley took the side door into the hall. The gym emptied in a slow wave. Some parents had already come and lined the corridor, asking if their kids were okay. Faces pinched. Voices low.

Ethan stood near the front office, one hand on his chest, the other holding a folded handkerchief. His shirt was crisp. His eyes were red, but not puffy. A secretary spoke to him, head tilted in sympathy.

"I tried to help her," he said. His voice dipped at the end of the sentence. "I told the officers she had been pulling away. I did everything I could."

A mother touched his sleeve. "You did your best."

He nodded and looked down like the words hurt. When he lifted his head, his eyes slid over the crowd and landed for a second on Riley. The look was flat, almost bored. It vanished as soon as he noticed her watching. His mouth pulled into a thin, pained line. He dabbed at his eye with the cloth.

Another parent asked, "When did you find out?"

Ethan blinked slowly. "Just now," he said. "Officer Miller called." He placed his hand on the counter to steady himself. "I could not breathe."

Riley watched the small details. The way he timed his breaths. The way his shoulders rose during the loudest whispers. The way his voice broke right after someone said Danny's name. None of it looked like shock. It looked like a script.

Ms. Porter stepped from the office and placed a hand on Ethan's arm. "Please sit down. You don't have to keep talking."

"I want people to know she was loved," Ethan said. He lowered himself into a chair and stared at the floor. Tears welled and did not fall. He wiped them anyway.

Riley felt cold. The corridor swelled with murmurs, with promises of casseroles and prayer lists, with the soft sound of comfort given freely to the man who had made the rules. She backed away until the wall pressed between her shoulders and the lockers. Ethan lifted his head again and searched the hall like a man checking the time.

He found Riley once more. This time he did not look away. He gave the smallest nod, polite and empty. Then he folded his hands and waited for the next person who needed to comfort him.

After the Van

Night pulled a gray lid over town. Streetlights buzzed on and made halos on wet pavement. Riley walked along the curb until she reached the far side of the lot. Danny sat in his truck with the engine off. The cab was dark. His silhouette bent over the wheel.

She tapped the window. He did not move. She opened the passenger door and climbed in. The air smelled like coffee and rain.

"I'm sorry," she said. The words felt small.

He kept his forehead on the wheel. "They found her where we used to meet." His voice was quiet and rough. "He put her there. He wanted them to find her there."

Riley stared at the empty road ahead of them. "They will say you did it."

"They already do." He sat back and wiped his face with his sleeve. His eyes were raw. "I loved her. I did not keep her safe. I did not even keep her from being used to hurt me."

"That isn't your fault," Riley said, but it sounded thin, even to her.

He let out a breath that shook. "He stood in the school today like a hero. People patted his arm. They told him he was strong. You saw it."

"I saw it," she said. She thought of the timed tears. She thought of the calm eyes. "It felt wrong."

Danny's hands tightened on the wheel. "They took her journal from me. It was the only thing I had left that was hers. Now they will twist that too." He let out a short, sharp laugh. "Maybe they already have."

Riley closed her eyes. The ceiling light cast a soft white ring on the dashboard. "What do we do?"

“I don't know,” he said. “If I talk, I break my promise. If I don't, I look guilty.” He stared at his knuckles. “Maybe that was the point. He made a game I can't win.”

They sat in the quiet with the windows fogging. Somewhere a train horn called, long and low, then faded. Riley felt the sound press through her chest.

“I can't lose you too,” Danny said. He did not look at her when he said it. “Do you still believe me?”

Riley thought of Olivia’s shoes. She thought of Ethan’s nod. She thought of the green bubbles that told a story that fit too well. “I'm trying,” she said. “I'm trying every minute.”

He nodded once. It looked like it cost him something. Then he looked down at his hands. Dirt still clung under his nails and across his knuckles. "I can't even wash it off yet," he said. His voice had gone flat with shock. "Not yet."

Riley looked at the grit pressed into his skin and said nothing.

“Tomorrow,” she said. “We keep moving tomorrow.”

Danny turned the key. The engine caught and then settled. He looked at the road. “I won't stop.”

They pulled out of the lot and drove into a town that already believed it knew the truth. The streetlights hummed. The night held its breath.

Chapter Twenty-One

The Weight of Chains

The Arrest

The lot was half empty and wide with morning light. Wind pushed wrappers in a lazy circle near the curb. Danny's truck sat in its usual place at the far edge, angled like he was ready to leave but never did. He slouched behind the wheel, head tipped back, eyes closed.

Riley saw him from the library steps. She lifted a hand, then let it fall. Before she could decide whether to go over, two squad cars rolled in. Their tires hissed on grit. Doors opened. Officer Miller stepped out first, jacket zipped to his throat. Officer Reyes followed with a small, unlined notebook.

Students paused mid-step. Heads turned. Phones rose without a word.

Miller stopped at the driver's side window. He spoke low. "Danny, step out of the vehicle, please."

Danny flinched awake. He squinted into the sun, then at Miller's badge. He opened the door slowly and slid down to the gravel. "For what?"

"Stand by the hood," Miller said. "Hands where we can see them."

"Tell me what this is." Danny's voice had a hard edge, but it trembled at the end.

Reyes positioned himself to the side. "We need to place you under arrest for further questioning," he said. "We will go over your rights at the car."

"For what?" Danny repeated, louder now. "I didn't hurt her."

Miller took his wrist. "Hands on the hood."

Riley moved two steps closer without meaning to. Heat ran up her neck. The metal of the truck caught a white strip of sun. Danny placed his palms on the warm paint. His shoulders were tight. The cuff clicked and closed. The sound carried.

A boy near the crosswalk whispered, “Get it on video.” Someone laughed once and stopped.

“You know I didn't do this,” Danny said. He spoke to the air, to no one and to everyone. “You know it.”

Miller read the rights, clear and even. Reyes watched the crowd while Miller spoke. He didn't write anything down. Danny’s jaw worked while he stared at the wipers, at a nick in the rubber he had been meaning to fix. He looked up once and found Riley at the curb. The look on his face knocked the wind from her. It held fear, but it also held a dare: please hold on.

They turned him. The cuffs flashed. A girl near Riley made a small sound in her throat. Miller guided Danny toward the open back door of the squad car. Reyes stayed with the truck, eyes on the windows, waiting for anyone who thought they were brave.

“Riley,” Danny said. He twisted at the waist. “Tell them. Tell them he—”

The car swallowed the rest. The door shut with a soft, final sound. Miller nodded to Reyes. Reyes gave the truck one last look, then joined him. The cruiser pulled away slow enough for every phone to follow it down the lane.

Riley stayed on the edge of the sidewalk until the dust settled and the noise faded. Her hands shook. She tucked them under her arms and stared at the bright mark the cuffs had left on the morning.

The Verdict Arrives Early

The first bell rang, but no one rushed inside. The lot became a stage. Parents cut across the lane to stand with their kids. Teachers tried to herd the tide toward the doors and failed.

Mr. Cole stood near the entrance with his arms crossed. "Phones away," he said. Only a few obeyed. He watched the road where the cruiser had gone and shook his head once.

Ms. Porter moved from group to group with her voice low. "Give each other space," she said. "If you need to talk, find me." Her eyes were wet but steady. When she reached Riley, she stopped. "Are you okay?"

Riley nodded. The motion felt like a lie.

Behind them, whispers stacked and sharpened.

"They cuffed him right here."

"My cousin said the cops found more."

"Everyone knew he was bad news."

"Texts don't lie."

A boy in a letter jacket spoke like a leader. "They should have taken him sooner."

A girl answered, "Why did she even talk to him that much?"

Riley gripped her backpack strap until the webbing cut her palm. She wanted to say that love didn't pick the easy people. She wanted to say that none of them knew anything. The words stuck like stones in her throat.

Ms. Porter touched Riley's sleeve. "Don't read comments today," she said. "Promise me."

Riley couldn't promise that. She looked past Ms. Porter and caught Coach Rowland near the bus lane. He stared at the place where the squad car had been, like he could still see it. His mouth pressed thin. He looked older than yesterday.

Parents swapped quick, certain lines.

“They have enough now.”

“He brought shame to this place.”

"It's over."

Riley felt the ground tilt under all that certainty. She stepped back until her shoulder hit brick. Inside the glass doors, she caught her reflection. She looked like a girl who had not slept.

“Come inside,” Ms. Porter said. “Please.”

Riley followed. The hall hummed with something that sounded almost like relief. People like clean stories. This one had a villain now.

Ethan's Shadow

The second bell had not finished when a dark sedan turned into the lot. Ethan parked near the visitor spaces and sat for a moment with both hands on the wheel. Then he got out, smoothed his shirt, and walked toward the doors with a slow, careful pace.

He didn't ask any questions. He didn't raise his voice. He stopped near a knot of parents and stood with them like he belonged in their circle. "Is everyone all right?" he asked. "I heard the sirens."

A mother said, "They took him." Her voice carried a charge.

Ethan held very still. "I see."

Another parent touched his sleeve. "I'm so sorry."

He nodded once and looked down. When he lifted his head again, his eyes were wet. "I trusted that boy in my home," he said. His voice broke on the last word, only slightly. "I never imagined."

A soft shock moved through the group. Heads bent closer. The circle widened as more people heard and repeated it. Ethan didn't move to the center. He stayed at the edge, but the arc bent toward him anyway.

Through the glass, Riley watched from the hall. She saw the way he placed his hand against his chest. She saw the way he breathed in, slow, before he spoke. She saw him glance at the school camera above the doors, then lower his gaze like a man who wanted no attention at all.

He looked up and found her. His face emptied for a heartbeat. Calm slid into place again, smooth as a coin in a palm. He gave a small, sad nod, as if to say, *we're both hurting*. The nod felt like a finger pressed to her mouth.

Mr. Cole pushed the door open and stepped out. "We need to get students inside," he told the group. Ethan stepped back at once, posture perfect, hands loose at his sides.

"I only wanted to be sure they felt safe," Ethan said. The sentence landed exactly where he wanted it to. Parents repeated it as they turned away.

Riley couldn't stop shaking. She hugged her binder to her chest and made herself walk. As she passed the office, she heard a secretary whisper, "He's a rock," like it was a blessing.

Riley thought of rocks and rivers. A rock can stand still while a river does the work.

The Story They Chose

Night pressed against the windows early.

Riley lay on her bed with the light off and her phone bright in her hands. Her feed kept filling with the same image from different angles, different accounts, different captions. Danny against the hood. Wrists cuffed. Mouth open like he had been caught between a prayer and a curse. Every new post said the same thing in a different voice.

Justice for Olivia.

Finally.

We knew.

Riley stared until the words stopped looking like words.

Then came the old photos. Danny at a fall game, head tipped back, laughing at something outside the frame. Olivia in a hoodie with half her face hidden behind her hair. A grainy shot of them near the library steps. A blurry one from the edge of the parking lot.

The comments kept multiplying beneath them.

Look at the way he watches her.

He never let go.

He was obsessed.

Everybody saw it.

Riley's thumb hovered over the screen.

Nobody had seen anything.

That was the worst part. They had seen scraps. A look. A rumor. A few stolen moments from too far away. Now they were stacking them into something neat enough to live with. Neat enough to repeat. By the end of the night, half the town would be telling the same story like they had been there for all of it.

She locked the phone.

A second later, she unlocked it again.

Her bedroom was dark except for the weak light from the screen. The house had gone quiet hours ago, but that only made everything in her head louder. She saw the train yard tape snapping in the wind. The white sneaker near the edge of the gravel. Danny twisting toward her as they pulled him away. Ethan standing outside the school doors afterward, one hand pressed to his chest, wearing grief like he had rehearsed it.

That small nod he gave her came back hardest.

Soft. Sad. Controlled.

It made her stomach turn all over again.

She covered her eyes with her arm.

"Tell me you didn't," she whispered into the dark.

The ceiling fan clicked overhead and kept turning.

Her phone buzzed against her wrist.

She looked down.

Ms. Porter.

Checking on you. I'm here if you need me.

Another message came in almost at once from the track group chat.

Coach Rowland says we'll meet tomorrow. Candles at the track. Wear blue.

Riley stared at both messages for a long moment. The screen blurred, then sharpened again.

She typed back to the group chat.

I'll be there.

She almost opened a new message to Ms. Porter.

She almost opened Danny's thread.

Instead, she set the phone on her chest and stared up into the dark.

The town had picked a story. It had picked a villain and a saint. It had picked a shape for grief and shoved everything inside it until the edges stopped showing. Danny in handcuffs made sense to them. Ethan standing quiet in the middle of the parking lot made sense to them. People liked clean stories. They liked them even more when those stories let them stop asking questions.

Riley turned onto her side and pulled the blanket up to her chin.

She thought about all the times Olivia had looked over her shoulder before answering something simple. All the times she had smiled too fast. All the times she had gone quiet the second Ethan came up. None of it had felt simple then.

But the whole town had decided simple was better.

Her throat tightened.

She didn't know if she was strong enough to stand outside that story by herself. She didn't know if she could keep holding on to the thin, fraying line that still tied her to the idea that Danny might not have done this.

That thought scared her.

The other one scared her more.

What if he really hadn't?

Her eyes burned. The phone slipped from her hand to the pillow beside her.

"I'm trying," she said to no one.

The words came out thin.

"I'm still trying."

Outside, a siren passed somewhere far off without slowing down. The sound thinned, faded, and disappeared into the night. Riley lay still and listened to the quiet settle back into place.

The night kept watching.

Chapter Twenty-Two

The Hollow Candle

Hallway Verdicts

By the next morning, the whispers were no longer questions.

They had hardened into verdicts.

"He begged her to sneak out."

"He hid her body at their spot."

"They should lock him up forever."

Riley walked through Hollow's Edge High with her books pressed tight to her chest. Lockers slammed shut around her. Clusters of students shifted apart when she came too close, then leaned back the second she passed. Every laugh sounded sharp. Every glance stayed on her too long.

"Look who's still defending him," a girl muttered near the water fountain.

Another answered, "She'll end up just like Olivia."

Riley's face burned, but she kept walking.

In history, Mr. Cole stopped beside her desk when her attention drifted for the third time.

"Eyes on your work, Riley."

His voice was firmer than usual. Not cruel. Not cold. Just tired in that adult way that made everything feel worse.

Riley lowered her gaze to the page and nodded. She did not remember a single thing he said after that.

At the end of the day, Ms. Porter caught her outside English.

"You don't have to carry this by yourself," she said gently. "Let people help you."

Riley wanted to ask who, exactly.

The teachers who kept saying Danny's name like a fact.

The students who had already turned Olivia into a candle and a hashtag.

The parents trading certainty like gossip at checkout lines.

Instead, she gave the smallest nod.

Her chest still felt hollow.

Help meant naming something she still couldn't bear to say aloud.

The Town Divides

After the last bell, Riley shouldered her bag and followed the crowd toward the buses. The noise felt too close. The lane too tight. She stopped at the edge of the lot, turned away, and started walking instead.

The air was cool enough to sting her nose. Pavement stretched wide and open in front of her, a relief after the narrow halls. Bus engines rumbled behind her, but the sound faded quickly. Every step felt like space.

She cut along Main Street, passed the post office, then the library. Danny's truck was not there.

The grocery store doors slid open with a rush of cold air and fluorescent light. Riley grabbed a basket she did not need and drifted down the first aisle.

It found her anyway.

Two parents stood near the apples, speaking in voices they did not bother lowering.

"He always had a temper," one said.

Near the bakery, a boy held up his phone and showed his friend another post.

"Everyone's saying the same thing."

At checkout, the cashier glanced at Riley, then leaned toward the bagger.

"She was close with him, right?"

The bagger did not answer.

Outside, two teachers from school crossed the lot ahead of her without noticing she was there.

"Ethan showed them more proof," one said quietly.

"Poor man," the other answered. "No one should have to bury a child."

The words landed like a slap.

Riley kept walking until she reached the cart return, then sat hard on the curb with the useless basket beside her. Cars rolled past. Wind knocked loose carts together. Every open window seemed to carry another sentence, another clean little version of what had happened.

The town had learned its chorus.

It did not need a conductor anymore.

Riley pressed her forehead to her knees and breathed until the buzzing in her ears eased.

Then she stood.

The vigil would start soon.

She did not know if she could face it.

She did not know if staying away would feel any better.

False Flame

The track filled as the sun went down.

Candles clicked to life one by one, small flames cupped inside careful hands. Blue ribbons fluttered from wrists and fence wire. The chain link trembled every time the wind shifted. The whole track glowed with the kind of grief people trusted more when it looked organized.

Riley stood near the back with a candle from the kitchen junk drawer. Wax warmed her fingers. Her jaw ached from keeping it tight.

Ethan stepped to the center with a framed photo of Olivia and a tall white candle.

He waited until the crowd quieted itself.

Then he began.

"She ran with heart," he said. His voice was low and unsteady in exactly the right places. "She loved with everything she had."

A girl near the front started crying into her sleeve. Someone whispered a prayer. Candles lifted higher.

Ethan looked down at the framed photo and swallowed before he spoke again.

"We will carry her light."

The crowd softened around the words.

That was the part Riley hated most. Not that they believed him. How easily he gave them something to believe.

His timing was perfect.

He let his voice break only when the quiet had deepened enough to hold it. He paused long enough for people to lean in. He breathed in slow. Let his shoulders shake once. Then he gave them the line they were waiting for.

"That boy took her from us."

Agreement moved through the stands like one long exhale.

Riley felt cold all over.

Coach Rowland stood near the fence in his windbreaker, face drawn tight, eyes fixed on the lanes instead of Ethan. Ms. Porter held her candle low, lips pressed together like she was holding back something she did not trust herself to say.

Ethan lifted the frame slightly. Light caught the glass and washed Olivia's smile in gold. For one second, the whole track seemed to glow.

Then the wind bent the flames. Several went out at once.

Riley shielded hers with her palm and looked back toward Ethan just in time to catch it.

One small pause.

One tiny slip.

His face emptied.

Not grief. Not shock. Just stillness. Calm. Calculation.

Then the mask returned.

He lowered his head. Wiped at tears that had not fallen. Let the crowd love him for surviving this.

Riley's stomach turned.

To everyone else, he was a father brave enough to stand in the middle of his own grief.

To Riley, he looked like a man who had known exactly where to stand.

Cracks in Belief

The kitchen light was still on when Riley got home.

Her mom sat at the table with a mug between both hands. "You're late," she said softly. "Rough day?"

Riley set the grocery bag on the counter and shrugged. "Just school."

Her mom watched her for a second. "I saw the vigil pictures."

Riley froze for half a beat.

"Poor girl," her mom said. "Poor family."

Riley looked down at the bread in her hands. The plastic crinkled under her grip. She wanted to say something. About Ethan. About the way he spoke. About how grief had sat on him too neatly. About the tiny moment when his face had gone blank before the sadness returned.

Instead, she said, "Yeah."

It was easier.

Her mom stood and crossed the room, slow enough to give Riley time to pull away if she wanted. When she touched her shoulder, Riley nearly flinched.

"You don't have to carry everything by yourself," her mom said.

Riley nodded because that was easier too.

Later, in her room, she dropped onto the bed without turning on the lamp. Her phone lit the dark in her hands. More vigil posts. More blue ribbons. More captions talking about justice like justice had already happened.

Then she saw one new photo.

Ethan at the track, one hand over his chest, Olivia's framed picture in the other. His head was bowed. Grief caught in perfect focus.

Riley stared at it.

Then she zoomed in.

The candlelight had frozen his face in soft gold. Around him, everyone looked wrecked. Red eyed. Broken open. But Ethan looked arranged. Even the way he held the frame looked careful.

Riley's thumb moved without thinking. She saved the picture.

The second she did, her pulse jumped.

She did not know why she saved it.

Only that she could not make herself delete it.

Across the room, the house gave a small settling creak.

Riley looked back at the screen.

At Ethan's face.

At the hand pressed to his chest.

At the grief everyone trusted.

A cold feeling moved through her, slow and steady.

For the first time since Danny was arrested, her doubt stopped feeling shapeless.

It still was not proof.

It was not even a thought she knew how to say out loud.

It was smaller than that.

Sharper too.

A splinter.

Riley locked her phone and set it on the nightstand. Then she lay back in the dark, eyes open, staring at nothing.

Everyone else seemed relieved to be done looking.

Riley wasn't.

She kept seeing Ethan's face in the candlelight, too composed, too exact.

For the first time, her doubt had somewhere to land.

Chapter Twenty-Three

The Silent Verdict

The Halls Decide

The next morning, the splinter was still there.

Riley felt it the second she stepped into Hollow's Edge High. Nothing in the building looked different. Lockers slammed. Sneakers squeaked over the waxed floor. Someone laughed too loudly near the trophy case. The bell still rang with the same ugly buzz.

But the mood had changed.

The whispers were gone. People were speaking plainly now.

"He'll get life."

"My mom said they found everything in his truck."

"He probably thought nobody would ever catch him."

Riley kept walking with her books pressed tight to her chest. She didn't look at the faces around her. That was the trick. If she looked, she might flinch. If she flinched, they'd know they'd hit something.

A boy near the water fountain leaned back against the wall and watched her pass.

“Still talking to him?” he asked.

His friend laughed before Riley even answered.

She didn’t stop. She didn’t speed up. She just kept walking, heat climbing into her face.

At her locker, her fingers slipped on the combination twice. By the time it opened, she could feel two girls standing a few feet away, pretending to dig through their backpacks while they watched her.

One of them said, not quietly enough, “I swear, if that was my friend, I’d be ashamed.”

The other answered, “Maybe she already knew.”

Riley shut the locker harder than she meant to. The sound cracked through the hall. Both girls went quiet, but only for a second. By the time Riley turned away, they were whispering again.

History was worse because it was quieter.

Mr. Cole stood at the front of the room with a stack of papers under one arm and a line of notes already half written on the board. He looked tired. More tired than usual. The class settled slower than it should have, people leaning toward each other for one last murmur before they sat.

Riley took her seat and opened her notebook. She stared at the page without seeing it.

"Riley."

Her head lifted.

Mr. Cole tapped the corner of the worksheet on her desk. "Stay with us."

His voice wasn't harsh. It wasn't accusing. But every head near her still turned.

Riley nodded and lowered her eyes again. "Sorry."

He moved on. The lesson started. Dates, names, wars, maps. None of it stayed in her head. All she could hear were the scraps of talk that slipped around the room whenever Mr. Cole turned back to the board.

"He fooled everybody."

"Olivia trusted the wrong person."

"My brother said he saw the arrest video."

By lunch, Riley felt scraped hollow.

She took her tray to the end of a table near the windows and sat with nobody across from her. Outside, the practice field lay still under a pale sky. The track fence flashed silver every time the light hit it. For one second, she saw the vigil again. Candles. Blue ribbons. Ethan with Olivia's picture held carefully against his chest.

Then someone set a tray down across from her.

Ms. Porter didn't sit. She only rested one hand on the back of the chair and looked at Riley with that same quiet, searching sadness she'd carried since the news broke.

"You can come by after school if you need somewhere quiet," she said softly.

Riley looked up.

The words almost undid her, not because they were big, but because they were small. Human. Kind. Something not shaped like a verdict.

She swallowed. "Okay."

Ms. Porter gave a small nod and moved on.

Riley watched her go and thought how strange it was that kindness now felt almost as frightening as cruelty. Cruelty was easy. Cruelty asked nothing. Kindness wanted her to speak, and speaking meant naming the thing she still couldn't prove.

By the last bell, her shoulders ached from holding tension all day. Every stare had pressed the same message into her skin.

It wasn't rumor anymore.

It was a sentence.

The Whole Town Speaks

Riley walked home the next afternoon like she always did.

She needed air. Space. Movement. Something that didn't smell like floor wax and crowded bodies and people pretending not to stare. But once she reached Main Street, she understood the walk wouldn't save her.

The whole town had caught up.

At the post office, two men stood near the counter with folded envelopes in hand and voices pitched low in the way people used when they wanted to sound respectful while saying something cruel.

"They better not let him make bond on some technicality," one said.

The other grunted. "Not after what he did."

Riley kept her eyes on the row of boxes along the wall and walked back out before either one turned fully toward her.

Outside the church, the candles from the vigil were still piled in a crate by the steps. Wind pushed at the loose ribbons tied to the rail. Three women stood near the entrance in sweaters and sensible shoes, speaking with their heads bowed like grief and certainty had become the same thing.

"We've been praying for Olivia," one said.

Another answered, "And for that boy's soul, though I don't know what good it'll do now."

Riley felt her jaw tighten.

She kept moving.

At the grocery store, the blast of cold air and bright lights only made everything feel harsher. She grabbed a basket she didn't need and drifted past produce, past the bakery, past a display of paper towels stacked in a tower that leaned slightly to one side.

Near the deli counter, a mother held her phone where her teenage daughter could see it.

"There," she said, tapping the screen. "That's her father. Poor man."

The daughter glanced over and then, just as quickly, glanced at Riley.

Riley didn't need to see the phone to know what was on it.

Ethan's face had been everywhere since the vigil. Bent head. Hand to chest. Perfect grief. Hollow's Edge loved grief when it came dressed the right way.

At checkout, the cashier looked past Riley's shoulder and lowered her voice toward the bagger.

"That's the friend, isn't it?"

The bagger didn't answer, but silence could agree with people just as easily as words.

Riley took her basket back to the cart return without buying a thing. Outside, she sat on the curb for a moment and pressed both hands to the edge of the metal frame, grounding herself against the cold.

Across the lot, a community board stood beneath a plastic cover. Flyers overlapped in crooked rows. Lost dog. Yard sale. Tutoring. Church supper.

In the center was a fresh sheet of paper with a neat bold heading.

Protect Our Kids. Keep Him Off School Grounds.

Half the page was already full of signatures.

Riley stared at it.

They were acting like Danny might come strolling back into town tomorrow. Like he was some threat still moving loose among them, like the story had already been tried, proven, and filed away.

A woman stepped up beside the board and added her name without hesitation.

That was what finally got to Riley. Not the anger. Not even the fear.

The ease of it.

The whole town had accepted the same version because it asked nothing of them except belief.

Riley stood and backed away from the board.

By the time she reached the sidewalk again, one thought sat hard and clear in her chest.

The students had started it.

The adults had finished it.

The Man They Trusted

The next morning, Ethan was at the school.

Riley saw him before he saw her.

He stood outside Ms. Calhoun's office with two parents from the track stands and a booster club mother who still wore her blue ribbon pinned near her shoulder. Ethan held a manila folder in one hand. His posture was careful. Controlled. He looked exactly like what Hollow's Edge wanted him to be. A father still standing because he had no choice.

Riley stopped short near the corner.

She was far enough away that she shouldn't have been able to hear much, but Ethan's voice carried in that measured, broken way some voices did when the speaker knew exactly how to use silence.

"I just wish I'd pushed harder," he said.

One of the parents touched his arm. "You couldn't have known."

Ethan lowered his eyes. "I knew enough to worry."

The other parent shook her head slowly, already aching for him. "You were trying to protect her."

He gave a hollow little laugh that sounded like it had been dragged out of him. "I thought I was. She thought I was being unfair. I didn't want her near him. I told her that more than once."

Every word landed cleanly.

Not too much. Not too dramatic. Just enough.

Riley could see Ms. Calhoun through the small office window, head bent over paperwork, face drawn and serious. Coach Rowland stood a few feet away near the trophy case, one hand braced against his hip, jaw tight enough to show even from across the hall. He wasn't part of the circle, but he was near enough to hear it. Near enough to let it stand.

That hurt more than Riley expected.

Ethan glanced up then, as if some part of him had felt her staring.

His eyes found hers at once.

He didn't flinch.

He didn't look startled.

He only held her gaze for one calm, unbearable second. Then he gave the smallest nod. Polite. Public. Empty.

Anyone else would've read it as acknowledgement.

Riley felt it for what it was.

A warning.

Stay quiet.

Let this stand.

Her pulse kicked hard against her ribs. For one sick second, she couldn't move. The hall around her blurred with passing students and slamming lockers and the rustle of paper.

Then Ethan turned back to the parents and bowed his head just enough to make them lean closer.

The performance went on without her.

Riley forced her legs to move.

She walked past the library doors, past the vending machines, past the writing lab where Ms. Porter's door stood cracked open. Her throat burned with all the things she couldn't say.

To everybody else, Ethan looked broken open by grief.

To Riley, he looked practiced.

What His Voice Carried

The next afternoon, Riley was in the station lobby when Miller and Reyes led Danny past the front desk in cuffs.

She hadn't meant to be there. Or maybe she had. By then even she couldn't tell the difference between accident and need. She'd told herself she only wanted to ask whether there was anything else she could add. Some detail she'd missed. Some small thing that might matter. But once she stepped into the station and smelled old coffee, floor cleaner, and copier heat, she knew that wasn't the whole truth.

She stood near a row of bolted plastic chairs with her arms folded tight across her chest while a deputy at the desk flipped through paperwork without looking up. The lobby was too bright. Too still. Every sound seemed sharper than it should've been. A ringing phone in the back. The soft crackle of a radio. The scrape of a chair leg across tile.

Then a door opened deeper inside the station, somewhere beyond the front desk and interview rooms.

Miller came through first.

Reyes was half a step behind him.

Then Danny.

He looked worse than he had the last time Riley saw him. Paler. Thinner. His hair needed washing. Shadows sat bruised under his eyes. The cuffs on his wrists flashed under the station lights as they guided him past the front desk.

Riley's breath snagged.

"Danny."

His head snapped up.

For one second, something alive broke across his face. Not relief exactly. Something rawer. More desperate.

"Riley."

Miller kept a firm hand on his arm, but Danny still leaned toward her. Reyes glanced once between them and said nothing.

Riley took one step forward without meaning to.

Danny's voice cracked on the first word. "You know me."

The sound of it hit her harder than she was ready for. There was no smoothness in it. No careful placement. No control.

Only fear.

"Please," he said. "Riley, please. You know I didn't do this."

The deputy at the front desk looked up. A woman filling out a form near the wall went still.

Even here, Danny looked exposed.

Danny didn't seem to remember any of that.

His chest heaved. His eyes stayed locked on hers with a kind of terrified honesty Riley had not seen once in Ethan.

"I didn't hurt her," he said. "You have to believe me."

Miller tightened his grip. "Keep moving."

Danny resisted for half a second, not fighting, just trying to stay turned toward Riley.

"Tell them," he said, voice fraying even more. "Tell them I'm not lying."

Riley opened her mouth.

Nothing came out.

The bright lobby, the crackle of the desk radio, the scrape of shoe soles on tile, the low murmur from the front desk. All of it seemed to fall away beside the sound of Danny's voice tearing itself apart.

Reyes put a hand against Danny's shoulder and urged him forward.

Danny twisted once more to look back at Riley.

Not angry.

Not manipulative.

Just scared.

Then Reyes turned him toward the back hall, and the heavy door swallowed him.

The sound it made when it shut wasn't loud. That was what Riley remembered later. Not loud. Just final enough to land in her chest like something dropped down a well.

She stayed where she was in the lobby for several long seconds.

A phone rang once in the back. Miller said something low to Reyes that Riley didn't catch.

Life went on around the station the way it always did after other people's worst moments.

But Danny's voice stayed with her.

Ethan's grief always sounded prepared.

Danny's fear had sounded like it didn't know anyone was listening.

That was the difference.

Not proof.

Not yet.

But it was something.

The Last Thread

That night, Riley lay on her bed with the lamp on and her notebook open beside her.

She hadn't written a full page in days.

Her phone lit her face from below as post after post slid past on the screen. Vigil photos. Blue ribbons. Candle flames caught in soft focus. Ethan with his head bowed. Danny in cuffs. A grainy clip from the school lot. Comments piling under comments until they all started to sound like one mouth.

#Justice for Olivia

Monster.

He never should've been around her.

Lock him away and throw out the key.

Riley scrolled until her thumb hurt.

Then she stopped on the photo she'd saved from the vigil.

Ethan in candlelight. Hand to chest. Olivia's framed picture held at exactly the right angle. Grief arranged so neatly it almost glowed.

She stared at his face.

Then she saw Danny again at the station. Hair falling into his eyes. Cuffs flashing. Voice breaking apart in real time.

One face built for witnesses.

One face forgetting he had any.

Riley locked her phone and set it beside the notebook.

For a long moment, she only listened to the house. The old heater clicking on. A car passing outside. Her mother moving around in the kitchen and then going still again.

Finally, Riley picked up her pen.

Her hand shook once before it steadied.

Then she wrote one line.

Danny sounded scared. Ethan sounded ready.

She stared at the line until the ink dried.

It wasn't proof.

It wasn't enough to carry to the police station and slap onto a desk.

But it was honest.

More honest than anything the town was saying.

A soft knock touched her door.

"You okay in there?" her mom asked.

Riley swallowed and looked at the page.

"Yeah," she said, though her voice came out thinner than she wanted. "Just tired."

Her mother lingered on the other side for a second, then moved away.

Riley leaned back against the wall and looked at the line again.

The town had made its decision.

The school had made its decision.

The grown ups had made theirs too.

But the thread inside her hadn't snapped.

It had frayed. It had burned. It had gone thin enough to hurt.

Still, it held.

And for the first time since Danny was taken away, Riley understood something clearly.

Everyone else was done looking.

She wasn't.

Chapter Twenty-Four

The Last Candle

What They Decided

By morning, the whispers had changed.

They didn't hide in corners anymore. They moved openly through Hollow's Edge High, carried in plain voices, passed from locker to locker like something settled and done.

"He'll rot."

"My uncle says they've already got enough."

"I heard he confessed."

Riley shoved books into her bag harder than she meant to. The zipper caught, then slid shut. Around her, students kept talking without lowering their voices. Nobody glanced over a shoulder first. Nobody sounded unsure.

That was the worst part.

The town had stopped wondering.

At her locker, a boy near the water fountain looked her way and said, "Still defending him?"

His friend laughed before Riley could answer.

She didn't stop. She didn't look back. But heat climbed into her face and stayed there all the way to class.

In English, students dragged their desks into loose circles for group work. Riley stayed near the edge of the room with her book open in front of her, though she had not read a single line. The voices around her drifted and crossed until Danny's name kept finding her anyway.

"He always had that look."

"Quiet ones are the worst."

"Olivia was too nice to see it."

Riley stared down at the page until the letters blurred together.

Ms. Porter moved between the desks, setting down papers in neat stacks. When she reached Riley, she paused. Her hand rested against the corner of the desk for one brief second.

"Focus on your work," she said softly.

There was care in her eyes.

No defense, though.

Not when everybody else had already decided.

At lunch, Riley took a table near the windows and lasted less than two minutes before Danny's name found her there too.

A boy from track said the police would not have arrested him without proof.

A girl from yearbook said people had always missed what was right in front of them.

Another voice, farther down the table, said Olivia had probably been scared for a long time and just never told anyone.

Riley kept her eyes on the milk carton in front of her and said nothing.

Every silence felt like agreement.

By the time the bell rang, her food was untouched, and her jaw hurt from keeping it shut.

The rest of the day moved around her in hard little pieces. Locker doors. Bright hall lights. Shoes squeaking across waxed floors. Every sound seemed sharper now, as if the whole building had lost patience with doubt.

By the last bell, Riley felt hollowed out.

Her books were weightless in her arms. Her steps dragged anyway. She kept her head down and held tight to the one thing she had left.

A thin, fraying thread of belief.

It should have snapped by now.

It had not.

Ethan's Shadow

The grocery store hummed with the low drone of coolers and fluorescent lights.

Riley had gone there because home felt too small and school felt worse. She drifted past stacked fruit, paper towels, frozen dinners, and sale signs she never read. The whole place smelled like coffee, lemons, and cold air pushed through vents too hard.

People talked around her like she was not there.

Near produce, a woman said Ethan Harper had tried so hard.

A man by the freezer case muttered that some boys were rotten before they were grown.

Riley kept walking until Ethan's voice reached her from the next aisle and stopped her cold.

"A father should keep his daughter safe," he said.

He stood near the bread display with a woman clutching tissues in one hand. His shoulders sagged in just the right way. His voice carried enough to be overheard, but not enough to seem meant for anyone else.

"But how do you fight someone who worms his way into her trust?" he went on, shaking his head once. "I saw it coming, and I still couldn't stop it."

The woman's face crumpled at once. "Poor girl. You did all you could."

Ethan bowed his head.

From where Riley stood, grief had carved itself deep into his face. The pauses were perfect. The silence after each sentence landed exactly where it needed to. Even the slight shake in his shoulders came at the moment her hand touched his arm.

Riley froze at the end of the aisle, a basket hanging from two fingers she did not remember picking up.

His words felt aimed at her even though he had not looked her way yet.

Then he did.

Just once.

His eyes met hers across the distance. Calm. Measured. A grieving father carrying pain the town wanted to reward.

Then came the smallest nod.

Not for the woman beside him.

For Riley.

Stay quiet.

Don't move.

Her chest locked so fast it hurt.

She turned sharply, left the basket on a shelf beside canned soup, and pushed through the front doors into cold air.

Outside, she bent beside the cart return and dragged in a breath that did nothing to steady her. Through the glass, Ethan still stood with his head bowed while the woman dabbed at her eyes.

From out here, it looked holy.

That was the worst part.

He was not just lying.

He was giving them a version of grief they wanted to hold close.

No one else saw it.

No one else ever did.

What Fear Sounds Like

The next afternoon, Riley cut past the station steps and told herself it was only because it was on the way.

That lie lasted until she saw Danny.

A patrol car idled at the curb. Officers Miller and Reyes guided him toward the entrance, one on each side. Danny looked thinner already. His hair was a mess. The cuffs on his wrists flashed once in the fading light.

He moved like someone who had not slept right in days.

"Danny!"

The word tore out of Riley before she could stop it.

His head jerked up.

For the first time in days, something alive hit his face. Relief. Shock. Need.

"Riley."

Miller tightened his grip, but Danny leaned forward anyway, the movement clumsy with the cuffs.

"You know me," he said. His voice cracked hard on the last word. "Please, you know I didn't do this."

The desperation in it ripped straight through her.

Not smooth.

Not careful.

Nothing like Ethan.

Danny's chest heaved as Reyes tugged at his arm, but he kept fighting for one more second of eye contact.

"I didn't hurt her," he said, louder now, raw enough to turn heads. "You have to believe me."

A few people on the sidewalk slowed.

Not many. Just enough to look, decide, and keep moving.

Miller muttered something low. Reyes pulled harder.

Riley tried to speak.

His name made it to her throat and died there.

Danny's eyes stayed locked on hers until the steel framed door cut between them and he was gone.

Silence rushed in after him.

Riley stood frozen on the steps with shame burning through her chest. She had called his name. She had made him look up. She had given him one second of hope and done nothing with it.

But his voice stayed with her.

Not the words. The sound under them.

Fear.

Real fear.

Not public grief polished into something easy to admire.

Not the careful sorrow Ethan wore like a suit.

This had been different.

Ragged. Human. Barely held together.

What fear sounded like when no one wanted to hear it.

The Last Believer

That night, Riley lay curled on top of her blanket with the lamp on and the notebook heavy on her chest.

She had not written a word.

Her phone kept filling with the same images from different accounts and different angles. Ethan in candlelight. Danny in cuffs. Olivia smiling in an old track photo pulled from happier days and turned into proof for people who had already chosen the story they wanted.

Below one post, somebody had written, Everybody saw it.

Riley stared at that line until her stomach turned.

No, she thought.

Everybody chose the easier version.

She scrolled farther.

The same vigil photo kept coming back. Ethan in candlelight. Head bowed. Hand to his chest. Olivia smiling from the frame beside him while comment after comment buried Danny under words that all sounded the same.

Predator.

We all missed it.

Thank God her father fought for her.

Riley stopped scrolling. The photo stayed on the screen, glowing in her hand, and all she could think was how neatly Ethan fit inside their grief.

A knock sounded at her door.

"You okay?" her mom asked.

"Yeah," Riley said.

Her voice sounded thin even to her.

The footsteps moved away.

Riley unlocked Danny's thread and stared at the blank message box. Trust me would have made her throw the phone. I'm sorry would have been worse. She locked the screen instead and pulled the notebook into her lap, but even then the pen would not move.

She kept hearing him on the steps.

You know me.

Please.

I didn't hurt her.

The whole town believed they had the answer. Teachers believed it. Parents believed it. Students repeated it until it no longer sounded like rumor and started sounding like memory.

Riley pressed the notebook harder against her chest.

"If I'm wrong," she whispered into the room, "then I've already lost."

The house gave her nothing back.

Outside, wind rattled the gutter once and passed on.

She stared at the ceiling until her eyes stung.

She was the last believer now. The last candle in a town that had already blown every other light out.

She felt it flicker.

But it didn't go out.

Part IV

The Home Stretch

Chapter Twenty-Five

The Trap

Crossing the Line

The streets were quiet, but Riley felt seen with every step.

Porch lights glowed up and down the block. Curtains shifted once or twice in the dark windows. A dog barked somewhere behind a fence, then stopped. Every small sound made her feel more obvious.

She pulled her arms tight across herself and walked faster.

Danny's voice stayed with her. The raw crack in it outside the station. The way he had looked at her like she was the last person on earth who might still believe him.

You know me. Please. You know I didn't hurt her.

She needed something real.

Ethan's house waited at the end of the street, bigger than it ever looked in daylight. The siding caught hard shadows. The windows looked black and flat. Nothing in it felt like a home.

Riley climbed the porch steps and tried the front door.

Locked.

Of course.

She stepped back down and moved around the side of the house, keeping close to the wall. Gravel shifted under her shoes. The yard smelled damp and cold. At the kitchen window, she stopped and tested the frame with careful fingers.

It gave.

Not much.

Just enough.

Riley stared at the narrow opening for half a second, breathing through the rush in her chest. Then she pulled it wider and hauled herself through.

She landed on the kitchen floor with a soft thud and froze.

No shout.

No footsteps.

No sudden light.

Only the house around her.

The air smelled faintly of woodsmoke and lemon cleaner, but something sharper sat under it. Something metallic. Something wrong.

Riley stayed still and listened.

The refrigerator hummed. A pipe clicked once inside a wall. Somewhere deeper in the house, wood settled with a sound like a held breath being let out.

She was inside now.

There was no backing out clean.

The Staged Room

Riley crossed the kitchen slowly, then moved toward the stairs.

Each step gave a soft groan under her weight. She stopped after every one and listened again. The house stayed quiet, but it didn't feel empty. It felt watchful.

At the top of the stairs, the hallway stretched ahead in dim, colorless light.

Olivia's door stood shut.

Riley went to it and put her hand on the knob. Her palm had gone damp. She turned it anyway.

The room beyond looked neat at first.

Too neat.

Track medals hung in straight rows. The bed was made so tightly it looked untouched. A stuffed rabbit sat against the pillow with its ears fixed upright; its face turned toward the room as if it had been posed.

Nothing in it felt natural.

Riley stepped inside and shut the door partway behind her. Not all the way. Just enough to cut the hall a little.

The room smelled like old paper, polish, and something stale under both.

She went first to the dresser.

The top drawer opened with a soft scrape. Shirts folded in clean stacks. Socks paired too carefully. Nothing shoved aside. Nothing lived in. She checked the rest of the drawers, then the desk, then under the bed.

Nothing.

Her breathing got shallower.

She crossed to the closet. Shoes lined the floor in even rows. A sweater hung with the sleeves folded inward just so. The space looked less like a girl's room and more like a picture of one someone had tried too hard to keep perfect.

Riley crouched near the bedframe and that was when she saw it.

A dark fleck in the carpet.

So small she almost missed it.

She leaned closer.

Blood.

Dried. Old enough to darken. Small enough to be scrubbed around instead of fully lifted.

Her stomach turned.

Riley stood too fast and looked at the window. Her fingers went to the sill. There, near the lower edge, a deep scratch cut through the paint. Another beside it. Not random. Not age. Something had clawed there. Hard.

She turned toward the bookshelf.

A gap between two framed photos and a stack of books. Not a big one, but wrong enough to stand out once she saw it. Her eyes moved over the shelf and stopped.

The track trophy was gone.

The one Olivia had shown off. The one she kept where she could see it.

Riley looked around the room again, slower this time.

The straight ribbons.

The made bed.

The rabbit.

The drawers.

Everything looked cleaned, corrected, arranged.

Not preserved.

Managed.

Like somebody had stripped the room down to the version they wanted other people to see.

Something cold settled in Riley's chest.

Danny hadn't done this.

Caught

A floorboard creaked behind her.

Riley went still.

She turned slowly toward the door.

Ethan stood there, broad shoulders filling the frame, one hand still resting on the knob. His face gave almost nothing away at first. Then his mouth curved slightly, not warm enough to be a smile.

"You shouldn't be here, Riley."

His voice was calm.

That calm hit harder than yelling would have.

Riley backed toward the dresser without meaning to.

"You killed her."

The words ripped out before she could stop them.

Ethan tilted his head a little, studying her like she was a problem he had expected sooner or later.

"That's a serious thing to say."

"You cleaned this room." Her throat had gone tight, but she kept going. "You cleaned all of it."

His eyes moved once over the room, then back to her. "You've always been observant."

Riley's hands shook at her sides. "You killed Olivia and blamed Danny."

Something flickered in his face then. Not guilt. Not fear. Mild disappointment, maybe. Like she had finally reached the answer and bored him by doing it.

"Do you have proof," he asked softly, "or just suspicion?"

She looked toward the half open door behind him, then back at his face.

He saw it.

Of course he did.

He stepped into the room and shut the door behind him with a quiet click.

Riley's body screamed at her to run.

Ethan took another step.

"Olivia thought she was clever too," he said, his voice dropping lower. "She thought secrets could keep her safe."

Riley pressed back into the dresser. "Stay away from me."

But he was already too close.

The truth arrived all at once then, not just as knowledge, but as shape.

The unlocked window.

The quiet house.

The open path in.

This had not been a discovery.

This had been the door closing behind her.

Bound Silence

Riley lunged sideways.

She almost got around him.

Almost.

Ethan caught her wrist so fast it made her stumble. His grip was brutal and certain. She twisted, kicked, clawed for his face, but he moved like he had already pictured every version of this.

He drove her back hard enough to knock the breath out of her.

"No," she gasped, but the word barely formed before he slammed a hand over her mouth.

The room blurred into pieces.

The bed.

The desk.

The rabbit.

The floor.

Riley fought anyway. She drove her heel down, thrashed, tried to bite through his palm, but he was stronger and colder than she had prepared herself for. Not frantic. Not clumsy. Just efficient.

By the time rope bit into her wrists, panic had turned hot and white behind her eyes.

He forced her into the chair by the desk.

The same chair Olivia must have used for homework. For writing. For all the small quiet things a person did when they believed their room still belonged to them.

Now the wood dug into Riley's back while the rope cut deeper each time she jerked against it.

A gag came next. Rough cloth pulled tight and knotted hard behind her head. The taste of it filled her mouth. Sour. Dusty. Used.

Ethan stepped back to look at her.

Riley's chest heaved. Her wrists burned. Her eyes flicked wildly around the room, searching for anything she could reach.

Nothing.

The room had become a trap, fitted into the house as neatly as everything else was.

Ethan crouched in front of her. "You almost stayed quiet," he said. "That would've been smarter."

Riley made a sound through the gag, full of fury and fear and nothing he needed to understand.

He slipped a hand into his pocket and took out a brass key.

Her stomach dropped.

Her name wasn't on it.

Olivia's was.

The letters had been carved deep and ugly into the metal. Not engraved. Cut. Jagged enough to look violent even now.

Ethan turned it between his fingers, almost thoughtfully.

"She thought this meant freedom," he said. "She always wanted symbols. Little stories she could tell herself."

He leaned closer and touched the cold key to Riley's cheek.

"But it was never freedom."

Riley squeezed her eyes shut for a second, then opened them again. Tears blurred the room, but not enough to hide him.

"It was a chain," Ethan said.

He let the words sit there.

Then his hand caught Riley's chin, forcing her to keep looking at him.

"And now," he said quietly, "the chain belongs to you."

Riley strained so hard against the rope that the chair legs scraped across the floor. The locked window flashed in the corner of her vision. Too far. Useless.

Ethan stood, calm as ever, and straightened the edge of the desk as if that mattered too.

Then he looked down at her once last time.

"You were clever," he said. "But clever doesn't win."

The room went colder around her.

Riley had not just walked into Ethan's house.

She had walked straight into Olivia's prison.

And now the trap was shut.

The Chair

For a long time after he left, Riley could hear nothing but her own breathing.

The rope bit deeper the more she fought it. The gag held the taste of dust and old cloth against her tongue. The chair gave a small groan every time she moved, as if even the wood remembered who had sat there before.

Olivia's room.

That was the part Riley could not stop feeling.

The track medals still hung in their tidy rows. The rabbit still watched from the bed. The desk lamp threw a weak pool of light across papers that had been arranged too carefully to be real. The whole room looked frozen in place, preserved for strangers, cleaned down to a lie.

But Riley knew better now.

She could see Olivia in it too clearly.

Sitting in this same chair, shoulders tight, writing in quick secret lines. Looking over her shoulder at every sound in the hall. Trying to carve out one small corner of the house that still felt like hers.

Riley jerked hard against the ropes again.

Pain shot up both arms.

The chair dragged an inch across the floorboards and stopped.

Not enough.

She forced herself to go still.

Think.

Breathe.

Listen.

The house answered in small sounds. A faint hum from below. Pipes ticking inside the wall. The soft movement of old wood settling into night. Beyond the door, somewhere farther down the hall, a floorboard gave a tired creak and went quiet again.

Ethan was still there.

Of course he was.

Riley looked toward the window. Locked. Too high to reach from where she sat. She looked toward the desk, then the dresser, then the bed. Nothing close enough. Nothing loose enough. Nothing she could pull free without her hands.

Her eyes landed on the rabbit.

Its stitched face looked blank in the dim light.

The sight of it made something twist deep in her chest.

Olivia had lived in this room.

And Riley had still failed to understand how bad it was until the ropes cut into her own wrists.

A sound rose in her throat behind the gag. Angry. Broken. Useless.

She swallowed it and tried the ropes again, not wild this time. Small movements. Careful ones. Testing.

The knot at one wrist did not give.

Neither did the other.

But one of the chair legs shifted slightly on the floor.

Riley held still again, breathing hard through her nose, and listened to the silence gather itself around her.

Not yet.

But not nothing.

She fixed her eyes on the door and forced herself to stay awake.

Because if Ethan came back, she needed to hear him before she saw him.

And if there was even the smallest chance to get out of that chair, she couldn't waste it panicking.

So she sat in Olivia's room with the ropes burning her skin, the carved key still cold in her mind, and the whole house closing around her one quiet inch at a time.

Chapter Twenty-Six

Captive Silence

The Room That Isn't Empty

Riley didn't move, even when the house creaked and something shifted faintly down the hall. The rope had cut deep enough into her wrists that her fingers had started to go numb, but stillness felt safer than panic. For now, safe meant quiet. She kept her eyes on the door and listened.

The room pressed in around her, too clean and too controlled. At first glance it looked untouched, like any normal bedroom frozen in time. But the longer she stared, the more it felt wrong. The track medals hung in perfect rows along the wall, each ribbon straight, each edge aligned. The bed was smooth, the pillow untouched. Even the stuffed rabbit sat upright, its ears fixed in place as if someone had adjusted them recently.

Nothing in this room had been allowed to fall out of line. Her gaze drifted slowly to the desk. At first, it looked just as controlled as everything else, but then she saw the faint scratches along the surface. They were shallow, deliberate, and close together. Not random. Not careless. The kind of marks someone made when minutes started to feel physical.

Riley's stomach dropped as the realization settled in. Olivia hadn't just sat here to study or read. She had been watching the clock. Waiting in a place that was never really hers.

The thought hurt worse than the ropes biting into her wrists.

Riley pulled once without thinking. Pain tore up both arms, sharp enough to make her vision blur. The chair scraped an inch across the floor before catching. The sound felt too loud, too sudden, and she froze instantly, her breath catching behind the gag.

She listened until the silence settled again. Nothing came from the hall. No footsteps. No movement. Not yet.

Her breathing slowed again, forced back under control. Panic would get her nowhere. Not here. Not with him still in the house.

She swallowed hard and kept her eyes on the door, forcing herself to think instead of panic.

The Man Who Watches

The door opened without warning. Riley dropped her gaze instantly and let her body go slack against the chair, tipping her head forward as if the weight of everything had finally worn her down. Ethan stepped inside and shut the door behind him with a soft, deliberate click.

"You're learning," he said.

His voice was calm, almost thoughtful. Not angry. Not rushed. Riley didn't react as he moved around her slowly, his steps quiet against the floor. He wasn't trying to hide his presence. He wasn't cautious. He was comfortable and that made him worse.

He stopped near the desk, and Riley felt his attention shift before she saw his hand brush lightly over the surface. His fingers passed right over the scratches. Her pulse spiked, but she kept her body still.

He paused there for a second, fingers resting against the wood, then moved on without a reaction or question. Either he hadn't noticed, or he had and it meant nothing to him.

"She used to sit here," he said. Riley's stomach tightened as his fingers rested on the desk. "She thought this room was hers." He paused, just long enough to let the words settle. "She liked to pretend."

Riley's nails dug into her palm.

Ethan stepped closer, not crouching fully this time, just enough to lower himself into her space.

"People need that," he went on. "Small illusions. Control. Privacy. A place they pretend is safe."

His eyes flicked briefly toward the desk before returning to her. "They think if they carve out something of their own, no one can reach them there." He held her gaze long enough for Riley's stomach to tighten. "But they're wrong."

Riley forced herself not to react. Not to look. Not to give him anything he could use.

Ethan studied her for a moment longer, something almost clinical in his eyes.

"You're smarter than she was," he said.

It didn't sound like praise.

It sounded like a warning.

He straightened, smoothing his sleeve with slow, careful movements, as if resetting himself.

Then he turned and walked out.

The door shut.

The lock clicked.

The Rope Gives

Riley moved the second the sound settled.

She twisted her wrists against the rope, forcing her thumb into the knot and ignoring the sharp burn as the fibers tore into her skin. Pain shot up her arms, but she didn't stop. She pushed harder, teeth clenched behind the gag.

The rope held. Her breathing picked up, fast and uneven, but she forced herself to stop before panic took over. Force wasn't working. Not yet.

She had spent too long watching Olivia run to misunderstand pain. Pain did not always mean stop. Sometimes it meant adjust.

She shifted her weight slightly, testing the chair beneath her. One leg sat uneven against the floor from where she had dragged it earlier. It wasn't much, but it was something.

Carefully, she leaned her weight again, just enough to tilt the angle of her wrists.

The chair creaked, and Riley froze. She counted in her head, waiting for footsteps, for the door, for anything that meant he was coming back. When nothing came, she moved again. This time she didn't pull. She pressed.

She worked the rope against the rough edge of the chair back, guiding it instead of fighting it. The fibers scraped and tightened, biting deeper into her skin. The burn was immediate, sharp, and relentless, but she held steady.

The rope still didn't give at first. She adjusted her angle and tried again. This time the fibers shifted slightly, not enough to break, but enough to feel different.

She pressed harder this time, careful, controlled. The rope tightened, then dragged across the wood.

A faint snap sounded beneath the rope, so small she almost thought she imagined it. Riley stilled, breathing hard through her nose. Then she felt the change: a slight looseness. Not freedom, but enough to matter.

What He Missed

A faint sound drifted up from below. A door closed somewhere in the house, followed by slow footsteps moving away from her, not toward her. Riley froze and listened until the sounds faded.

Her mind raced. Where was he going? Why now?

Another sound came through the floor, softer this time. Metal shifting. Keys, maybe. Something being set down.

Her eyes moved to the door. It was locked, of course, but not everything in this house was perfect. Not everything had been accounted for.

She forced herself to look at the room again, this time with purpose. It was not a bedroom anymore. It was a problem she had to solve.

The window was too high and too far from the chair. The dresser was heavy, solid, impossible to move while she was tied down.

Her gaze shifted to the desk. One drawer sat slightly uneven in its frame, barely noticeable unless someone was looking for it. Riley hadn't noticed it before. Now it stood out. Something had been opened, forced, or hidden there.

Her wrists shifted again inside the rope. The looseness was still there. Small, but real.

Her breathing steadied.

Everything in this room had been controlled, adjusted, and forced into place, but not perfectly. Not completely. Ethan believed he didn't need to be careful. That belief might be the only mistake he had made.

The Last Run Begins

Riley pressed the rope against the chair again, harder this time, working the fibers against the rough edge instead of wasting strength on the knot. The rope scraped deeper into her skin, but she kept the pressure steady. Pain spread through both wrists, hot and sharp, until her hands shook from holding still.

Another strand gave, more felt than heard beneath the rope.

The binding shifted against her wrist, not loose enough to free her, but no longer fixed in place. Riley froze, her pulse slamming so hard she could feel it in her throat. For one wild second, she wanted to yank until the whole knot came apart. She wanted to tear free, rip the gag from her mouth, and run before Ethan came back.

But wanting wasn't the same as surviving.

She forced herself to stop. The rope had changed, but it had not failed. If she rushed now, she would make noise. She would scrape the chair again. She would give him a reason to come upstairs before she was ready.

Downstairs, something moved again. A step, a door, then a faint scrape of metal. Riley held her breath and listened. The sound came once more, softer this time, followed by the low murmur of Ethan's voice. Not words she could understand. Just his voice, calm and close enough to remind her that the house still belonged to him.

Her eyes moved across the room one more time. The window was still too far. The desk drawer still sat uneven. The floor between the chair and door looked impossibly wide. None of it was enough yet, but it was no longer nothing.

She curled her fingers slowly inside the loosened rope, testing the space she had made. Her skin burned where the fibers had cut her, and something warm slid down toward her palm. Blood, probably. She didn't look. Looking would make it real, and real would make her panic.

She kept her eyes on the door and forced herself not to rush. Panic would waste to only chance she had made for herself.

The house wasn't quiet. It was waiting, and Riley forced herself to wait with it.

The next time she moved, it would be for the door.

Chapter Twenty-Seven

Splintered Chains

Breaking Point

The rope burned her wrists raw. Each twist carved deeper, the strands sawing her skin open. Riley pressed her forearms against the chair's edge, then pulled until her shoulders shook.

The wood creaked under her weight, a long groan that made her freeze. She held her breath and listened. Ethan's footsteps drifted faintly from below, steady and unhurried. He thought she was secure. He thought she was beaten.

The air was thick with lemon polish and dust. Under it was something worse, an iron tang that clung in the back of her throat.

Riley shut her eyes. For one dizzy second, she could almost see Olivia here. Olivia bent over the desk, pen in hand. Olivia curling up with her rabbit. Olivia alive.

Riley twisted again, pain spreading like fire. The strands cut deeper, but she welcomed it. Pain meant she was fighting. Pain meant she wasn't done.

The gag tasted of sweat, cloth, and old fear. She bit it until her jaw ached, forcing her teeth against the rough weave. She pulled harder, harder, until the knot shifted a fraction. Her heart leapt. She pulled again, her wrists screaming. The rope groaned. Threads frayed.

Her body shook, but she didn't stop. Another strand split. Then another.

The Window

The chair toppled sideways with a violent crack. Riley hit the floor hard, wood slamming into her shoulder. The sound thundered in the house, echoing like a gunshot.

She froze, chest heaving. Her ears rang with silence, then the muffled thud of Ethan moving below.

Her panic snapped into motion. She twisted, dragging her body until her knees hooked the chair rung. She forced her wrists forward, shoving into the slack she'd earned. Blood slicked her skin. The knot slipped loose with a wet snap.

She yanked the gag loose, coughing air into her lungs. The taste of metal and cloth lingered. She spat, wiped her mouth, staggered up. Her legs wobbled like dead weight, but she lurched toward the window.

For one second, she almost screamed Olivia's name. She swallowed it back. Noise could kill her.

The latch stuck. She clawed at it, nails splitting, palms scraping raw. She threw her shoulder into the frame. Black spots burst across her vision, but she shoved again. The wood groaned, then broke open.

Cold air surged through the gap. It smelled of wet earth and distant smoke. It smelled like freedom.

She hauled one leg over the sill, skin ripping against splintered wood. Pain tore through her, but she shoved forward until her chest cleared the frame.

Her feet hit grass. She stumbled, her knees biting mud, then pushed upright. The yard spread wide, dark and empty. For the first time, there was no rope on her skin.

She ran.

The House Wakes

“Riley!” Ethan’s voice erupted from below, sharp at last, the calm stripped out.

She bolted across the yard. The front door banged open behind her. Light washed over the grass. His boots struck wood, then dirt.

“Riley!” Closer.

Her breath tore through her throat. The ground was slick, mud pulling at her bare feet. She slipped, caught herself, drove forward.

The world blurred—black sky, pale moon, trees clawing at the horizon. The tree line loomed like salvation, like jaws waiting to shut behind her.

Behind her, his boots pounded steady, deliberate. He was not rushing. He was pacing.

"You can run," his voice carried, low and sure. "They always do."

For a split second, she heard it the way Olivia must have heard it, calm and certain, impossible to outrun.

Riley’s chest clenched. Her mind flashed to Olivia’s rabbit, still perched on the bed. To the medals gleaming on the wall. To Ethan smoothing them with his hand like they were trophies of his own.

She hurled herself harder, lungs burning, legs screaming.

She hit the tree line. Branches whipped her arms as she plunged into shadow.

Into the Night

Branches cut across her arms. Roots hooked at her feet. She stumbled, caught herself, pushed forward again. Bark scraped her palms raw when she caught a trunk to steady herself.

The shadows pressed tight, moonlight bleeding through in fractured ribbons. Every step felt blind. Every sound exploded. The snap of twigs, the hiss of leaves, the thunder of her own heart.

“Clever,” Ethan called. His voice was steady again, calm as death. “But clever doesn’t win.”

Her legs screamed. Her chest split with fire. She ran anyway.

Her mind circled back, fragments replaying in a fevered loop. Danny’s face. *Trust me.* Olivia’s laugh. Olivia dragged away.

Riley shoved harder, each step agony. She wasn't running only for herself anymore. She was running for Olivia. For Danny. For every warning she had ignored until it was almost too late.

The ground sloped downhill. Momentum carried her too fast. Branches tore her shirt. Mud streaked her arms. She didn’t care. She let the slope hurl her forward, reckless and wild.

The house glowed behind her, a box of fire in the trees.

For the first time since she stepped into that house, nothing held her but the dark.

But freedom still had footsteps.

Chapter Twenty-Eight

The Last Run

Into the Thicket

The forest thickened around her like a trap. Branches slapped her arms, sharp lines of pain striping her skin. Roots curled from the ground like claws, tearing at her bare feet with every step. Her lungs clawed back at her, each breath scraping raw, as though she were sucking broken glass into her chest. She didn't care. She kept moving.

Her vision swam with sweat, her eyes burning. The sting blurred the path, but stopping wasn't an option. If she slowed, even for a second, the woods would take her. They'd cradle her like they had Olivia's body at the train yard, bury her beneath their silence.

The air carried the stink of damp rot; wet earth mixed with a faint smoke that drifted from somewhere far off. Chimneys. Houses. Normal life she could never reach.

Behind her, Ethan's boots struck dirt. Not rushed. Not panicked. Each impact steady, like a drumbeat that didn't belong to him but to something older, a predator's rhythm. He wasn't chasing. He was pacing. Waiting for her to fall.

Riley's legs buckled. She caught herself on a tree, bark ripping her palm. Her knees begged to fold, but she forced them back, locking them straight. She wouldn't collapse. She couldn't.

Her body screamed, but she shoved harder. She wasn't just running from Ethan. She was running toward something, light, survival, proof. The chance Olivia never got.

Through the branches, moonlight spilled in broken slats, silver stripes across the ground. They looked like a track lane, pale and unreal, and she drove her body forward as if the finish line waited just ahead.

Predator's Voice

"You can't outrun me, Riley."

His voice slid through the trees, cold and certain.

She stumbled. Her stomach knotted, nearly dropping her to the dirt.

"She tried too."

The words slammed into her chest. Olivia.

Her foot caught on a root, and she went down hard, knees skidding on stone and soil. Skin tore, hot blood slicking her shins. Pain rang in her bones.

Ethan's boots did not quicken. He didn't need to.

"You've got fight," he called. His tone was calm, steady. "She had fight too. But fight always runs out."

Her throat burned. She spat dirt, pushed herself up on shaking arms. Tears blurred her sight, but rage burned them back.

"Shut up," she whispered. Her voice cracked, but she said it again, louder: "Shut up!"

A chuckle answered her. Low. Cruel. It crawled along the trees. Then silence.

The quiet pressed down heavier than his voice had. The woods seemed to lean closer, listening with him. Every rustle of leaves, every pop of branches overhead became his hands reaching for her.

Her breath came harsh and uneven. She hated that he had stolen her silence. She hated that even the dark obeyed his pace.

Riley clenched her jaw, forced her legs to move. She refused to give him her fear. She would not let his voice become her finish line.

Breaking the Loop

Her body rebelled. Her calves trembled violently with each stride, warning of collapse. A stitch stabbed her side, knifing sharp and deep with every inhale. Her chest burned with fire that clawed into her throat.

Her thoughts wanted to unravel, to sink into the same loop she had fought before. Danny's eyes wide at the station. Olivia flying down the track. Olivia falling silent. The images came, pulling at her, trying to drag her down with her failing body.

No.

She seized the loop and crushed it.

Olivia had finished every race she'd ever run. Danny had begged her not to give in, his voice desperate but sure. Riley couldn't betray either of them. Not now.

She forced her body to listen. Breath in. Breath out. Count each stride. One-two. One-two.

The forest blurred to shadow. She didn't see trees anymore, only obstacles to clear, hurdles to push past. Her arms pumped, legs fired, every ounce of her reduced to motion.

Her mouth tasted of blood, copper pooling on her tongue where she'd bitten her lip. Her throat burned like she was swallowing fire.

Behind her, boots struck louder. Steady. Gaining.

Fear tried to crack her. She gritted her teeth and turned it into something sharper. Defiance. Every step was rebellion now.

No Finish Line

The trees thinned. Moonlight spread across a clearing, pale and merciless.

Her heart lurched. She hurled herself forward, the last of her strength breaking through her stride.

Ethan crashed into the clearing. His hand reached, fingers grazing the back of her shirt.

Her legs buckled. She staggered, nearly falling. But momentum hurled her forward, a wild, broken sprint.

Her throat ripped with each gasp. Her heart pounded like it would split.

"You can't win, Riley," his voice cut across the night. "You never could."

She didn't look back. She didn't speak. She ran.

The ground sloped hard. Her feet flew too fast, half-controlled, half-falling.

Olivia's unfinished race blazed in her mind. Danny's plea drove her forward. Her own voice cut through them both.

Live. Live. Live.

One last stride. One last chance.

She vanished into the trees.

Ethan's boots crashed behind her, relentless.

The last run was not over.

Chapter Twenty-Nine

The Evidence

The Call and the Threshold

Riley ran until the woods thinned, gravel cutting her bare feet. A porch light glowed ahead, a lonely square of yellow in the dark. She stopped there, trembling, and fumbled her phone. Twice her thumb slipped, once she hit the wrong button. The third time, the call went through.

"Reyes," a tired voice answered.

"It's me," Riley gasped. "He—he had me tied up in Olivia's room. I got free. I need help. Please, Birch and Miller. Hurry."

Silence. When Reyes spoke again, his tone had sharpened, clipped and hard. "He had you *what*?"

"Tied up," Riley said. "I got free."

"Are you okay? Are you injured?" Reyes asked.

"I'm scrapped, but okay. Please come now."

In the background, she heard the scrape of a chair and the crackle of a police radio. Another voice cut in, rough and urgent. Miller. "If that's true, we're not waiting. Stay on the line. Don't hang up. We'll bring you back to the station for a statement."

Her breath hitched. "Don't take me to the station. If we don't go back, he'll clean it up. You'll miss it."

"What will we miss, Riley?" Reyes asked.

"The room," she said. "There was blood in her room."

Low voices passed between the two men. Then Reyes again, firm: "Stay where you are. Do not move."

After what felt like an eternity, red and blue washed through the pines. The cruiser stopped, gravel spitting under its tires. Reyes stepped out first, his coat slung over one arm. He set it on her shoulders without a word. Miller climbed out slower, scanning her face, sharp eyes probing like he could weigh truth from lies.

"You understand," Miller said, "this isn't by the book. You just escaped a possible crime scene."

"I understand," Riley said, her voice raw, "but let me show you where to look."

Reyes gave one short nod. "You stay close to us. No wandering."

Together, they walked the short stretch back. The house rose out of the dark like a crouched figure that hated light. Reyes killed the headlights before the drive. They approached on foot, gravel crunching soft under their shoes.

Riley clutched the coat tight around her shoulders. The air was cold enough to sting, but the deeper chill came from what waited inside.

The Trophy Gap

The porch boards gave a low groan as Reyes rapped on the door with his fist. A moment later, the knob turned. Ethan appeared in the frame, water glass in hand. His shirt hung loose, his hair slightly mussed, like he had been asleep. His eyes flicked from the badges to Riley, hunched behind them.

"What's this?" he asked, voice flat. "It's the middle of the night."

Reyes lifted his badge higher. "We got a call. Riley says she was restrained in this house against her will."

Ethan's jaw twitched. "That's absurd. You can't just come in here without a warrant."

Reyes didn't move. "A minor reported unlawful confinement. That gives us exigent circumstances. We're stepping inside."

Miller's tone dropped low. "And until this is cleared, you're staying in sight."

Ethan didn't budge. He gripped the glass tighter, his knuckles pale. For a heartbeat, the doorway seemed locked. Then, slowly, he shifted aside, leaving a sliver of space. His voice was measured, too smooth. "You're making a mistake."

Reyes went first, flashlight sweeping. Miller followed, keeping Ethan in view. Riley hovered at the threshold, her feet rooted but her voice clear.

"Left wall," she whispered. "Past the desk. The case."

Reyes angled the beam. Rows of trophies gleamed in neat ranks. Between them, a clear gap stood out, the dust framing a square where a base had once rested.

"There used to be one here," Riley said. Her voice steadied as she spoke. "North Ridge meet, last fall. I have a picture."

Reyes asked, “Describe it.”

“Tall,” Riley said. She lifted her hand, measuring the air. “A gold runner on top. Her name plate at the base. She kept it in the middle—he made her dust them.”

Miller leaned closer, tracing the outline with a gloved finger. Dust swirled. “The outline’s clear,” he said. “This sat here for months. Moved recently.”

Ethan shifted, jaw tight. “She could have taken it to school. They display trophies sometimes. Check with her coach.”

Reyes’s gaze didn’t waver. “We will. But you dust this room, don’t you?”

Ethan’s lips pressed thin. “I keep my house clean, yes.”

“Then you’d know what sat here last week,” Reyes said evenly.

Ethan’s eyes flicked to the shelf, then away. “I don’t account for every item. You’re wasting your time.”

Riley’s stomach knotted. The empty dust square glared louder than his voice.

Reyes let the silence hang after Ethan's deflection about the trophy. His notebook closed with a snap that sounded louder than it should have been. Then he spoke flat, leaving no room for argument.

"Miller, keep him here. Riley, show me what else you saw."

Ethan's eyes tracked them as Reyes guided her toward the stairs. His grip on the glass tightened, muscles in his forearm straining.

The sound came sharp and sudden. A crack like a gunshot. The glass split in his hand, water spilling down his wrists. Shards tinkled to the floorboards.

Riley flinched hard, her pulse lurching. For a moment she thought he'd come at them. But Ethan didn't even blink. He lowered what remained of the glass onto the table, then lifted his gaze again. His face was calm, too calm, as if nothing had happened.

Reyes froze halfway up the stairs. His hand hovered over his holster, eyes narrowing. "That supposed to mean something?"

Miller shifted his stance, shoulders broadening to block Ethan's line of sight. "Careful with your hands, Harper." His voice dropped, sharp enough to bite.

Ethan wiped his wet palm on his jeans. "Accident. Thin glass. Don't read into it." His voice never rose, but the chill in it cut deeper than shouting.

Riley pressed closer to Reyes, her skin crawling. If he could crush a glass barehanded and not react, what else could he do?

Reyes gave Ethan one last hard look, then turned back to Riley. "Show me." His tone was calm but clipped. Urgent.

The smell of lemon polish grew sharper as they climbed, masking something darker. Riley's stomach twisted, but she kept moving. The room waited at the top of the stairs, neat and quiet, like it had never held a scream.

The Stain

The lemon-polish smell grew stronger the higher they climbed. Riley's leg shook as she reached Olivia's door.

The room was pristine: bed made, medals glinting, rabbit propped neatly on the pillow. It looked untouched. But Riley knew better.

Reyes entered first, sweeping the light in slow arcs. "Show me," he said softly.

Her throat closed, but she forced her feet across the carpet. She stopped near the bedside table, pointing to the floorboards. A faint discoloration marred the grain, darkened and uneven oval. "There. He tried to scrub it."

Reyes crouched low, steady as stone. He leaned close, flashlight fixed, his gloved hand brushing the edge. The mark drank in the light instead of reflecting it. He pulled a swab from his pocket and pressed lightly.

"Could be blood," he murmured. He didn't commit, but the crease in his brow deepened.

Riley's breath came quick. "It is. I know it."

From the hallway below, Ethan's voice carried up, calm but edged. "You done snooping? Or are you planning to camp in my daughter's room all night?"

Riley flinched, her shoulders jerking. Reyes didn't look away from the floor. He capped the swab and slid into a vial. His voice stayed level. "Ignore him."

He rose, taking one last sweep of the room: the medals, the rabbit, the faint stain at their feet. He closed his notebook with care and gave a short nod toward the door.

"Let's go," he said.

Riley stepped back into the hall. The air felt colder out there, heavier, pressing close. Miller stood at the landing, his stance firm, Ethan's shadow visible at the bottom of the stairs. Riley's pulse hammered in her ears. Something was about to break.

Weight Shifts

The hall closed in as they stepped out, colder than the room behind them. Riley pressed her back to the wall, her pulse loud in her ears. Miller waited at the landing, squared between them and the stairs. Below, Ethan leaned against the doorframe, one hand resting on the broken glass he'd left on the table. His shadow stretched long across the floorboards.

Reyes slid his notebook into his coat pocket. His voice stayed calm, controlled. "Explain the stain on the floor. It looks like a hand pressed down."

Ethan's jaw tightened. "You're reaching."

"Maybe," Reyes said, voice even. "Where's the missing trophy?"

"I told you. I don't track her things."

"Who dusts the room?"

"I do."

"Then you'd know what sat there last week," Reyes said. His tone never rose, but it pressed harder than shouting.

The mask cracked. Ethan's voice snapped sharp. "Get out of my house."

Miller didn't budge. "We're not finished."

"You are finished." Ethan's voice rose, brittle and ragged. "You had your look. You got nothing."

The house held still. A clock ticked somewhere, steady as a metronome. Riley's heartbeat matched it, fast and uneven.

Reyes's voice cut the silence. "We'll be back. Don't leave town. Don't touch that room."

Ethan's glare sharpened. "You don't speak to me like that."

Reyes's tone hardened. "Do you understand?"

After a long pause, Ethan gave a short, furious nod.

Miller shut his notebook. The empty square on the shelf and the faint stain by the bed said more than words.

Reyes turned to Riley. "You're leaving with us. A nurse will look at you."

Her legs shook, but she moved. Passing Ethan made her skin crawl, but she kept her head forward, her jaw tight. Not yet.

The porch air hit cold against her face. The wide night sky stretched above the trees. Reyes followed close, his voice lower now. "You did well."

"Will it be enough?" she asked.

"It's weight," he said. "Weight shifts cases. Keep breathing. We'll carry the rest."

Riley glanced back once. Through the doorway she could still see the neat rows of trophies, gleaming. The gap stared back, louder than all the others.

For the first time, she believed the truth might be heard.

Chapter Thirty

The Confession

The Warrant

The fluorescent lights at the station buzzed faintly as Riley sat on the cot in a small side room. A nurse dabbed antiseptic across the cuts on her arms, and the sting snapped her back into her body.

"You'll bruise," the nurse said. "But nothing's broken. You'll be sore for a while."

"Okay," Riley murmured.

Her voice sounded flat to her own ears, like it belonged to someone standing across the room.

At the doorway, Miller spoke low into his phone. "Mrs. Mercer? This is Officer Miller. Riley's safe. She's with us now at the station."

He paused, listening.

"Yes, ma'am. I know this is a shock. She's shaken, but she's holding strong."

Another pause.

"She was found at a residence connected to the investigation. I'll explain everything when you get here."

He listened again, his expression tightening just slightly.

"I understand. You can come to the station. We're filing for a warrant now, so things are moving quickly."

When he hung up, he glanced at Riley. "Your mom is on her way."

Her chest tightened. Relief and dread tangled together until she could not tell one from the other.

Down the hall, Reyes's voice carried through the open door. It was clipped and firm.

"Yes, Your Honor. We have probable cause. An escaped witness, previously held captive, has provided details consistent with the victim recovered at the train yard. Her account gives us strong reason to believe further evidence remains inside the residence. Time matters. The scene needs to be secured before anything can be moved or destroyed."

A pause followed.

Riley stared at her hands. The dried blood around her wrists looked darker under the station lights.

Then Reyes said, "Thank you. We'll meet you at the courthouse."

Minutes later, the cruiser moved through the quiet streets. Riley sat in the back with a blanket around her shoulders and her knees pressed tight together. The town outside the window looked wrong in the early dark. Storefronts. Stop signs. Empty sidewalks. Normal things pretending nothing had happened.

The courthouse sat nearly deserted. The judge looked exhausted, his eyes shadowed from a long night, but when Reyes laid out the facts, he did not hesitate.

"This is exceptional," the judge said, signing with a heavy hand. "Make it count."

The stamp cracked down on the page.

Riley flinched.

They had it now. The right to strip Ethan Harper's house open.

Minutes later, the cruiser tore back through Hollow's Edge, lights flashing, siren splitting the quiet. Reyes held the warrant tight against his chest. Backup was already moving toward the Harper house. Each turn of the wheel dragged Riley closer to the place she had barely escaped.

A Mother's Plea

Red and blue lights washed over the Harper house as the patrol cars pulled in. Officers moved toward the porch. Two handlers followed with dogs straining at their leashes, eager and restless. The house stood still beneath the flashing lights, its windows dark except for the faint glow from inside.

Riley froze when she saw her mother's car at the curb.

The driver's door flew open.

"Riley!"

Her mother rushed forward, but two officers stepped into her path.

"Ma'am, stay back."

"She's my daughter!" Her mother's voice cracked. "You are not dragging her back into that house."

Miller came down from the porch, one hand raised. "Mrs. Mercer. She'll be safe. We have a warrant. We need her to walk us through what she saw."

"You can't ask that of her." Her mother's eyes were wet, but her voice was fierce. "She has been through enough. Let her go home."

"I know you want to protect her," Miller said. "But Riley knows where to look. Without her, this house stays a lie."

Her mother looked past him to Riley.

"You don't have to do this, honey. Let them handle it."

Riley's throat tightened. Part of her wanted to run to her mother and let the whole world close around that one safe place. But Olivia's room waited inside. The vent. The desk. The place Ethan had turned into a cage and called it home.

Riley forced the words out. "I need to. For Olivia."

The air went still between them. Her mother's shoulders sagged, the fight breaking under the weight of Riley's face.

"You come straight back to me when it's over," she whispered.

"I will," Riley said.

The promise felt too large for her mouth.

Reyes gave Mrs. Mercer a small nod. "We'll take care of her."

Then he turned and led Riley inside.

The Grate

The air inside smelled sharp with lemon cleaner. Under it lingered something sour. Something wrong.

The dogs moved fast, nails tapping against the floor. Their handlers gave short commands as they swept through the living room, then the kitchen. Riley stayed near Reyes, her arms folded tight around herself. Every creak of the floor made her skin pull tighter.

Ethan stood near the living room entrance with his arms crossed.

He looked patient. Too patient.

"This is ridiculous," he said. "She had her silly hiding spots. You won't find anything important."

No one answered him.

One dog sniffed near the kitchen cabinets, then pulled hard toward the stairs. The handler followed, and the second dog darted after them. Riley's stomach dropped as they climbed.

Olivia's door stood open.

The handlers stepped inside first. The dogs moved over the room, noses low. One went straight to the bed, then to the vent near the floor. It pawed at the grate and whined, claws scraping metal.

"Alert," the handler said.

Ethan's voice cracked sharp behind them. "It's junk. She shoved things in there all the time. Nothing that matters."

Riley turned.

His jaw had clenched. His fingers twitched at his side. The calm mask was thinning.

Reyes crouched beside the vent. "Open it."

Miller knelt with a screwdriver. The first turn squealed. Rust flaked loose. The second screw groaned, and dust sifted into the air. With a sharp tug, the grate came free.

A stale breath spilled from the dark space behind it. Little scraps tumbled out first. An old receipt. A broken pen cap. The corner of a folded note Olivia must have hidden long ago.

Then something clinked softly onto the floor.

Riley's key.

Her chest caved at the sight.

The small worn piece of metal lay in the dust, dull under the flashlight beam. She had given Olivia that key like it could mean safety. Like it could mean a door. Like it could mean there was still a way out if Olivia needed one badly enough.

Olivia had never used it.

Riley stared at it until her eyes burned.

I should have pushed harder.

The thought hit so cleanly it felt like a wound.

Miller reached deeper into the vent. When his hand came back out, he held the weight they had been hunting for.

A track trophy.

Its base was dented. Dark grooves stained the metal near the edge.

For one second, no one spoke. Then Miller slid it into an evidence bag. The plastic crinkled loud in the silence.

Riley barely heard it. Her eyes stayed on the key.

"That was her safe place," she said, voice breaking. "Where she kept things he wasn't supposed to touch."

Ethan's fists curled at his sides.

"She had no right," he muttered.

Reyes stood with the bagged trophy in his hand. "No right to what?"

Ethan's eyes flashed.

"To keep things from me."

The words hung in the room. Plain. Ugly. True.

Reyes held up the evidence bag. "Then explain this."

Ethan stared at the trophy. His face shifted. The last of his control cracked, and something dark moved through the opening.

The Confession

Ethan laughed.

It came out brittle and wrong.

"She took it herself," he said. "Always sneaking. Always keeping pieces of herself away from me."

His eyes stayed locked on the bag in Reyes's hand.

"She sat there with it in her lap, smiling at it like it mattered more than her own father. I told her to put it back. I told her to respect me. To respect this house."

Riley pressed back against the wall. Her heart hammered so hard it hurt.

When Ethan said this house, it sounded like he meant every wall, every room, every breath Olivia had taken inside it.

"She wouldn't listen," Ethan said.

His voice changed. Lower now. Rougher.

"She never listened. Not when it mattered. She had all these plans in her head. Little secrets. Little people whispering to her, telling her she could leave me."

Reyes said nothing. Miller stood near Ethan's right side, watching him closely.

Ethan's gaze dragged back to the trophy.

"I snapped," he said.

Riley stopped breathing.

"I hit her with it." His voice trembled, but not with grief. "Once. Then again. She kept looking at me like I was the monster. Like I was the one destroying her."

His mouth twisted.

"So I made her stop looking."

The room went silent.

Reyes's voice cut through it, steady and cold. "You killed Olivia Harper with this trophy?"

Ethan looked at him.

"Don't call it murder."

Riley's stomach turned.

Ethan's eyes shone now, bright with something that was not regret.

"She forced it. She betrayed me. She thought she was clever. Hiding keys. Hiding notes. Running to him. Running to her." His gaze flicked to Riley. "She thought I wouldn't know."

Riley's skin went cold.

Ethan leaned forward slightly, voice dropping. "I knew everything."

Reyes held his stare. "Everything?"

Ethan smiled faintly.

"She wrote things. Hid things. Thought Danny was the only one she could trust." His voice sharpened. "She thought I wouldn't see what she was planning. I knew where she went. I saw her sneak out. I saw who waited for her."

Riley's breath caught.

He was not confessing to care.

He was confessing to possession.

Reyes's face hardened, but he did not press. Not yet.

"Ethan Harper," he said, "you are under arrest for the murder of Olivia Harper."

Miller stepped forward and cuffed him.

The click of metal sounded final.

Ethan did not resist. He looked past Reyes, past Miller, past the evidence bag in the detective's hand. His eyes landed on Riley one last time.

"You all thought you were saving her," he said.

Riley stared back at him.

"No," she said quietly. "We were too late."

For the first time, something in Ethan's face moved.

Not guilt.

Not shame.

Just anger that she had said it out loud.

Miller turned him toward the door.

The Finish Line

Riley stood frozen as they led Ethan out. His boots thudded across the porch, each step pounding through her chest. He never looked back.

Morning air cut cold across her skin. Her mother stood at the edge of the yard, trembling behind the police line. When she saw Riley, she pushed forward.

An officer moved to stop her.

Reyes noticed. “Let her through.”

The officer stepped aside, and Riley’s mother ran to her. She wrapped both arms around Riley, holding on as if the whole night might still take her.

Riley folded into the embrace and clung to the one safe thing left in reach.

“I’ve got you,” her mother whispered. “I’ve got you.”

Riley tried to answer, but only a broken sound came out. For a moment, the house behind her was only a shadow.

Inside, officers laid evidence bags across the table. The dented trophy sat sealed in plastic, marked and tagged. Nearby, Riley’s key rested in its own bag.

Small. Plain. Too late.

Reyes glanced toward the doorway where Riley stood with her mother.

“She gave us the weight,” he said quietly.

Before anyone could answer, Miller came down the stairs, face drawn.

“We found something else.”

Reyes turned. “What?”

“Room upstairs. Monitors. DVR. Looks like years of footage.”

Riley's stomach dropped.

Ethan's words came back.

I knew everything.

She whispered, "He was watching her."

Reyes's jaw tightened. "We'll take it all in. We'll review everything."

He looked at the house, then back toward the street where Ethan was being placed into the cruiser.

"For now," he said, "this part is over."

The sky was lightening, streaks of dawn breaking across the trees. But no warmth touched Riley.

Not yet.

The News Breaks

The holding cell hummed with a tired buzz.

Hours had passed since dawn broke over the Harper house. Danny sat on the bench with his elbows on his knees and his head in his hands. The concrete smelled like bleach, metal, and old air.

He had stopped asking what time it was. He had stopped expecting answers that meant anything.

Every sound made him look up. Every set of footsteps carried the threat of another round of questions. Another officer. Another look that said they had already chosen the shape of him.

Keys clinked. The door slid open.

Reyes stepped in first, Miller behind him. Their faces were the same, but the air had changed. Less edge. More weight.

Danny stood. "What now?"

Reyes met his eyes. "It was not you."

Danny stared at him.

Reyes took one step closer. "We have his confession. We have the weapon. We have more."

Danny did not move. The words did not reach him all at once.

"Say it again."

"It was Ethan Harper," Reyes said. "You are being released."

Danny laughed once.

The sound came out raw and painful.

"So I rotted in here while he walked free."

Miller's voice stayed even. "Not anymore."

Danny looked down at his hands. His knuckles were scraped. Red lines circled his wrists where the cuffs had bitten too long.

"What happens now?"

"Paperwork," Reyes said. "Then you walk out the front door."

Danny looked up.

The word front sounded almost cruel, like doors still meant something simple.

Out the Door

They moved him through two locked gates and a hall that smelled like metal. At the front desk, a clerk slid a plastic bag across the counter.

Phone. Wallet. Keys.

A few small things that belonged to a life he no longer recognized.

Danny stared at them before picking them up. His phone felt strange in his hand. Too light. Too ordinary. He had imagined getting it back a hundred times. Now that he had it, he did not know what to do with it.

Outside, cameras flashed.

Voices rose at once.

"Danny, did you know?"

"Do you have a statement?"

"Did you hurt her?"

"Were you framed?"

The questions crashed into each other until they became heat and noise. Danny kept his eyes on the concrete. Cracked paint lines. Oil stains. A cigarette butt flattened near the curb.

Anything but the cameras.

A man near the lot spat on the ground. "He should still be inside."

A woman folded her arms, mouth tight. "I don't care what they say. He did something."

The words slid under Danny's skin and stayed there.

He kept walking. Every stare felt like a hand. Every phone felt like proof that freedom did not erase what people had already decided.

"They'll never forget my face," he said.

His voice was low, meant for no one and everyone.

"They'll never let me outrun this."

The wind moved across the lot, cool and empty.

Freedom felt like a hole.

What Remains

Riley stood near the edge of the parking lot with her mother. She looked small inside a too big hoodie, eyes rimmed red, arms wrapped around herself like she was trying to hold something together. When she saw Danny, she lifted a hand, then let it fall.

He stopped a few feet away.

"You came."

"I wasn't going to let you walk out alone," she said.

Her mother stood beside her, tired and watchful.

"You're free now," she said gently.

Danny glanced toward the street, then at the phones still pointed his way from behind the police line.

"Am I?"

No one answered right away.

Riley stepped closer. "They'll move on."

He gave a small nod that held no belief.

"Maybe not today," she added.

His mouth twitched, but it was not a smile.

"He confessed?"

Riley swallowed. "Yes. And they found more."

Danny looked down.

"It's over," she said.

He wanted it to feel like air.

It did not.

For a second, neither of them moved. Then Riley stepped into him, and Danny folded his arms around her. The hug started stiff, all sharp edges and careful space. Then something in both of them broke enough to let them hold on.

"I'm sorry," he said into her shoulder. "For everything I couldn't stop."

Riley shook her head. "You tried."

"So did you."

The words hurt her.

They let go at the same time. The space between them felt heavy with what neither of them could fix.

They walked toward the far side of the lot to escape the last of the cameras. Traffic moved beyond the curb. Somewhere overhead, a plane cut a white line across the morning sky.

"What now?" Riley asked.

Danny looked at his hands again. "I don't know. Job's gone. Friends too. People see my face and decide."

"We'll prove who you are," Riley said. "We won't let this be the last word."

His smile came small and cold.

"They already decided who I am."

Across the street, a bus sighed to a stop, opened its doors, then pulled away again. Danny watched it go like it might be a way out.

Reyes and Miller stood near their car, giving them room. When Reyes caught Riley's eye, he lifted one hand.

Not a wave.

A quiet promise.

We'll finish this.

Danny looked back at the station doors.

He was free. But it felt like exile, not home.

He turned away from the building and started toward the road. Riley fell in beside him.

They did not talk. The sound of their steps was steady and thin against the pavement.

After a while, Danny said, "Thank you for coming."

"Always," Riley said.

They kept walking. Behind them, the station shrank. The cameras faded. The voices thinned into traffic and wind.

The town did not soften.

The truth had not healed anything.

But each step pushed the building farther behind them.

It was not peace.

It was not forgiveness.

It was only forward.

For now, forward was all they had.

Epilogue

The Finish Line

The Trail Begins

The courthouse brimmed with faces before the doors even opened.

Reporters waited in the hall with cameras held low and notebooks ready. Neighbors filled the benches with stiff rows, dressed like they had come to church instead of court. Some whispered behind their hands. Some sat silent, eyes fixed on the front of the room as if looking away might make them guilty too.

Riley, sat beside the mother with her hands folded in her lap. She had tried to keep them still, but her fingers kept tightening against each other until her knuckles ached.

At the defense table, Ethan sat in a dark suit that didn't quite fit him right.

The cuffs were gone now, hidden from the jury, but Riley could still fill them in the room. She could hear the hard click from the night they put them on him. His hair had been cut shorter. His face looked thinner. But the calm had stayed.

That was the part she hated most.

Ethan looked almost comfortable, his hands folded on the table, his mouth resting in a faint line that could become a smile if he wanted it to. He glanced once toward the gallery, and for one second his eyes passed over Riley like he barely knew her.

Like she was only another witness.

Like Olivia had only been another problem.

The prosecution opened with the shape of the case first. They built it slowly, piece by piece, as if the room needed time to understand how long the truth had been hiding in plain sight.

Witnesses came and went.

Ms. Porter spoke about the changes she had seen in Olivia. The tired eyes. The careful answers. The writing that had grown darker before anyone understood why. Her voice stayed steady until she said Olivia's name the third time. Then she paused, pressed her lips together, and started again.

Coach Allen admitted he should have noticed sooner. He said Olivia had run like every race mattered more than it should. Like stopping was the one thing she could not afford.

Riley took the stand after lunch.

The walk from the gallery to the witness chair felt longer than it was. She could feel every eye on her back. Reporters. Neighbors. Teachers. People who had whispered Olivia's name for months as if grief gave them ownership.

She sat, raised her hand, and promised to tell the truth.

Then she did.

She told them about the rules. About the check ins. About the way Olivia always looked toward doors and windows before answering anything. She told them about the key she had given Olivia and how giving it had felt like help at the time.

Her voice almost broke there.

Almost.

The prosecutor gave her a moment. Riley looked down at her hands until the room steadied around her. Then she looked back up.

"She was scared," Riley said. "And we all kept waiting for her to say it in a way we could use."

No one in the courtroom moved.

At the defense table, Ethan watched her with that same flat patience.

The evidence came next.

Ethan's confession recorded and clear from body cam footage. His voice filled the courtroom, calm at first, then cracking into something uglier as he spoke about obedience, secrets, and betrayal. No one coughed. No one shifted. Even the reporters stopped writing for a few seconds.

Then came the trophy.

Blood stained. Sealed. Undeniable.

Riley could not look at it for long.

Beside her, her mother reached for her hand and held it under the bench, out of sight from everyone else.

The surveillance archive came last.

Years of footage pulled from the hidden room upstairs. Files cataloged by date. School mornings. Late nights. Olivia alone in her room. Olivia sitting on her bed. Olivia walking from one small corner of her life to another, never knowing how closely she had been watched.

The jury did not look away.

Some of them flinched.

Riley did not blame them.

She had lived with the images for months, and still every mention of them made her feel like the walls were closing in again.

Across the aisle, Danny Holt sat near the back row with his head lowered. He had come every day. He never sat close enough to draw attention, but attention found him anyway.

It always did now.

People still looked at him like they expected guilt to show on his face if they stared long enough.

Riley glanced back once.

Danny did not look up.

The trial went on for days. The town listened. The cameras waited. The courthouse filled and emptied and filled again.

Olivia remained everywhere.

In testimony.

In photographs.

In silence.

In the empty space no verdict could ever fill.

The Verdict

The jury filed back after hours of deliberation.

The courtroom changed the second they entered. Every whisper died. Papers stopped rustling. Someone in the back row drew in a sharp breath and did not let it out.

Riley sat straighter.

Her mother's hand found hers again.

Ethan stayed still at the defense table. His attorney leaned close and said something too low for anyone else to hear. Ethan gave one small nod, as if the words meant nothing to him.

The foreman rose with the paper in his hand.

His voice was steady.

"Guilty."

The word moved through the room before the rest of the sentence could follow.

First degree murder.

Unlawful imprisonment.

Evidence tampering.

Obstruction.

The list went on, each charge landing with its own dull weight. Riley heard them, but not cleanly. Her pulse roared too loudly. Her eyes burned. Her mother squeezed her hand hard enough to hurt.

No one cheered.

That was not what this was.

A few people cried softly. Someone behind Riley whispered Olivia's name. The judge's gavel struck once, sharp and final, and the room pulled itself back together.

After the sentencing arguments, the judge looked down at Ethan Harper.

For the first time all day, Ethan's smile faded.

Not because he was sorry.

Because the room was no longer his.

The judge's voice carried clearly.

"Life without the possibility of parole."

Riley closed her eyes.

The words should have felt bigger. They should have split something open. They should have given Olivia back a measure of what had been stolen.

They did not.

When Riley opened her eyes again, Ethan was watching the room.

His gaze drifted over the jury, the attorneys, the reporters, the neighbors. Then it landed on Riley.

His mouth curled into the faintest smirk.

Not defeat.

Not shame.

Only another turn in a race only he understood.

Riley held his stare until officers moved between them and blocked him from view.

After the Verdict

The courthouse did not empty right away.

People lingered in clusters, speaking in low voices like they were afraid normal volume might crack the place open. Reporters waited near the doors. Cameras flashed outside against the courthouse steps. White ribbons fluttered along the railing in the cold wind.

Riley stayed inside with her mother for a while.

She sat in the gallery, hands clasped so tight her knuckles burned. Relief flickered somewhere inside her, but grief drowned it before it could spread.

Justice was too small a word.

It sounded clean. Finished. Like a door closing.

Nothing about this felt closed.

She could still picture Olivia's empty seat beside her in English. The untouched tray at lunch. The way Olivia used to smile when she almost let herself be happy and then seemed to remember she was not supposed to.

Riley's mother leaned close. "You ready?"

Riley nodded, though she was not.

Near the back row, Danny lingered with his shoulders rounded and his head lowered. He had been released months ago. Cleared in every way that mattered on paper.

But paper had not followed him into grocery stores.

Paper had not stopped people from crossing the street.

Paper had not given him back the job he lost, the friends who vanished, or the version of himself the town had buried before the truth came out.

The verdict had cleared him.

Hollow's Edge never fully would.

Riley walked toward him.

Danny looked up when he heard her steps. For a second, his face tightened like he expected another accusation. Then he saw her, and the look softened into something tired.

"It's done," Riley said.

Danny gave a small nod. "For him."

She knew what he meant.

Teachers dotted the benches around them. Ms. Porter sat with a white ribbon pinned to her chest, her face pale and still. Coach Allen stared hard at the floor. Ms. Calhoun wiped at one eye, then folded the tissue in her hand until it was too small to fold again.

Their silence said more than any testimony had.

The community had not healed. It had cracked open. Some people wanted the truth to make them feel better. Some wanted it to excuse how long they had looked away. Some wanted it to turn Ethan into a monster so they would not have to ask why nobody saw him clearly sooner.

Riley had no patience left for any of them.

Outside, candles lined the courthouse steps. Their flames shook in the wind but did not go out. Photos of Olivia rested against the stone wall. Track photos. School photos. One picture of her laughing with her head turned slightly, like someone had called her name just before the camera flashed.

Riley stopped in front of it.

For a moment, the noise faded behind her.

Reporters.

Traffic.

Whispers.

All of it thinned until there was only the small sound of candle flames moving in the cold.

Riley bent and touched the edge of the frame.

“I’m sorry,” she whispered.

The words were not enough.

They never had been.

She stood there with Danny a few feet behind her and her mother waiting nearby, and she let Olivia’s name sit in the air without trying to make it easier.

Not a headline.

Not evidence.

Not a case.

Olivia.

Only Olivia.

The Transfer

The prison hall was dim, and Ethan Harper's footsteps echoed like a slow drumbeat.

A guard walked on either side of him. Chains clinked at his wrists and ankles, steady and dull against the concrete. The sound did not seem to bother him. He moved with the same careful control he had worn for months, shoulders straight, chin level, eyes bright with cold patience.

The walls smelled of bleach and old stone.

Somewhere farther down the block, a man laughed once, then went quiet.

Ethan did not look toward the sound.

He kept his eyes forward.

The guard on his left stopped at a cell near the end of the row. He checked the number, then unlocked the door. Metal scraped and groaned as it opened.

"Inside," the guard said.

Ethan stepped in.

The cell was narrow. Two bunks. A toilet. A sink bolted to the wall. A small window too high to see through unless a man stood on the bed.

Someone already sat on the lower bunk with his back turned.

His posture was straight and still, hands resting loosely over one knee. He did not look up when Ethan entered. He did not need to.

The guards removed Ethan's restraints, gave the usual warning, and stepped out. The door shut with a heavy clang.

For a moment, neither man spoke.

The hallway noise faded into a low hum.

Then the man on the bunk said, “So.”

His voice was low, smooth, and almost pleasant.

“What are you here for?”

Ethan studied the back of his head. The pressed shirt. The neat hair. The strange stillness of him.

Then Ethan smiled faintly.

“My daughter forgot what I taught her,” he said. “She mistook disobedience for freedom. I corrected that.”

Silence filled the cell.

Not shocked.

Not empty.

Interested.

The man on the bunk turned at last.

His face was pale. His eyes were sharp and calm, with intelligence simmering just beneath the surface. He looked Ethan over slowly, not with fear and not with judgment.

With recognition.

Then he smiled.

“Dr. Leonard Caldwell,” he said softly. “Pleasure to meet you.”

His gaze settled on Ethan’s face, steady and almost kind.

“Correction is such an interesting word, isn’t it?”

Acknowledgements

Thank you to Miblart for the beautiful cover design for *The Last Run*. They took the heart of this story and turned it into an image that feels haunting, emotional, and unforgettable.

A great cover does more than decorate a book. It gives the story its first breath before a reader ever turns the page. Miblart captured the mood, tension, and darkness of Olivia's journey in a way that truly feels perfect for this novel.

I am incredibly grateful for their talent, care, and professionalism. They truly are amazing.

Thank you for helping give *The Last Run* the face it deserved.

www.ingramcontent.com/pod-product-compliance
Lightning Source LLC
La Vergne TN
LVHW100501110826
845146LV00002B/479

* 9 7 9 8 9 9 3 3 8 0 8 0 3 *